Gratitude

Christopher Beck

LEAF BY LEAF

Published by Leaf by Leaf
an imprint of Cinnamon Press,
Office 49019, PO Box 15113, Birmingham, B2 2NJ
www.cinnamonpress.com

Print Edition ISBN 978-1-78864-893-6

British Library Cataloguing in Publication Data. A CIP record for this book can be obtained from the British Library.

Designed and typeset in Adobe Caslon Pro by Cinnamon Press.
Cover design by Adam Craig © Adam Craig.
Cinnamon Press is represented by Inpress.

About the Author

Chris realised a long-held ambition to write when, owing to health problems, he was forced to give up a career as a medical practitioner. In 2007 he won a regional play writing competition with *The Lesson* and had it performed at The Little Theatre, Wells. In 2010 he obtained an MA in Creative Writing at Southampton University. He had two short plays performed at the café, Nuffield Theatre, Southampton. He self-published a novel *The Summertime Blues* in 2015. Throughout his writing career there has been a steady output of poetry, some of which has been published. In 2021 his poem *Still some way to go, Mother Rosa* was short-listed for the Wells Literary Festival Poetry Competition. Other interests include music, playing classical guitar and sailing.

Gratitude

Chapter 1

Under some protest Mel was told she could take her place a little early. She'd learned that playing the dumb tourist would loosen up the most tight-assed official, even at the Ritz Hotel. She was early because of the tall woman who'd begun to waylay her at Green Park Tube Station. Hardly realizing it, Mel had fallen into the habit of allowing extra time to complete her journeys.

She sashayed past the grand piano then glided up the short rise to claim her table for afternoon tea, this time taking more notice of the décor. She supposed it grand in a museumy sort of way. For the year 2016 the word passé didn't seem out of place. Despite, or because of this it gave—she imagined—ordinary folks a sense of occasion and style, not to mention the chance of observing how the posh took their tea. That the noisy crowd of women to her left were revelling in, and at the same time, defying their surroundings was quite okay with her.

She was waiting for Helena, not just any Helena, *Lady* Helena. They were both recent alumnae of the same Harley Street clinic. In just two or three meetings their sorority was sealed. Defying post op instructions they had deserted their rooms to wander the corridors and get some air. They compared notes, bandages and leisure time, discovering a mutual aversion to daytime TV. Helena needed little persuading to come back to Mel's room and assist with a bottle of Prosecco.

A large woman in a ruched maroon gown approached the piano, adjusted the stool and began to play. *Chopin* Mel thought, remembering early days with her piano teacher. But, at times, the soloist could barely rise above the orchestra of loud women—out-of-towners on a spree, all sporting more or less the same labelled shopping bags. Mel wondered what pricy flights of fancy were stashed away in those gaudy bags. They were all overdressed, as most likely she, in her chambray pantsuit, was.

Close enough to the appointed time her clinic buddy appeared as if she'd just come on at the Old Vic. Wearing Cashmere and pearls, she tipped the pianist a respectful glance then took the short flight of steps as if she owned the place. There was a microsecond of silence from the tables as she approached. Mel waited until she could just see the azure of Helena's irises, then stood up.

'Hello, Blue Eyes.'

'Hello, Green Eyes.'

Mel was quick to convert her companion's intended handshake into a high five, and for several seconds they stared into one another's faces, observing in their different styles of speech what a favourable result each had achieved. Lady Helena's perfume reeked as much of class as of money.

'You heal real fast, Helena.'

'Just luck,' she replied, touching her face. 'I envy you your complexion, so delicate and pale.'

'You shouldn't, it's high maintenance.'

'Forgive me… you're much younger than I remember. Too young to need…'

'Show business,' Mel replied. It seemed as good an explanation as any.

For a while they continued to smile conspiratorially at one another until the waiter appeared and offered them an extensive choice of tea. The order completed, Helena's expression was unmistakable: who are these awful women?

'It's a package. The coach does a store-crawl then tops it off here. They'll talk about this forever in Dullsville. Sorry, I thought it'd be quiet… even familiar.'

'Never been. I told you we were country bumpkins.'

'But aren't you married to a Sir, live in some ancient hall.'

'Oh dear, Mel. You've got that look I like to see only when I'm working. I'm the girl next door, brought up in Aylesbury, won a scholarship. I actually voted Labour once.'

Aside from a maverick giggle, Helena looked and sounded nothing like the girl next door. It was those schoolgirl splutterings as much as anything that had endeared her to Mel in the first place. Then there was the voice, unfettered now by dressings: a rounded alto register that would not have been out of place in a certain play by Oscar Wilde.

'So, what is your actual… role?' Mel asked.

'I extort money from the rich and hand it over to charity.'

'Robin Hood!'

They laughed, their voices melding into something softer than the crescendo and forte of the brassy orchestra. The pianist, meanwhile, soldiered on with *An English Country Garden*.

Eyebrows raised, a note of faux exasperation stealing over her face, Helena asked, 'Am I so amusing?' She'd placed her cup and saucer down on the table and returned a tiny half-eaten sandwich to her plate.

'I just love all that refinement—the English etiquette. I'm jealous, that's all. It comes over so natural. Has to be in your DNA.'

'But not in yours, I think.'

'Now let's not fall out over a little thing like tea cups.' Mel went on, 'You know, I nearly asked for coffee just to see what'd happen. Would the waiter deconstruct on the spot or show me the door?'

'Probably both, you wretched *gel*.'

They were back at the clinic where keeping a straight face carried more than one meaning. They could always rely on their cultural differences for an inexhaustible repertory of jokes. They'd even begun to talk clinic style— side of mouth.

'You'd have been great with a burger, Helena. Maybe that's where we shoulda gone.'

'You're impossible!' Helena protested.

'That dainty way you hold your cup and saucer. See— critical use of the pinky finger, both hands. That's just how to keep your burger's content from decorating the Versace, the Gucci or just the sidewalk.' Mel demonstrated the technique with her mouth wide beyond the cause.

Helena erupted, dabbed her eyes and kept saying, 'I'd never…' but got no further. Finally, her convulsions subsided.

'I'd never manage one. It does seem to require a rather large mouth.' Helena was exercising her jaws, to which she kept drawing up the modesty of a hand.

'And what's that supposed to mean?' Mel replied with mock offence, thinking, so far, so good.

She'd been here once before, the guest of a media personality. His niece was going to be the next stage

10

sensation. Daisy was still her client but now majored in stage design. For a while he kept turning up at the agency with flowers and an ego the size of which she'd not met with since her trips to Hollywood.

After scones and cakes, they left together for a stroll through the park. It brought Mel down to earth with a thump. She'd assumed that beyond the jokes they'd discover common ground. She hadn't been anywhere near a horse since she was a girl and Helena rarely went to the theatre. They were town and country.

Over tea they'd put a little more flesh to their individual resumés, or rather Mel had. Helena was more reticent about her personal life. The estate was involved with weddings and corporate events. There were two teenaged sons who roared about the top field on motor bikes in the school holidays. Noble hubby was a 'hands on' farmer and the family occupied only a small section of the Jacobean house, which was in need of extensive repairs. To her relief Mel gained the impression an invitation to stay was not a realistic expectation. She had no wish for an entrée into 'high society'. Eccentricity aside, all she'd read and heard was negative.

A country estate is something I'd hate, sang a voice in her head.

Helena became animated recalling her forays into the mathematical worlds of corporations and industry. It was where she'd worked before her marriage, where she could 'talk the talk'. It led Mel to guess that not just charm but a dose of bullying went into her charity pitches. Behind all that jolliness and blue eyes there was clearly some steel.

'Anything wrong?' Helena asked as soon as they were

completely on their own. There was something about her friend: Mel could only describe it as a finely tuned instinct.

'I'm crazy, that's what. Going on stage again after such a long break. It's no big deal, a rock musical, four soloists. And I *really* like the people running the show. They're younger, ten years or so. My last boyfriend was younger still. You get the picture?'

'You'll be fine, I haven't the tiniest doubt,' Helena said. 'I can imagine the self-questioning, but this little trick,' she added, touching her face, 'works as much on the psyche as the physical. I can't wait for my next assignment.' Helena knew nothing of the stage yet what she said made some sense. It sounded like the sort of flummery aristos are born to pull off, but no, this woman—maybe just fifty—was even older in wisdom. Mel was half-expecting her companion to use an algorithm and come up with a figure close to her own 44 years.

They kissed goodbye near Buckingham Palace, Helena in a taxi to her 'office'—an apartment near Russell Square, Mel returning through the park, a familiar emptiness taking hold. Helena promised to be in touch when next in town. Then her expression had changed—the *Lady* Helena was constantly on guard against the attentions of the press and social media.

'So, could we keep this …' she breathed, 'entirely *entre nous?*'

It was as if her face was still swathed in bandages, her mystery preserved while Mel's mask had been removed—she'd talked too much about Henry and the divorce.

The daffodils were a blaze of gold through the lattice

of bare trees as Mel wandered back through the park, convincing herself of nature's restorative powers before the hustle for the Piccadilly Line. She almost willed the crazy woman, a stylish, some would say loud, dresser to appear but there was no sign of her lofty presence on Mel's route through the crowded station. Retaining her sunhat, she felt at least partially disguised.

Green Park was where Mel often changed lines when visiting her stepdaughter in North London. She could make the transit by the corridor or the escalators, turning it into a sort of hide-and-seek game where you were never quite sure how it would play out until the last moment. Even losing could be graded—*minor* if the woman just held a photo in front of you, *major* if she tried to engage you in conversation.

Emerging from Hammersmith Tube station Mel felt the chill of a cold wind go straight through her silk pantsuit. Weathering New York winters seemed a lifetime ago. In four years, she'd adjusted, in mind as much as body, to the London climate.

Upping her pace, she arrived at the one-and-a-half room, second floor office, warmer and breathless, the combination of exercise and cold having made her wheeze a little. She'd kept away from health issues with Helena, though the cues to respond had been out there. Mel had still talked too much and, come their next meeting, that would have to be turned around. She couldn't quite escape the notion that Helena, despite her status and need for nothing, still wanted something more from her.

'Holly, you get outta here right now,' Mel said sternly, but in a whisper.

The sound booth was still in use. Jared, one of their

regular narrators, a client no less, was yet to finish recording all his chapters. Creating files for audiobooks was a useful side line for the agency. They had access to some of the finest voices.

'Will there be flowers from a certain uber-smooth personality?' Holly teased in her flat northern vowels.

'Like fuck! She was a she, a lady. A *real* lady. Only you gotta keep schtum.'

Chapter 2

The northbound Jubilee line was its calm Sunday morning self, the cars rattling along in that hollow, empty manner that seemed to beg the question: where *was* everybody? It always came with a subtle change of mood when the train hit broad daylight—part of the ritual and excitement Mel felt when visiting her English family. Only this time it had cost her some sleep. Today, a decision had to be made about who was to care for Billy after preschool when Jess was at work. Mel was armed with a sticker book full of different scenes and a wealth of adhesive characters and animals. She'd also brought her small guitar to sing to him.

As soon as he saw her enter the soft play café he waved and shouted. His mum, on all fours, turned and beamed at Mel. Jess had attractive almond eyes and good bone structure, her blond hair now short and stylish. Even before they kissed, Mel knew something was wrong. She hoisted Billy up, cuddled him then kissed his head. He too had had his hair cut short—much to her disappointment.

'Can I play too?' Mel asked.

'He wants you to play with him outside. Don't you, darling—the pirate ship, or maybe the fort. Wow! You look super relaxed, Mel. You must *so* love that job of yours.'

'Matter of fact I've had a short vacation.' Mel instinctively touched her face and tried not to guess the cause of Jess's anxiety. This on top of the nerves she'd been nursing about whether she'd be offered 'the job'.

'Go anywhere?'

'Only walked the river and read.'

'I'd be like that if I could *just* design.'

'Oh, had a facial too.'

Jess worked three days a week in a West End clothes shop that had once sold a dress she herself had designed and made.

'Come on little big man, let's go play,' Mel said, handing Jess her phone, the book and the guitar, then leading her young charge out through the open café door where he gave her the slip and scampered off towards the blue and white pirate ship. As ever, he was wearing his striped soccer shirt.

They'd done the swings, the ropewalk, the revolving saucer as well as playing pirates—good and bad. Now all he wanted was to play in the fort that stood in the older kids' section.

'Okay, pirate man, but we'll have to lift you over the ramparts. Then you be careful.' The steps and ladders were higher and steeper here and once he was installed, she didn't take her eyes off him for a second. At least it was quiet and not teeming with older ones. Billy suffered from a degree of clumsiness that Jess preferred to call *dyspraxia*.

He was issuing urgent instructions to his imaginary minions. Together they fought off two waves of enemy attacks in quick succession when a plane banked overhead, the sun flashing off its wings. Mel looked up and was about to say something when the air suddenly reverberated with noise. Billy covered his ears, his little face contorting with distress. She leant over the fort, plucked him up as if from the jaws of a fiend then rushed him back to the café. Jess was already at the door.

'Alright my baby. Alright now,' she soothed in his ears. Billy had a problem with sudden, loud noises, Jess explained, and wherever they went she carried a supply of cotton wool to protect his ears. As soon as he was pacified, he turned his attention to the book and began attaching figures with unconscious surrealism to the various scenes. Mel's phone had chirped only once. She and Jess cradled large cups of coffee.

'It's about Dad,' Jess began.

'Oh?'

'The consultant says he's showing signs of dementia.'

'Surely he's *much* too young,' Mel said with conviction.

'They're calling it pre-senile dementia.'

'Shit!' Mel gasped, then checked that Billy hadn't heard. Her mind was struggling to come to terms with the diagnosis, its ugliness, and then thinking about the implications for Jess and for Billy. Weren't some cases hereditary?

'There's something else one of the doctors keeps asking about: the time you two met. They seem to be saying that on that particular day the air was so full of toxic stuff, the gases, the dust, there might be long-term effects. Dad never talked about it. Now I think…' Jess reached for a paper napkin on the table, 'he can't…'

'Remember?'

'He can… but he needs a lot of prompting. Then we— I mean Davina and me—aren't the best prompts. We don't know the right questions to ask. I'd hate to ask something that'd upset him.' Jess's face was taut, her lovely eyes grave and a little evasive. Mel caught her stepdaughter's drift and took refuge in Billy.

'Love that dinosaur on the farm, babe. He's really

gonna give those other animals a hard time. Unless he's vegetarian.'

'T-rex only eats meat,' Billy said with enormous conviction.

'Too bad for the farm then,' Mel replied looking at Jess and coaxing a brief smile. 'Okay, whaddya want?'

'Could you meet and talk? Just once.'

'About what?'

'Oh, I don't know. If you could just *see* him I'd be... it would be so right. Even if nothing... I'd feel a lot better getting your input. A big ask, I know.'

'Just your dad and me, right? *No* Davina.'

Jess nodded enthusiastically and was about to launch into unconstrained gratitude when Mel felt a sudden urge to bring up the past, then wished she'd kept quiet. 'Don't know if there's any connection. Suppose that doctor ought to know we used to do stuff. But then so did the rest of New York for heaven's sakes.' A change of expression spread over Jess's face. 'Nothing way out, just the usual suspects. God! Why did I open my big mouth?'

'And why did the happy couple need drugs?' Both women glanced towards Billy as if the topic might affect him but he was fully absorbed with his sticky figures.

'Because, you know, it makes you feel... you can do anything. You're rich and beautiful.'

'And now?' Jess enquired, looking serious, hostile even.

'I'm much more responsible now,' Mel said.

'So it's only now and then, is it?' Jess's sarcasms were getting louder and Billy's concentration had at last been broken.

'Mummy sad.'

'No, no, babe. Just grown-up talk,' adding, 'well, some

of us think they're grown-up.'

'Ouch! Don't do *any* of that stuff these days. It has zero relevance to your dad. It's just there was something back awhile in the press. Fizzled out pretty quick I recall.'

'What about booze?' Jess probed.

'*Negative*, leastways we were only occasional users.'

'Dad drank after the divorce. Now Davina's quite hard on him. What about you?'

'Hey, what is this?'

'Mel, you look fantastic, you've got this amazing job that *you* alone created. But I know there's a back story.'

'Uh-huh, there's ups and downs. But I can be hard on me too. Can we change the tape, my dear stepdaughter?'

On the way back the train was busier—ideal for Mel to cut off into daydreams of Billy, having him all to herself in Chiswick, playing mom. She almost shivered at the thought of bathing his perfectly proportioned body, putting him to bed, reading him stories and singing to him. When the train went underground, she was confronted by her reflection in the opposite window, hugging her guitar and smiling stupidly. She hastily adopted a more neutral expression but the bubble of joy inside her refused to burst. It didn't matter that Jess had never so much as mentioned Billy sleeping over in Chiswick. It was pure speculation, of course, but might caring for Billy lead to certain changes in her own chemistry? She prayed it would.

Mel was to pick up every Tuesday and Wednesday lunchtime, maybe sometimes staying over. The current child-minding arrangements—never satisfactory—had been eating into her stepdaughter's meagre earnings. Her own mother lived in Sussex and rarely came to London.

The 'interview' had turned into something like a poker game, Jess keeping her weak cards close to her chest while Mel put down her invincible ace—the promise to see her ex-husband. Even then Jess had taken a final swipe at Mel's chemical past.

'And I always thought how brave you two were after 9/11, how well you'd coped. Now I know—you were in La La Land.'

'Never said I was brave. We *were* in love. It was just parties and concerts. Molly and coke.'

'*Who? What?*'

After a tedious explanation about MDMA, e and amphetamines, Jess calmed down but not before Billy, once again distracted, asked, 'What's e, Mum?' With great emphasis Jess replied, 'A baddy' and then followed this with, 'e's a baddy' and everyone laughed. With that, Jess became serious, even melodramatic.

'Not made a will—yet. But if shit ever happens, Mel, you rank above my mum, right?' It was as if Jess had just pinned a medal on her. She was choked.

But Mel would need some basic instruction—what exactly *were* pull-ups? And only when the part-time mom checked all the right boxes to Jess's satisfaction would she begin her scariest job.

At Green Park, she'd almost made it to the Piccadilly Line when she heard a familiar voice.

'Do you busk?'

There was no way anyone carrying a ¾ guitar could be mistaken for a busker. Mel was too taken aback to reply. In any case the tall woman—appearing from nowhere—

went on, 'My sister, Jo-ju, used to have a regular pitch right here.'

'Oh, okay,' Mel said, feigning some interest.

'I showed you her photo once.'

Two or three times, Mel half recalled to herself.

'You think I'm loony, don't you? Asking total strangers if they've seen Jo-ju. I was working abroad, lost contact.'

'Missing Persons?'

'They said social media was best.'

Mel had an uncanny sense she knew where the conversation was heading. It had never progressed this far before.

'Hope it works out for you,' she said and scuttled off to the west-bound platform where a wall of sound indicated the next train's imminent arrival and her escape. Or so Mel thought. The woman had kept pace with her and, as the train noisily pulled up, began to shout, 'Do you *know* anyone, I don't do social media. I'm desperate.'

The car doors were opening. Mel had only to make a few yards of ground at speed and lose her pursuer. Then it dawned—there was nothing to stop the woman doing the same, maybe even following her all the way to her house. There was only one thing to do. She took out her card and thrust it into the woman's hand and, without waiting for any reaction, turned and ran for the train. Not daring to look back, it was a while before she was confident her pursuer had not boarded the train. She still felt shaky and now regretted giving this anonymous person the means to go on harassing her. The 'game' had got a lot more serious, and how quickly it had all happened. She couldn't help thinking she'd been singled out, that the woman had inside information. She'd dressed, by her standards, drably today in jeans and sweater. Mel must have walked right past her; now she felt robbed of her reveries—in their place anger and unease.

As soon as Mel made it home, she got out the Mason jar, her treasury of Gratitudes, and tipped out all the little strips of card. She read several at random before unscrewing the top of the fountain pen and filling out a blank one with the words: *Playing Billy's Mom*. She made sure there were always a few left blank in the jar. Did that make her an optimist or a fantasist?

After their brief Monday morning conference, Holly rolled her eyes as she handed Mel an airmail letter.

'Our man in Hollywood. I'm dying to know—does he still do those pencil sketches?'

'He has so far,' Mel replied.

Six or seven weeks earlier, Holly had 'mistakenly' opened and read the first two letters of the correspondence before realising their personal nature. She had a theory; Holly always had a theory. 'One day they're going to be worth serious dosh. *That's* why he sends them here. Security.'

In the circumstances—each letter headed, *Please file all correspondence*—it was not an unreasonable guess and Mel agreed. Holly curtsied, cleared her throat and said, 'Sir Royce, your sirship.'

'Whatever. He's earning us bucks,' Mel replied.

It took a good forty minutes to go through the various actors' 'Spot' files, fire off emails and send text messages. Revivals were in the air, and the New London Theatre was casting for *The King and I*. Only then did she read the letter, his fifth, bearing sketches like the others, then place it with the rest in the only drawer in her desk with a lock. She was about to turn the key when she sought out the first airmail, in particular the pencil sketches, the subject a hooded figure whose face was a little obscured, a woman's face.

My Dear Irish, A little problem and all because I paid no heed to your tender admonitions and now I'm paying something else—the price. 'Don't go to Venice Beach after dark' was your almost casual PS. Was it a joke or did you know something?

Mel had no recollection of ever giving him any advice about Venice Beach.

I'd forgotten how quickly the sun goes down here so I was coming back in the dark when I made out this tall figure silhouetted by the surf. There was something familiar too—dark hood and streamers—straight out of the RSC's wardrobe for the Scottish play! Sorry, that was not our best period, was it? But we did seem to salvage something after all…

Mel didn't go much on the word 'salvage' nor was she crazy about 'not our best'. She'd done nothing wrong aside from letting him out of her sight and had told him so in her reply, adding one sad emoji, and then another. Stratford, that summer season of 2014, was a steep-sided roller-coaster, forcing her to come to terms with a relationship that was always going to be 'nuanced'.

'Sorry, I talk too much, don't I?' Holly had gone around the back of the sound booth and stood by her boss's desk.

'It's okay.'

'And I'm nosey… all I want to know is, has that witch woman still got the hex on him?'

'Seems so,' Mel replied, manufacturing a smile.

Holly nodded, smiled weakly then returned to her desk. Mel hadn't the heart to tell her that the 'witch woman' was probably dead. She'd snuck up on Royce in the dark, blown some powder in his face and he'd been sneezing ever since—a 'spell' had been put on him. A few days later a woman's body, full of methamphetamine, had been brought ashore at Malibu. Mel returned the letter to the drawer.

Five minutes later, with a steady hand, she poured the coffee into two mugs—hers a Jackson-Pollock design, Holly's covered in Van Gogh irises. She'd bought them at MOMA as presents but never got around to sending them.

Chapter 3

Mel hadn't a clue what she was going to say to her ex-husband.

Their meeting suddenly felt absurd, and what if he wanted to meet again? She was afraid he would stumble over her name, worse, call her by his first wife's name. How she must love Jess and Billy if this was the measure of it—a train ride through Kent to a Friday lunch date with a man she'd once loved, a man who might not remember too much about that love. But wasn't that what she was quietly hoping for? No, not if it meant he had something wrong with his brain. It was important to get Davina out of her head. God only knew what *she* thought of the visit. That would come later through Jess, carefully filtering her words, softening the barbs with a wine or two. On the Tube Mel had avoided her reflection; apart from a pink scarf and beige shoulder bag she was in grey—leggings, skirt and top. She might be visiting a maiden aunt.

After leaving the city's gritty air, the atmosphere and outlook improved—woods and gentle hills—but nothing came near distracting her from her mission, whatever that was. She'd resisted the idea of running a list of questions past Henry to see how they squared with what she'd learned online. The last thing she wanted was to stir up anything painful. There was no expectation of point-scoring or blame games—that wasn't how they'd parted—but could she trust his wife not to start calling her names again, and what effect that might have on Henry, especially now?

As the train slowed for the village, the last thing she expected was any sense of familiarity. But having rushed to her feet and peered this way and that, she began to see clapboard houses in spacious lots that reminded her of places in New England she'd visited or passed through as a child. Her carriage coasted slowly past Henry before coming to a halt; now he was looking in the wrong direction. She hadn't quite been able to wave to him, but she'd seen his face, checked his bearing and concluded he was simply a slightly older version of the person with whom she'd spent ten years of her life. He was half leaning on a golf umbrella.

She tapped him on the shoulder and, spinning round, he looked briefly stupefied. 'God! You're looking well, so young. How are you?'

'I'm good, Henry. And you?'

'Old, as you see. Now I feel even older,' he said with a thin laugh.

'You're looking good. Must be all that golf.'

There was a polite exchange of smiles, and as they came out of the station Mel tried to guess which car was Henry's. After their move to England, he'd evolved at weekends into a sports car enthusiast. The quandary was resolved when he told her it was less than a half mile walk to the house. What a good plan to have chosen to wear boots for the occasion; he made a joke about them, said they reminded him of Minnie Mouse, then offered to carry her bag. There was some patchy mist about and the threat of rain but only the odd drop had fallen. She still seemed to be looking about convincing herself this was *old* England.

'Bet you could walk miles in those boots,' he said.

What had he in mind? she wondered.

The cottagey house with mullioned windows was set back from the lane by a well-tended lawn and a few small trees. Inside was a rash of wood panelling and every room they entered appeared tidy to a meticulous degree. She failed to imagine Billy playing here, failed too to spot any of Henry's old prints—no Hoppers or Jackson-Pollocks in sight. Maybe they were upstairs but Mel had her doubts— what passed for art on the walls was either pure kitsch or dark biblical scenes.

'I think all this gloomy woodwork'll have to go. It's getting on Dav's nerves, mine too,' Henry explained.

It was clear Henry was now a bunch more fastidious under the third wife's house rules. In New York and London, they had only ever rented apartments, and in all that time they'd barely been able to keep their rooms clear of junk and dust. It was as if they could never quite shake off the debris that had so entirely informed the day they met. Coming to the UK, there were too many changes at once, the exception being their mutual untidiness. Although it increasingly got to them, they never quite learned to deal with it other than citing some bohemian tendency, more his in New York, hers in London.

There was something exaggeratedly self-conscious about the way Davina's lasagne and salad selection deputed for her. But it was too good for Mel not to utter *delicious* and, still hungry, ask for more. She kept waiting for his jibe about her poor attempts at fine cuisine but he'd either forgotten or wanted to spare her. In New York it had never been an issue, but in the London apartment, without a job, she was expected to produce meals when

Henry returned exhausted from Canary Wharf.

After they'd cleared their plates and drunk half the bottle of red, Henry's mental machinery seemed to go into slow motion.

'You're living with this nice guy now, Antony, isn't it?'

'No, Henry,' she replied, stifling a laugh, 'he's just a dear friend.'

'Dear friend? He's *got* to be gay. What does he do?'

'Writes the art pages and reviews in all the local mags.'

'Oh yeah, Jess did tell me. I forget things, then come up with a different version. Mind's not as sharp as it was. I have trouble with names. Who doesn't? Davina's a love, but a great worrier. And she's laid it on pretty thick to Jess.'

'Anything else?'

'Not really,' he said, sounding almost offended. 'Once, I cut off on the train, next thing I knew I was two stops down the line.'

'You did that on the subway.'

'Did I?'

It was her first screw-up. 'Don't bring up anything from the past' was in big letters in the rulebook she was supposed to keep in her head.

After the Twin Towers, Henry had got himself enrolled at short notice in Graduate School, Columbia. He'd take the Number One to the Morningside campus while she walked, more often ran, from their Village apartment to the Broadway office. A sponge to Art and the Humanities, Henry never entirely mastered the map of the New York subway nor the order of its stations.

'Well, only once or twice,' she said, backtracking and shrugging.

The apple strudel looked so cookery-book perfect it heightened all Mel's hostility towards Davina but, once in the mouth, its yummy flavour made her mad with envy. She was used to her cooking being described as fast and brutal, even taking a kind of pride in its lack of pretension, its throwback to a simpler lifestyle. In and around Greenwich and the East Village they'd curated their own medley of dining experiences—home, restaurants and everything in between.

'I hear you've made contact with some of the old crowd,' Henry said.

'The other way about, Henry. They're desperate for tickets for the shows when they hit town. I do my best— at short notice—and they take me out to dinner. They always ask after you. Why've you given them up?'

'Oh, I don't know… they're a bit serious. Davina's got a big family, nice folk.'

Serious was not a word Mel would have used to describe 'the crowd'. True, they didn't exactly let their hair down but they laughed at her cheesy jokes and liked their food and drink. She suspected they were way more fun than Davina's folks.

'Look, Henry, you've gotta keep up, stay in circulation. Meet people, new people. Have your *own* circle.'

'I was wondering when I was going to get the lecture. Last time we met *you* were the one finding it hard to make friends.'

'I took my own advice. I've some real good friends now.'

'Boyfriends?'

'No time for that right now. The agency and the audiobooks keep me busy.'

'What about your… the actor. Forgotten his name.'

'Royce. He's filming right now in Hollywood. It's *entirely* professional.'

Trying to fill the blanks in their conversation she'd talked too much about herself and couldn't get Henry to open up. All he kept saying was 'I'm boring. Your life's more exciting'. At last there was a breakthrough when she asked about his trips to the British Museum.

'It's that book I started on, you remember, at Columbia. Eco-economics. I have to make myself go into town. Some days I'm just not up to it.'

It was the best news she'd heard and she gave him all the encouragement she could muster, even asking 'technical' questions, which meant she was soon lost, but his enthusiasm was unmistakable. Why hadn't they gotten onto this earlier?

'Hear you're returning to the stage,' Henry said.

'We did five nights in our local theatre. I was just helping out some people I met in the pub. Such a fun time, it feels a bit flat now,' Mel said, remembering just in time not to make it sound such a blast. She tried to get him to enthuse about the book again but the glint in his eye had gone. It was time for direct questions. 'Truly, Henry, how are you? And Davina?'

He said he felt under a cloud, but that if he was patient enough it would pass. He said nothing about his wife or their relationship, which was a relief to Mel who'd only asked out of politeness. She stood up, started to fidget then tried to think of something nice to say about Supercook, suddenly getting inspiration from the wood panelling. Close up she could see it was quality oak but darkening unevenly.

'Davina's right…' she said, turning round, but didn't get any further. Henry, still at the table, head bowed, looked fragile and lost. He was moving his lips but she could barely hear him. She rushed over. Had she brought on a spasm, a stroke? Placing her arms around his shoulders, their heads touching, she whispered, 'Henry, you okay?' When there was no response, she repeated her question louder, unsure why she'd whispered before. His monotone went on without a break, slowly, softly but now it was possible to make out the words.

'…didn't know where I was, how I'd got there. No memory. Something really terrible had happened, but what. I was covered in something but couldn't work that out either. Could hardly hear a thing but there was someone out there coughing. Finally realised it was me. Felt like I was totally alone, the world had gone away. Then close to, a sound, a voice that wasn't mine. Frightened me at first. Then gradually, gradually…'

He turned to her, offered a bemused look, almost a smile. She held his hand and waited for the spell to pass. Eventually he stirred and said, 'Where was I?' Mel tried to revive the subject of the book but it seemed beyond Henry's reach so she stuck to safer, everyday things. When she volunteered to tidy the kitchen, he reacted with the ghost of a smile. Instead, they decided to walk out to the local wood.

Back on the train Mel concluded the visit had done neither of them any favours. Physically exhausted, she now saw more clearly how prominently she'd figured in the failure of their marriage, and perhaps, to a degree, in what has since become of her ex-husband. Suppressing tears, she divided her attention between answering texts and visiting her photo file—in particular, Jess and Billy. They'd pronounced him 'high functioning' at the last clinic assessment; the result being he'd go to mainstream school, probably next January. Poor Henry could barely come to terms with there being anything wrong with his only grandchild. He'd cashed shares, promising Jess a fund for the therapy he didn't quite believe in.

She left the train at Hammersmith, checked out some performance dates at *The Lyric,* then let herself into the agency office. Holly's message read, 'Everything sorted and up to speed. Hope trip was OK'. Mel sat down at her desk trying to find something to do. She got up, made a coffee, returned to her desk and then, beginning to think about Royce again, unlocked the drawer and re-read his latest letter.

Dear Irish, Let's call this episode five. I went to see the rhinologist—nose man to the stars. Nice but ineffective—the sneezing goes on. This and other things confirm to me I'm the victim of a curse, so I've started seeing Madame Ruth. Have also been to see the Santa Monica police in the shape of Lieutenant Dolores Del Rey. What eyes! And the way she carries her gun! So far, the LAPD have been unable to identify the body and the lieutenant is toying with the idea of seeing copies of the sketches I sent you of the creature on the beach. You may need to take them to my solicitor, witness copies, sign forms etc. In two days, we leave the studios for shooting in New Mexico…

The policewoman had made quite an impression—he'd included three sketches of her, including her gun, which seemed overly large. The sexual thing was only too obvious but something else in the letter struck Mel again. Royce was scared, the obvious culprit the 'curse', but she couldn't help thinking it had more to do with the lieutenant. There was also a nondescript sketch of the clairvoyant.

And then she saw it on top of the unsolicited mail: a small, buff envelope bearing neat handwriting. 'Private and confidential' had been enough to deter Holly from slitting it open and reading the contents. The letter was signed Maria de Kuyper, writing from somewhere in Northwood.

Dear Mel, First an apology for seeming to hound you at Green Park station. Not my style at all but we all know what desperate times can breed…

My mum was suddenly taken ill, which brought me back in a hurry from the US. It gave me only a little time to be with her before she passed away. Since when my time has been eaten up with the funeral, tying up her estate and trying to trace my sister. I've managed none of these things with any efficiency, least of all the search.

I'll be honest. I was never really close to Jo–ju. She's ten years younger and a wayward kid. She gave Mum such a hard time they gave up on each other. But the money from the house needs to be shared between us. There's another reason I need to trace her—one day I may need some of her cells.

I'd like to send you some money, on account, right now for your services—and to cover all nuisances incurred so far. Please invoice me…

The letter concluded with a brief description of Jo-ju, some photos and a time-line full of blanks and queries.

The sisters had not met in 5 years, maybe longer. Mel re-read the letter a couple of times and found no reason to doubt the story but again it felt like she'd been singled out. It seemed not to have occurred to the writer that Mel might refuse to be of any assistance. She messaged back, declining any payment, promising that Jo-ju would figure in her next blog as well as have her name flashed across the *Twittersphere*. Then Mel thought about the Facebook friend who worked in the music business. It was quite possible Jo-ju had cut some CDs, which, if so, might be traceable by someone in the know.

She left the office and made her way towards the river to find the tideway full and pearly white under the higher, brighter clouds. The familiar river walk between Hammersmith and Chiswick was, according to her friend, Anto, something akin to Zen, and sometimes her thoughts would zero there, her mind float, but not today. She half-wished there was a rehearsal tonight. Nearer home she bought a pizza and a bottle of Pinot Noir.

Tomorrow—Saturday morning—there was a group walk-and-talk by the river, all about William Morris. Anto would be there; he could probably give the talk himself. He knew everything about almost everything.

Chapter 4

Mel exchanged the solemn atmosphere of St Paul's for the bright daylight of tourist London. Scanning the scene, floaters swirled in front of her eyes and she fished inside her bag for her sunglasses. It was just after 12.30pm. On the Tube she'd punched away at her phone non-stop. Business, friends and family. The three were often crashing into one another. 'You've got to build a wall around that agency' a friend had recommended. Of course, they were right but how could she explain she was all things to all people now? With Henry, in New York, there'd been an impermeable barrier: work one side, leisure the other.

They waved at one another then Mel made her way down toward a stock-still Helena wearing a grey suit, pearls and a cloak. Was she cross because she'd been kept waiting a few minutes? But all in a good cause, if called upon, Mel would explain. She was dimly aware of some point of etiquette: *you* came over to a Lady, not the other way around. They kissed and complimented each other on their appearance. Mel wore a modest skirt and jacket.

'Sorry, lots of attenders today. It ran on a bit,' Mel explained.

'Oh, a service. Don't apologise.'

'The Eucharist. Lovely music and it only lasts an hour.'

'I envy you.'

'You were probably having more fun with your CEO. Nice huh?' Mel said, shooting Helena a look.

'*What?*'

'Come on, Helena, even I know money doesn't work on

a Sunday.'

'But, but…' Helena stammered before the look of shock on her face dissolved and she began to squeal softly as her shoulders shook and her ring-studded fingers flew up to her face. Mel was pleased not to have lost the trick of finding her friend's funny bone. She was still in thrall to Helena's title and could deal with it only by ignoring or sending it up. As they walked in the direction of the hazy sun, Helena held a handkerchief up to her face. Mel peered at it hoping to catch a glimpse of a monogrammed H. She'd watched too many period English movies not to imagine a corner full of elaborate gold stitchwork but her view was obscured.

'How about over there?' Helena suggested with a sweep of her hand, having returned the handkerchief to her handbag.

'Fine, I'm starving.'

But, having crossed the road, Helena, with the deftest touch, steered Mel away from the burger bar towards the bistro on the corner.

'You *were* hungry, weren't you?' Helena said, halfway through her meal, Mel having demolished her pasta.

'Sorry. Rude of me. I slept in, missed breakfast. Same thing Saturday; I was supposed to meet a friend for a walk-and-talk on William Morris. Not slept too good since Friday.'

'I thought you looked tired,' Helena observed.

'Truth is… I got a little hammered Friday night.'

Their table was by a window, allowing Mel some respite from her companion's hard gaze, and a view out while she recounted Friday's visit to Henry, her worries for him. How things had gone wrong after the move to London; her feelings of guilt.

'What did Henry do after the studying?'

'Worked for the New York City Tourist Board. Loved it.'

'Couldn't you have stayed?'

'He was desperate to mend things with his daughter. He kept on and on about being an absent father. He has no other children.'

'And now there's a grandchild… with problems?' Helena said, dropping her voice.

'In some ways Billy's really quite bright, but yes, he has some difficulties with movement and communication. He relates better now thanks to this rather wonderful place he attends. It's an American organisation, lots of one-to-one, very exhausting.'

'And your ex-husband pays, yes? What about the kids without a Henry?' Helena asked.

'Local authorities pay something. Families have to make up the shortfall. There's a charity they can apply to,' Mel replied, aware that Helena had begun to ask a lot of questions about her English family. She became defensive, recalling how she was supposed to make Helena do all the talking this time. But Helena was happy enough when Mel moved to neutral subjects: news headlines, celebrities, the Olympics.

'You disappoint me, Helena,' she said at last, determined to restore the earlier teasing mood.

'Oh, God. What have I done now!' The countess looked uneasy and Mel realised her pitch had been a little shrill.

'Oh, only got my hopes up,' she said, adjusting her

voice and curling her lips.

Helena's features relaxed and she arched her eyebrows.

'Just when I thought burgers and fries, I get this little nudge,' Mel complained.

Helena looked sheepish.

'One day I'm gonna take you to the best place there is. You'll love their gourmet burgers. You'll eat and hold them with perfect English refinement. I'll be *so* proud of you!'

Helena continued to shake her head and smile while Mel twiddled her fingers and ate another invisible burger just as she'd done at the Ritz.

Then she held up her phone and said, 'Of course, I'll want to video the event.'

'No! You mustn't do that. Ever!' Helena responded in one of her deeper registers. The cabaret was over, her face had darkened. Stammering, she repeated herself, attempting to sound less severe. Unusually for her she seemed to struggle with words, stranded as she was between an apology and the 'perils of adverse publicity'. And now, reading the total bewilderment on Mel's face, she seemed to be drowning in her own embarrassment.

'So sorry. You know I'm paranoid about publicity. I… I mean the family; the estate has been on the wrong end of it more than once.

'But I'd never…'

'I know. But if they can hack the royal family…'

Not for the first time Mel had become aware of Helena's Achilles heel and was keen to let her off the hook.

'I came in for some of that once. Found myself in the papers; if that wasn't bad enough, I got trolled. Felt like I was going insane,' Mel confessed.

After comparing brief notes and expressing mutual support, their lunch date recovered its bonhomie. They both sought refuge in trivia, avoiding any reference to unwanted publicity. Mel's relief went further. If she'd ever done so she no longer saw Helena as a type, an institution. Her friend had just revealed herself as a perfectly random human being. There was almost a feeling of disappointment about it.

They had just begun to go down the series of wide steps towards the river when they were overtaken by a squadron of loud teenagers on skateboards. The noise of their wheels crashing the steps was deafening and echoed between the buildings. The two women turned to one another with half-wistful expressions. As they descended further it seemed to Mel they'd ventured a little closer into one another's physical space. Before it went much further, she needed to come clean about attending the service at St Paul's.

'Want you to know I'm not super religious. It's just sometimes I need the buzz, the bells, the atmosphere.' As a child, Mel was always drawn to the music and theatre of the church, less to its discipline and faith. The grown-ups were inclined to mistake this for piety; it pleased her parents but not her brother. His teasing was cruel and endless—she would end up a nun.

'Neither am I. And don't be fooled into thinking I'm super moral either. The charity work is a sort of penance—I used to help rich people get even richer. That was my job. And I was very good at it.'

'Is that how you met your… the…?' Mel was trying to

find the correct term for her Lord and spouse. *Husband* didn't seem to carry the full pomp, and *Count*, she knew, was wrong.

Helena laughed. 'No, no. He was a merchant banker. We used to get on the train at the same station. We got talking about money one day.'

'How romantic!' Mel joked.

'Well, we had to start somewhere! Now we're both fully reformed characters,' she said, returning the irony.

They were on the flat concourse leading to the Millennium Bridge when a wave of loud music like stereo emitted from every direction: Abba. The music swirled between the buildings as if from multiple speakers at an outdoor rock concert. Then the volume plummeted, the source seeming to move away but remain just audible. Helena's lack of reaction spurred Mel into thinking up an idea she quickly rejected—the burger bar would be challenge enough.

The sun's diffuse glare had increased considerably but carried with it no warmth. A breeze was blowing down the Thames against which Mel's thin jacket was no match. She looked down at the swirling river and felt a shiver coming on. A large pleasure boat was heading east, its hull corkscrewing in the tide.

'I felt that,' Helena said. 'Come on, allow me to protect you from the elements.'

Mel was grateful for her friend's taller, fuller more sensibly dressed frame into which she snuck, escaping the worst of the wind. With their arms about each other they were still able to set a brisk pace to the south side of the river. On the way, Mel began to sing rather breathlessly, *London Bridge is Falling Down,* explaining that this was one of the many songs she sang to Billy, that bridges held a fascination for him. It brought on a fit of coughing.

'Oh, go on then. I'm such an old pleb, Mel. Give me portraits, landscapes, the Dutch golden age any day.'

Helena had shown little enthusiasm for Tate Modern but was finally persuaded to 'tag along' by Mel's imposing a time limit—forty minutes max. Then they could sit down again and enjoy more coffee before Helena had to return to another round of business.

'Sure, I do prefer the National,' Mel said, 'Billy loves it too but he's hard work. We take turns holding him up in front of the paintings. He spends an age looking at them. At home he talks non-stop about the colours, the detail. It's all there in his head but he hasn't quite got the words to express…'

'Don't we all have a bit of that?' Helena proposed.

Later, in the shop, Mel was surprised to find Helena buying a number of postcards all featuring modern art. Over coffee she scribbled notes on the back of her purchases. She'd also written down the name of the charity Mel had innocently referred to at the bistro. On reflection, it was clear it had been wheedled out of her with a certain professional expertise.

Returning Mel's earlier enquiry, Helena asked how she'd met her husband.

'Henry was working in the South Tower. He got out minutes before it collapsed. The agency where I worked wanted someone to go see what was happening. At the time the best guess was a movie or a terrible accident. I volunteered. Don't ask me why.'

The way Helena was nodding said *please tell me more*.

'I still get mixed up about how things came out. My therapist always said I was caught between consciously forgetting and unconsciously remembering.'

'I'm so sorry. It was clumsy of me to have asked about that.'

'It's okay. Henry? I saw this bunch of grey stuff sprawled out on the ground. Turned out he was covered in a thick layer of dust. Did what I could to get it off of him. The doctors said he'd be fine apart from some amnesia. They were right in a way. After beating his height phobia, he drew a line under the whole thing. Never went back to being a broker. We married in 2002.'

'Ever been?' Mel asked, thinking *enough of me*.

'Yes, it was before all that, the 90s,' Helena said, her voice dropping a little, her eyes contracting as if she was having trouble recalling some aspect of the busy three or four days spent there with her husband. Perhaps it wasn't their favourite place, Mel thought. But when quizzed, the must-see sights got good ratings.

'And what about dear ole Broadway? Did you catch a show?'

'Yes. I'm trying to remember… It was… I'm sure it was *Mamma Mia*. Yes, that's right. A lovely show. We really ought to do more in our quiet season.'

Mel was about to offer her services as a ticket agent when she remembered Helena's description of herself and hubby: *country bumpkins*. Did that mean that nothing in the theatre would interest them? The thought of luring her aristocratic friend into a rock concert now seemed totally absurd. Then Helena remembered Mel's show and asked how it had gone.

'Magic! The last night was a full house.'

Just before they parted—by the Millennium bridge, Helena was apologetic again about her 'plebeian tendencies.' She was indebted to Mel for the opportunity to discover some 'modern stuff' she actually liked. Whether or not she was building on this, what followed came right out of the blue.

'Next time we meet, it's a burger, right? And there's something I want to talk over with you. Don't look so shocked.' She laughed then took Mel firmly by the shoulders. As they kissed goodbye, Helena's taut arms held Mel rooted for a while. On her release she could register little more than sounds of surprise and intrigue and while she twisted about in her confusion her friend reached inside her cloak and produced a colouring book.

'For Billy. Give him a kiss from me.'

With that she turned and strode up the approach, waved, then mounted the bridge. Mel watched the upright figure sail through the crowd until it was lost in the mass of people crossing the Thames. Her instincts told her to run after Helena and demand to know what was wrong and not wait until 'next time' for an explanation. Instead, she began to walk west towards Southwark Tube station trying to analyse her friend's memory lapses, hoping to chance on some innocent explanation.

It had all started with talk of the opening ceremony of the 2012 Olympics. Mel had watched it on TV and, four years on, could still recall most of the scenes and their chronology. Helena had been there in person but could remember little of the stardust moments. Only two days on from Henry and Mel was again disguising her leading questions, hoping not to catch her subject out. And then the sketchy date for *Mamma Mia*! If there was one occasion Mel knew something about it was that particular opening night—October 18 2001, the famous Winter Garden Theatre. Not that she was able to get her hands on tickets for the premiere, but a few nights later she'd taken Henry to the show.

She texted Jess, saying she was on her way. Her mind had become a battleground between two preoccupations—what to say about Henry: what to think about Helena. Perhaps there was a connection.

Chapter 5

Mel would always be a hostage to her unruly imagination. With it came a never-ending range of desperate scenarios and pulse-racing finales while routine life went on around her. They played out the 'worst of all possible worlds', to misquote *Candide*, occasionally, the best. There wasn't much middle ground among her fictive thoughts.

Helena's fate appeared to hang in the balance—until Mel, on the spur of the moment, decided to intervene by googling 'memory lapses, age 50'. By the time she got off the train at Willesden Green, the possibility of a more upbeat explanation for Helena's confusion had materialised. Her friend might be a sufferer, she'd read, of stress, insomnia or some side-effect of medication. She was so relieved not to have made a fool of herself on the Millennium Bridge. There was still some cause for concern but the shadow cast by Henry's condition—her faithful companion these last two days and nights—had lifted a little. Now there was just the small matter of reporting back to Jess.

She had only a short walk to the small apartment but the wind that had blown all day was now laced with a fine, swirly rain. The drop in temperature and the smell of wet streets was apparent as soon as she stepped off the train. In her morning muddle she'd come out without an umbrella. After untying her chiffon scarf, she improvised a head dress and set off up the High Road at a rate of knots. By the time she reached the Victorian terrace, her carefully coiffed side bangs were wet and threatening to curl. In the weeks before the face-job she'd grown her bob long to camouflage the suture lines. Waiting at the door she was aware of her breathing and an ache in her chest.

'You're soaked! Come in the kitchen, I'll light the gas, get you a hair dryer.'

'Feels like I ran here.' Mel gasped, 'Doing my asthma no favours.'

'All right?' Jess asked, sounding concerned as she took charge of the wet scarf.

'Just upped the inhalers. Not kicked in yet,' Mel said, following Jess into the tiny kitchen diner. Once the oven was lit Mel drew up a chair and waited for the towel and hairdryer. When Jess returned alone, she asked about Billy.

'In Legosphere I call it. He's building a robot for you. You're not allowed to see it, or him, until it's complete. He needs a bit of help with the really small pieces, gets frustrated. We've had tears and… words he doesn't really understand.' Jess grimaced briefly before her smile returned. 'I love your hair. The lob makes you look so young.'

'Ah, come on, Jess, you must have worked out by now I've had a face job. Nice to hear you say *young* though. *That's* why I grew my hair long. See, I need to fight back— my MD says I'm nearing the perimenopause.'

'What the hell's that?'

'Don't really know. She just said get as much sex as you can.'

They laughed.

'It was just a mini, and I got rid of some moles at the same time.' Mel explained, 'They don't even put you out. That's where I met *her*, the lady I've been telling you about. Titled. We had identical bandages. She's kind of awesome, but nice with it, got this presence, you know, like a stage actor. We get on fine but she terrifies me. Or did so until today when she came over sort of fragile. The estate's in Hampshire.'

'Bet you get an invite: Do come down and kill some poor, harmless creature.'

'She knows I'm not into that. She likes to escape to town. Does some business in the city. You're giving me such a hard stare, Jess.'

'You look great, but you looked great before,' Jess said.

'I work around young people all day.'

'I swear it's more the hair. Bet Dad was wowed. So… how did that go?'

It had come at last, the moment that Mel had over-rehearsed. She wasn't cut out for this messenger malarkey and yet Jess would expect, *deserve* nothing less than the truth, whatever that was. By the time the oven was turned off in the tiny room she'd become feverishly hot. She switched off the hair dryer and began, 'Right. OK…'

She started by saying how much younger Henry appeared than she'd expected. With greater honesty she said she could vouch for the fact he was mostly on the ball—except for trivia, she'd caught him out a few times there, but discreetly. It was unfortunate they'd irritated each other towards the end of the meeting. It was an easy decision not to mention the 'flashback'.

'My impression is—for what it's worth—your dad's depressed. But that might just be a reaction to the other thing. He seems to have retreated into his shell, cut out the old crowd. The vibes I got were all coming from Control Headquarters – Davina. Sounds bitchy, huh? See I'm not so sweet after all. I should feel sorry for her, but don't. Think I made myself unpopular by lecturing him on getting out more. Was I fighting him or Davina, or both? The one bright spot is he's gone back to writing the book, which I took pains to encourage.'

'So grateful to you, Mel. It was a big ask, I know. Thank you. I need to speak to the GP, catch Davina on her own, then quietly sit down with Dad.'

Mel began to smile while, unknown to Jess, Billy came stealing into the room triumphantly holding up the completed robot.

'Look. And I did all the little bits.'

'Did you, sweetheart. Come show me.'

It was classic Billy – head on one side, the opposite arm outstretched as though he was about to dance or fly. When he got really excited, he'd go up on his toes but today, as he lunged towards her, he kept his heels down. She gave him a hug before taking possession of the figure. After articulating its head, arms and legs she met his palm with hers in a high five, praising his handiwork.

'Got something for you. A friend of mine sent you this.'

She pulled out the colouring book. Its pages were full of well-known icons of modern art in outline. Billy flicked through it and registered puzzlement.

'You remember all those pictures in the big art gallery,' Mel explained. 'Well, these are pictures *without* any colour. That's where *you* come in. You can use any colours you want. Shall we get your crayons out and do some together?'

'Great idea!' Jess announced, suggesting the two artists move to the 'studio' next door while she did a quick tidy before getting the supper ready for five o'clock.

In the far corner of the lounge stood the dressmaker's dummy, now clothed—Jess had been busy—with a half-worked wedding gown. It was a rare coup now for Jess to get a commission; most of her work was alterations.

For the next hour, Mel's sense of time stalled and her energy levels ebbed out of her. She played with her charge by the low table, on the floor and on the settee. Together they coloured in their Miros, Picassos and Rothkos. Billy was diverted for all of ten minutes before he bunked off to his favourite card game, making up his own version of the rules. After dealing, he laid out his cards, face up, in a long line while Mel held hers close to her chest promising not to look at her opponent's hand. The rules seemed to change with every game, which Billy always won. Next, they played with cars and trains, then he showed her his collection of football stickers. Mel's knowledge of soccer was such a void, Billy decided the best way to make up for this was to start a game on the carpet there and then. It was a relief when he declared himself the winner and asked Mel to hum tunes to him instead. This was their unique intimacy – Mel singing or humming while Billy, fascinated by the vibrations, took gentle hold of her nose. It was after this interlude that Mel became aware of a question forming on her step-grandson's face.

'Did you ever delete anyone, Mel?'

Struggling to intuit the question, she briefly thought of the art colouring book and then, with a shock, an altogether darker interpretation.

'No, no, Billy! That is a terrible thing, which I would never do. No. Never. Let's not talk about this anymore.'

What was this leading up to? Guns in America? Terrorism? Crime? To her immense relief he appeared satisfied with her answer although he showed neither relief nor disappointment that she was no killer. And then with flawless timing Jess commanded them to wash hands and come for supper – pasta again!

Set for three, a small table with folding legs had materialised out of the kitchen cupboards. Billy sat between Mel and his mum. He didn't eat pasta of any description, much less pasta with a spicy sauce. His plate was compartmentalised into four and contained alphabet 'fries', carrots, small dices of cheese and a pile of blueberries. As per usual he was making heavy work of his modest compartments when Mel delved into her bag and produced a chocolate wafer cookie. Jess's reaction was a mix of shock and surprise.

'Sorry, I should've cleared this with you first. Can he just have a taste?'

Jess appeared to give her assent and Mel placed it in front of Billy after first taking a tiny bite and going, 'Mmm.' He picked it up, smelt it then followed Mel's example. The two women held their breath while he was trying to decide whether he liked it or not. Jess took it out of his hand.

'You can have the rest when you've finished this lot,' she said, pointing to his compartments.

After the meal Jess ran the bath while Mel, having discovered a second wind, read Billy a story. Upstairs, once she'd helped him out of his clothes, he jigged about in a selection of his mother's hats, modelling each one in turn in front of Jess's bedside mirror, evidently pleased with his appearance and fluent performance. Finally, the mania passed and he submitted to his bath and Mel's supervision—her first.

His slender, perfect body, blond hair and gabbling playfulness brought a lump to her throat. As long as she sparred and fooled with him, she was saved from analysing her emotions too deeply. She was well aware she was seeing the best side of him today; he could kick off when deadlines approached. As it was, he allowed her to assist with teeth cleaning, towelling him dry and getting him into his pull-ups and pyjamas. It seemed he was giving the new hand an easy ride, and after hugs and kisses he was ready for Mum and more bedtime stories.

When Jess joined Mel in the lounge, they exchanged expressions of quiet exhaustion.

'I'm knackered. How do you cope *and* work?' Mel asked.

'I tell myself it'll get better, easier. It *has* really since he started at the centre. Thanks to dear old Dad's help. And you were a star today.'

'Have I still got the job, then?'

'Afraid so. Did he… say anything weird?'

'No,' Mel replied. 'Sorry about the cookie. I used to love them as a kid.'

They talked a while about fashion, the news, the week ahead. Mel was due to visit a two-day networking event and had a meeting lined up with a casting director. Otherwise, apart from giving a talk to some drama students, her daybook was quiet, which was good news for the asthma. She phoned for a taxi and when it arrived felt a twinge of guilt as she hugged Jess goodbye. As she'd hoisted Billy out of the bath he said quite casually, almost like a jingle, 'Daddy's dead. Daddy's dead'. She'd pretended not to hear and soon he was rabbiting on about anything and everything else.

Chapter 6

Mel got off at Turnham Green and made her way to the corner flower stall. Everywhere was slipping into darkness, hard edges were blurring, lights were going on. But looking up, pastel clouds drifted across a twilight sky.

Scanning the blooms, she realised she'd forgotten the name of the flower but knew exactly what it was she wanted—two bunches of the exotic-looking, stripy ones.

'Alstroemerias! One of my favourites,' said a voice behind her as she was completing her purchase. She spun round to find Anto beaming at her. They hugged and joked about Mel's C minus in horticulture.

'One's for you,' she said, 'for that lovely revue in the Herald.'

'Thank you. It wrote itself.'

Anto looked better than when they'd last met. After Marty left, he became a recluse and would rarely answer texts or the door when she called. He went to stay with his parents before Christmas and didn't come back for a couple of months. Fortunately, there didn't seem to be much art, culture or entertainment worthy of his pen while he was away. Now he was back to writing his columns and posting his blogs.

'Fancy a drink?' he asked.

'Can we make that eats as well. I'm starving. Don't feel like cooking.'

While Anto collared one of the waiters Mel found an unreserved table, set down the flowers on it and studied the menu. The bistro was full of loud voices and laughter.

Anto rejoined her, bringing two makeshift vases to the table then got into the groove with a medley of silly voices and political satire. She'd missed his comedic turns. A bottle of red arrived with some olives. She might have preferred something long and cool.

'Cheers! Mel, you were pitch-perfect, but to single you out would have gone against all my journalistic principles.'

'I'm relieved you didn't. Cheers.'

Before the food arrived, the conversation, or rather Anto's, moved to weightier matters: the EU referendum, the opposing camps, their campaigns.

'Not so long ago the EU was barely an issue. Then it was all those poor migrants on the move and what crawls out of the woodwork? Whatever you call it, it's no way to decide economic policy.'

It was vintage Anto—sieging from minor to major and back without taking breath. Whether or not he'd stopped hurting over Marty was what she really wanted to know about—not boring Brexit. She was only too relieved to be on the side lines, a complete neutral. She said nothing and he took the hint.

'Your voice is in great shape. How d'you manage that?' Anto asked.

'Still do regular exercises *and* sing to my little man.'

Mel described her new role-to-be in Billy's life, how she was half panicking, half excited about the responsibility. If she lost control of her charge, or rather *when* she lost control, she'd just sing his favourite song.

'Which is…?' Anto enquired.

'Can you believe it—*Bewitched, Bothered and Bewildered.* I think it's the sound of the words as much as the music.'

'Then a very sophisticated four-year-old,' Anto said as the waitress brought their dishes to the table and conversation took a back seat for a while. Mel's hunger was almost painful but she willed herself to empty her plate a little at a time. She still hadn't gotten over the embarrassment of speed-eating her lunch in front of Helena. She was also careful to sip her wine slowly; Anto was ahead by two or three glasses and might want a sober ear later to listen to 'life after Marty'.

Last summer they were the fun foursome. Marty and Pretty Boy were stagehands at the National. Floyd, not even his real name, was known to everyone but Mel by his nickname. He moonlighted as a model. Mel and Floyd, still in his twenties, were an inconstant item. By contrast Marty and Anto seemed well on the way to shaping a future together. The four would often wind up at Mel's, her rooftop terrace the perfect setting, weather allowing, for barbecues and drinks.

The split, she guessed, had to be down to their age difference, having had at least one such relationships fold that way. Did her intuition go further? It seemed like Anto had quite often brought the word 'adoption' into the conversation, but unobtrusively like the passing notes in a piece of music. Underneath the bluster he was quite a private person but then, for reasons she'd admit to nobody, so was Mel Giammetti. Perhaps she was beginning to read him better. Did that mean he could read her too?

As it happened there was no talk of Marty. On the walk back the conversation never got above mundane. Anto offered to give her lifts again to the supermarket; they talked briefly about a possible make-over for her roof top terrace and parted at Mel's, Anto's house only two streets away. Then, before she could open her door, he'd backtracked and was asking, 'You free at the week end?'

'A trip to the gym, otherwise, yeah, not much on.'

'That walk-and-talk you missed. How about I rehash the lecture but we go the other way? In fact, all the way to Kew Gardens, then back by train. There's lots to see.'

'Didn't really take it in last year, did I? Count me in.'

She thought it a good sign—Anto returning to didactic mode. He'd enjoy bringing William Morris to life, and thinking about Kew, she couldn't help smiling— he'd said something about her knowledge of plants being in special measures. Last time, she and Floyd had behaved badly and irritated him.

After checking her media feeds and watching TV she began to wonder what Marty had seen—sexual attraction apart—in Anto. Thinking back to what had first struck *her*—the pop-eyes behind the glasses, the podgy baby-face, the slightly eccentric walk. It all read of a need to conceal some inner flaw. Then his twin, the entertainer, would step from the shadows and be condescending and funny at the same time. Tonight, she realised, he'd worn his vulnerability lightly.

Asking about trains for *Bi-ces-ter* had drawn a lost expression from the face at the ticket office until Mel indicated somewhere a little to the north of Oxford.

'You mean *Bicester*.'

'Do I? How're you spelling that?'

The old saw about the disjunct between English spelling and pronunciation occupied her thoughts for barely a minute of the journey. She had more important things on her mind, chief of which was a run-through of her spiel. Her pitches to drama students followed an established formula: resumé, presentation, sprinkling of anecdotes, questions from the floor, Amen. Lots of questions meant she was doing fine and the stories might even spill over into coffee time. Her performance was *'school of the heart'*, and in that vein she'd disclose meeting her English husband in New York, September 11 2001. A student once observed that it came over like flash fiction and asked, 'Were you anywhere near the Twin Towers?'

Looking out her window she reflected once again that, outside London, England was a green country of low hills and, depending on season, leafy woodlands. You never went for long before passing through a town. In between lay tidy villages centred round ancient churches and old, if not always ancient, buildings. The hills were just beginning to shrink and level out onto a wider plain when a déjà vu coldly informed her she'd ridden this track before, seen these hills and woods roll by in a previous life. She turned to the car interior for clues, stared at her ticket, scanned fields and hedges. Somewhere between catching her breath and thinking she was about to wheeze, a light came on. *This* was the route the Stratford train had taken that day, only she'd gotten off somewhere and waited for a connecting train. Her uncertain grasp of English geography and railroads had made no link between today's trip and the telltale day return to Stratford-upon-Avon. Had she given a recent biography of Will Shakespeare a thought she might have recalled that from his horse he'd have been familiar with this stretch of country as he rode from London to Oxford and beyond into Warwickshire.

Her brain had all but wiped the journey to and from Stratford. What remained as sharp as a woodcut were her meetings with Royce, his prevarications, the realization there was someone else, there would always be someone else. Until then she'd warmed to the town's timber frames, old brick, its riverbank scenes and boats. She was there and back in a day that rivalled any of the days—and nights—Lennie had shown late or not at all. She no longer visited jazz clubs and had no plans ever to return to Stratford. She chewed gum and meditated on the innocent docility of cows and the mindlessness of sheep.

'After all you know, you're still in love' Holly had recently remarked, never afraid to air her point of view. 'Don't be ridiculous' didn't sound convincing enough. For sure, she didn't *love* him, but 'in love' might not be so far from the case. She was arguably the actor's greatest fan and still capable of conflating the man with his more sympathetic roles.

Just before boarding the train home, Mel, after making enquiries, decided it was only right to break her journey and tell Jess exactly what Billy had said. She'd tried talking it out with herself but the unease that had beset her last Sunday showed no sign of letting up. Billy's reference to homicide had so alarmed her she was scared to tell Jess *and* wanted to protect her at the same time. How rational was that? Ever since the white lie, Mel had been nagged by the possibility she'd glimpsed some dark corner of Billy's mind that needed to be drawn out into the open.

More alarm bells rang when she read Jess's text dissuading her from visiting. Billy was out of control and a neighbour had complained.

She got out at Wembley but it wasn't the right Wembley station for Willesden. She'd have to walk or get a cab. There were none in sight. She texted:

So sorry. Am close. Need to tell you something. Won't stay. M x

There was no response, and Mel trudged on towards the other Wembley station trying to carry in her head the best interpretation of Jess's silence.

The apartment was quiet, the door ajar. She gave it a nervous push and entered the tiny space realtors like to style a hall. Jess was stooped by the flimsy concertina doors to the lounge, listening intently. She indicated to Mel to keep hush and make some tea, which came as some relief and made her feel instantly useful, if confused. If Billy was asleep, why couldn't his mum be with him?

The kitchen smelt of ripe melon. She looked for teacups and, finding none, rinsed two mugs and squeezed a teabag between them. She thought of the Ritz and smiled—Helena's masterclass in the art of tea drinking it wasn't. Jess joined her; she looked worn and red-eyed.

'Thanks, Mel. Lou's here.'

'Who?'

'From the centre. I panic-phoned and they could hear him. *We're coming right round*, they said.'

The protocols, she explained, didn't always work and today her patience and cool were in short supply. She'd given Billy several countdowns to hand-washing and tea. Absorbed in a game he'd remained non-compliant and the trouble that followed was all down to *Mister Bugger.* Jess explained that this silent, invisible person was the bane of Billy's life, his bogeyman and an arch-baddy who often stole from Billy. Her son had no doubt heard the word on her lips more than once, and out of that the fiend, Mr B had come to life to torment them both.

'Then it got out of hand. I should have handled it better. He started smashing things and—we've been there before—scratching and biting himself.'

'Poor boy! Poor you!' Mel said, sandwiching Jess's hand in hers, their conversation collapsing into a heavy silence. And then there was Lou announcing his presence with a discrete *ahem*. He wore jeans and a kids-friendly T-shirt, his hair sandy and short. He gestured to Jess to follow him back to the lounge. He had an easy, bouncy manner into which Mel read a whole chapter of hope.

Left alone, she felt redundant and looked around for something to do. After opening a few cupboards, she located the dustpan and brush then turned her attention to the mess in one corner of the kitchen floor. Billy's potato 'alphabets', blueberries and little carrot pieces were a colourful collage against the grey lino. It resembled appliqué art and, without thinking, she took out her phone and snapped it.

She got out more fruit, chopped up a carrot and de-frosted some 'alphabets', guessing they included some of his favourite letters. Mel was hoping against hope that Billy would be calm enough to eat. His appetite was not good at the best of times, and this time round she had no chocolate cookie to offer him.

'You can't be Mel. She's a grandma,' Lou said, returning and introducing himself.

Mel responded with, 'Thought I'd start early.'

He laughed and seemed to look her up and down, his athletic frame never entirely still.

'Billy tells me you can sing through your nose.'

'Would that help?'

'Sounds like a great idea. Might keep that in mind.'

As well as dipping into the surreal, they were both trying to sound English when it was quite obvious, they came from opposite ends of the same continent. How would *he* pronounce *Bicester?* This was her big chance to flag up her concerns about Billy and she went about her mission at some pace. The psychologist neither reacted nor interrupted, just nodded professionally until she'd finished. Then he asked if she'd ever met Billy's dad.

'Never. He lives in Germany. Rarely visits.'

'About Billy—we think it's mainly linguistic. For instance: say he's not seen someone for a while, then they're 'dead', but they can still show up again and it's all right. Sometimes he ranks the sound of a word above its meaning. *Delete* could be one of those words. I guess he might get into poetry one day.'

He thanked her for her concerns, apologised for being unable to stay longer and, after inviting her to visit the centre, picked up his cycle helmet and left for volleyball training. Her default surveillance system recorded a wedding ring.

In no time Mel and Billy were giving each other a long hug, after which he was so sweetly apologetic, she struggled with her emotions, turning his contrition into something positive.

'You know Mum loves you. You gotta eat to be strong.'

Deals were struck; high fives enacted, and with less prompting than usual Billy ate the simple tea Mel had prepared. Any other night he might have insisted she bathe him and read him a story but tonight he was pleased for Mum to reclaim her rights. In the bath he blew off what Jess called 'botty pops,' and the bubbles caused everyone to laugh.

'Saw Dad on Tuesday,' Jess began after they'd both scoffed half a pizza and re-filled their glasses.

'Did you discuss…'

'It wasn't like that. He turned up at the shop, walked from the museum. We had a quick lunch break. He was into himself, rambly like. Talked about you.'

'Oh, heaven…'

'Why *did* you go to Hollywood so often?'

'What! It was my job. The agency sent me. Your dad was okay about all that. Look, we were happy then.'

'I know. It came across that time I stayed with you. It's just… he brought it up. He said, "Was that when it all started to go wrong?" I said he was into himself. I tried to put him right.'

Mel was stung into silence. She'd half expected something like this, some twisting of the truth with time and the loss of neurones from Henry's brain. It cast her in an unflattering light, one no doubt nurtured by the virtuous Davina.

'Out of interest,' Jess began again, 'what was the Hollywood business all about?'

'Movie stars on Broadway! It sounded crazy at the time but the agency did a lot of profiling, groundwork etc. and I was chosen to go out and sell it soft, hard, whatever. Not before they'd given me a makeover I might add—clothes, make-up, hair.' Mel sighed, remembering her Tinseltown days. 'Of course, the agency had a branch in Hollywood but no one there was much into musical theatre.'

'Dad was jealous?'

'No way. He loved to meet me off the plane like *I* was the movie star, when all I wanted was to kick off the heels and get into jeans and sweats.'

Jess was nodding and smiling. She seemed to want to hear more about this 'golden age' her dad had lived through, a period she'd had precious little to do with. But Mel was beginning to experience a familiar affliction and longed instead for the present tense.

'Hey, what a hunk. He can analyse me *any* day,' she said.

'He's a *child* psychologist,' Jess replied.

'Yup, he makes me feel so young.'

'Married to a beautiful wife, also a psychologist. She's Hispanic or Puerto Rican.'

'I hate her already.' Mel's deadpan responses suddenly gave way to infectious giggling.

Now they were both relaxed, it was time to go over, yet again, next week's dates and times—exactly when and where Mel would pick up Billy, occupy and give him his lunch. She'd been to the nursery, met the staff and had had her photo taken. Before she left, Mel deemed it polite to ask after Jess's mother.

'They're never at home! Always off cruising or it's dance holidays. We get down there when we can; Billy loves the sea.'

Everyone in her carriage, couples included, were occupied with phones, listening to playlists or making calls: into their own worlds. Mel closed her eyes and entered hers.

It was still a good call she'd made to break her journey,

even if the steep learning curve had been just that. Jess had lost her cool, but who was to say Mel would keep hers? One day Billy would likely trash *her* emotions, but she was family now and would have to learn to live with that. It was naïve of her to think her songs would magic away any meltdown. She looked out, fighting a compulsion to follow the cabling by the track that always tended to make her feel dizzy and nauseous. Relief came with the loss of light when the train went underground. She got out her ear pods, placed them and began to listen to her audiobook.

Chapter 7

The Lyric Theatre—just around the corner from the agency—was a handy venue. Meeting to do Friday lunch at the roof garden, Mel fancied, would settle all her intrigues about the woman—where was she working in the US, and why, if they weren't close, was she so keen to trace her sister?

Maria was sitting by a tree fern, an empty wine glass on the table. She had on dual colour jeans—blue and black—and a red leather top. Seeing Mel, she sprang from her seat, her long-lost-friend smile attractive, if slightly forced. The woman's cleavage and trim waistline more than complemented her six-foot stature. The bottle-blond hair gave her a Nordic look. There was something theatrical—Mel had suspected it before—about her demeanour.

'In anything at the moment?' Mel ventured.

'You guessed! Or did you look me up?' Maria replied, bemusement accompanying her smile.

'Negative. The voice, the body language…'

Finding they both worked in the same business, the need for further preliminaries swiftly disappeared, whereupon Maria picked up a menu and asked, 'What do you fancy for lunch? The avocado hummus and flatbread looks good.'

'I'll go with that.'

'Drink?'

'Soft, please,' Mel replied.

'Mmm… me too,' Maria said, heading for the bar.

Looking the woman up first would have sent the

wrong message; Mel was anxious to portray a degree of aloofness. She'd been more exercised about whether her hunch was right. It seemed the tables had reversed—her lunch date was arguably now the more apprehensive party.

The meal and small talk went down pleasantly enough. Lunch at work was, by contrast, minimal and quiet—nothing more than a sandwich, which Mel and Holly ate with a mug of tea at their desks.

'So, you've been working in the US, Maria.'

'Right. I was a day player at Universal. And then, *ahem*, I went to San Fernando Valley.'

'Porn?' Mel inquired without inflecting her voice.

'Just a look and see. It was all part of my grand scheme to direct erotic movies—shorts, and who knows, maybe one day a feature. I've got scripts, people, locations. In the middle of all this my mum gets ill and sadly dies. There'll be some money from the house, but it won't be enough. I've pitched to a few suits.'

'Is porn really the best way into erotica?'

'Good question, Mel. Put it this way: it was a perfect lesson in how *not* to do erotica. But I'm taking up your time and I still need to ask another favour. Sorry.'

So it wasn't *just* a thank-you for offering to trace her wayward sister! Mel braced herself for more demands on her services and—assuming she had any left—good nature.

'I wondered,' Maria went on, 'if you knew a film maker, really an auteur. Someone into shorts, someone I could tech-talk with. I'd pay for their time.'

'I know *someone*—but whether she'd be willing... I can only ask,' Mel replied. It was an unusual request, but then, how *did* actors successfully migrate from one side of the camera to the other?

'I'm so grateful to you. Say, didn't you play Mimi Marquez in that early production of *Rent*?'

'I have to work hard now to remember things like that,' Mel joked. It restored Maria's winning smile and for the first time she looked totally at ease. It was time to ask about what sort of cells she needed off her sister.

'It's an option I might never need,' Maria explained without really explaining anything, 'and then there's the money from the house I'll have to put aside. Tempting to call it a loan,' she added, her smile, once again deserting her.

There was one more big question to clear up. Had Mel been 'head-hunted'?

'No way! It's just I saw you once or twice with that little guitar and I knew you'd be good for me. What you thought of *me* I don't care to ask.'

Despite her earlier reservations, Mel found herself taking to this tall stranger, though not everything she'd heard added up. Maybe that was it—the woman had revealed as much of herself as she'd concealed: classic intrigue device.

Back at the agency Mel couldn't wait to ransack every source, file and reference relating to Maria de Kuyper, who must have already gone through a reciprocal process. The ensuing heavy silence was too much for Holly who started to cross question her about the mystery woman.

Maria had worked in provincial theatre, had had a few small roles in TV and appeared in two or three movies, one of which a critic had dubbed 'gonzo-erotic' and 'cultish'. And then, almost by accident, Mel unearthed an undated snippet linking Maria with an RSC production of the Scottish play.

Come Saturday morning the sun was highlighting the buds on the trees in the street as Mel made her way to Anto's house, a neat semi a little nearer the river. The front garden was all Zen—small statues in gravel. She'd never seen the back of the house and had barely set foot inside. They exchanged notes about the flowers she'd bought.

'What do they remind you of?' she asked.

'It's the whiskers—as if painted on. Cats, of course.'

'With me it's Cats, the musical.'

As soon as they joined the river path, Anto set the scene—1880s Hammersmith, time lines, local and national issues, then fleshed out the man, William Morris, of whom Mel pretended a little more knowledge than she possessed. She'd not even visited Kelmscott House, let alone bothered to look him up on Wikipedia. At times Anto would employ the first person, taking on the character of his subject.

He was the perfect didact and knew it, only no one was supposed to remind him he'd once been a schoolteacher, a *broken* schoolteacher was how he'd once put it, rebuffing any further enquiry or discussion of the subject. Except that Mel had, more than once tried with all good intentions to break the embargo and received short shrift for her pains. That didn't mean she'd stop trying.

The first stop on their itinerary of Kew was the Japanese garden, around which they moved with such languor it felt like a Buddhist meditation had settled over them, or rather Anto. He had once taught English in Japan and, from what little Mel could glean, it seemed to have been a contented, rewarding period.

In perfect silence they drifted some ways apart and occasionally Mel would look up to see her companion hunkered down to better contemplate the physical symbols and, for all she knew, enjoy communing with the spirits. Mel was capable of no such abstractions; she was blown away instead by the delicate white blossom which she photographed from different angles. It took her mind off Maria. There would have to be another meeting—and soon. Mel had lost no time making the connection: Maria and the Stratford 2014 RSC programme.

When Anto came out of his trance he announced that the Palm House was next on the list. Approaching it, they were greeted by a mass of deep red tulips that contrasted with the blue of the lake. When, last summer, the four of them had come on a trip to the gardens, she knew next to nothing about flowers. Neither she nor Floyd took much notice of them. He kept looking instead for somewhere to go dogging. Anto was uncharacteristically irritated, likening them to inattentive, badly-behaved children. Perhaps they'd reminded him of something from his 'broken' period.

After the scented sauna of the glasshouse rainforest, it was time for the cherry walk—an avenue of blossom, and a slow-moving procession of visitors that seemed to stretch forever. Small birds chirruped noisily, and once more, Mel angled her phone to capture ever better compositions of blossom and sky. Almost everybody else was busy doing likewise, to which Anto registered a harrumph of disapproval. Raising his voice, he said, 'Blossom time is revered in Japan, where it amounts to a philosophical and religious experience.' For the benefit of those within earshot, he gave the proper Japanese term, which Mel, however hard she tried, promptly forgot. She was trying to take a photo of a bird perched in a tree to show Billy.

'Enjoy while you may,' he said, coldly.

'Oh, *yeah*. These images will last forever, Mel countered, 'and what about all the art?'

'Life is not art.'

'Has a helluva lot to do with it,' she said, beaming at him. What was eating Anto? Instead of asking him or responding to his provocative remark, she gave him a little hug after which they both preserved silence for a while. She knew of course.

As soon as they sat down in the orangery and ordered soup, Mel lost no time in telling Anto about Helena.

'Why Mel, sounds like you're in love.' But before she'd risen to the bait he quickly added, '… with the aristocracy.' She was still left quietly fuming until he'd backtracked and she'd explained that titles meant nothing to her, that the woman was not so different 'from the rest of us'. She wasn't going to give him the satisfaction of being even half right.

Over soup, 'normal service' was restored and the talk turned to Billy and then Mel's terrace project. She confessed she had no idea about where to begin or what she really wanted.

'Think of an Italian garden, then scale it down,' Anto explained.

'A what?'

'Show you some pictures after lunch.'

At the station Anto disappeared for a minute then returned with a mix of magenta and orange tulips. She'd gone on a bit about the flowers by the lake.

'Gorgeous colours, thank you,' Mel enthused, giving him a hug.

While they waited for the train, Anto handed over his phone so she could view the sort of gardens he had in mind.

'Way too grand for my purpose,' she protested.

'Let me just take some measurements over tea, will you?'

It had only taken a few casual mentions—the idea of some greenery and flowers for her rather featureless roof terrace, and in a flash Anto was all over it. 'You want symmetry, statues, a water feature. Lavender's a must.'

'A lot to think about,' was all she could muster as their train arrived.

While Anto was busy with his phone for the short journey, Mel zoned out—or tried to. Disturbing her 'moment of Zen', as she sarcastically put it, he insisted she look at just one more garden.

'Don't scroll. Just guess who owns it.'

Mel had seen enough of horticulture for one day and, handing back the phone, made a face.

'*Thought* you'd be interested,' he said, returning the sarcasm, 'it belongs to your countess!'

Next Tuesday Mel went to work early with the idea of nailing as many of her 'to dos' as possible before starting her new career in solo child care. But it was hard to settle to anything without every other minute looking up the time, going into rehearsal mode or thinking the unthinkable. She checked and double-checked all the phone numbers she would ever, please God, *never* need to use. As yet she'd still made no decision on how to travel. What if the bus, train or taxi broke down?

In the end it was like tossing a coin, and although the journey was made by the slowest mode of transport—the bus, it still delivered her to her destination *early*. She walked up and down the road outside the nursery. *How could time be such a sloth?* That was the trouble with going to so many plays and musicals. You end up remembering little orphan lines you can't place. It sounded like Shakespeare, or maybe an actor waiting to go on.

Trudging a final 'there and back' she crossed the small forecourt and rang the bell, still a good quarter hour early. The diminutive Indian woman who answered the door wore a colourful beaded necklace, a plethora of rings and a confident smile. She was the hands-on proprietress, Rahni, about whom Jess had often spoken. Mel was invited to sign the visitors' book and then shown the kitchen and finally the cloakroom with its named pegs and low benches. They could hear voices everywhere— children singing and stories being read. Rahni seemed to be tuned to every room in the building while still attentive to Mel.

'How did you come today?' she asked.

'By bus, the 266. It took an hour. Think I'll get a taxi back.'

'Can't you stay over? Bring your office with you. Then you'd meet all the other mums and grans the next morning.'

'Maybe one day I'll do just that,' Mel replied.

Rahni seemed pleased with her suggestion then gave Mel a current edition of the Anita's House brochure before excusing herself. Her assistance was required in the kitchen—they were preparing a curry lunch for the children. Its complex aromas were making Mel feel hungry. She loved curries but they didn't always love her.

Left alone, five minutes to go, Mel sat on a low bench and read through the small booklet. It was full of kids' wisdom and cute illustrations of babies and toddlers. *And still time was a sloth!* Was it something Royce had said? His voice could sometimes turn ordinary conversation into something close to poetry. She was sure he could speak in pentameters when he wanted.

A crescendo of noise and voices arose in the nursery signalling the sound of excited, hungry children. And then Billy appeared with Lisa, the nursery assistant Mel had met once before. He ran up to her and, as if stuck by gravity, she enfolded him between her arms and legs.

'Had a good morning? What have you been up to, sweetheart?'

'Playing,' he replied as if she'd asked a dumb question.

'He's been playing very nicely with Timmy. They love that Lego set,' Lisa said. 'He's been saying all morning how Mel is coming all the way from London to see him.'

Mel kissed the small, blond head several times while listening to the rest of Lisa's report. Gathering up Billy's kit, not forgetting Wolfgang, his cloth monkey, she signed the book and suddenly, to her alarm, they were outside the main door. She gave him the option of walking or the buggy; to her relief he chose the latter. She began at last to feel more in control as she pushed him along at a pace. The priority now was to keep him awake and hope he'd come home with an appetite. It was time for some of the more sophisticated songs—he'd follow and repeat some of the words and maybe that way avoid dozing off. Jess hoped that one day he might stay on and have lunch with the others but right now his diet was too much of an issue. Arriving at the flat, Mel read Jess's brief note then sent her a text.

Making enthusiastic noises she got him into his raised chair then put his simple lunch together: alphabet fries, chopped carrots, pieces of cheese and blueberries—all in separate compartments, *and* a cookie, which she allowed him to eat before he'd finished the rest of his lunch. The leftovers remained so she tried offering some hummus but could see by now he was getting tired and yawning. She quickly laid him down in the lounge, put a nappy on him and watched him fall asleep while she snacked on a hastily made sandwich. Against all her efforts she began to doze.

By the time Jess arrived, Mel's second wind was waning. After the swings, slides and other distractions they'd played soccer. Home again and the time was passed with card games. As often as she thought decent, Mel made a mug of tea to pace herself and expedite the afternoon.

Hearing the key in the lock Billy deserted her and ran to greet his mum. Mel followed to find Jess kneeling and firing off lots of questions before Billy, too excited to get his words out quickly enough, could answer. Finally, Jess turned to Mel who gave her report for which her stepdaughter was overflowing with her praise. Then it was some time before the two women were able to talk at any length—Jess was commandeered to play cards on the floor while Mel made yet more tea.

'Think I've got Dad, Davina *and* the GP all pulling in the same direction,' Jess said after Billy had returned to solo play. 'The doc seems to agree with you. So... antidepressants.'

'Uh-huh.'

'Another thing. Dad's got this fear of going in lifts, high buildings. Said he had it for a while after 9/11.'

Mel nodded, explaining that the phobia had threatened to scupper their wedding day, that he'd worked on it, walked up and down miles of stairwells and finally beaten it. Jess appeared relieved and began to make a move towards the kitchen. Mel, having declined the offer of food, phoned for a taxi and hoped Day Two of this new life would be a shade less exhausting.

Chapter 8

While she waited for Maria, Mel tried not to picture her, reflecting instead on Billy and how well the first two days had gone. With little training or practice she'd played mom without going off her head or having her self-confidence trashed. It was Friday and the South Bank was a chequerboard of shade and sunlit concourses, all of which should have put her in a better mood. But Jess was taking Billy to her mother's place in Sussex for the weekend and Mel's green eyes were a shade greener imagining them all together by the seaside. She worried that Billy would be made such a fuss of he'd transfer his affections to his real grandmother.

Maria arrived late and, though a little flustered, still looked cool in an old summer dress and trainers. Before she reached the table, Mel was on her feet to greet and kiss her, noticing close up the gleam of tiny sweat beads on her face.

'Sorry, my solicitor called about the house, the money and in his words, "the pressing need to trace your sister—if at all possible."'

Mel agreed to put out more feelers. She'd not heard back from the CD search, she confessed, as she handed over the email address and phone number of Una, the film-maker she'd spoken to. Effusive thanks were followed by a guarantee to hold Mel to no more favours.

'It's great to see more and more women flashing a viewfinder. Movies are changing. Watch out Hollywood!' Maria said, adding, 'Like to think I can turn around some of your kindnesses.'

Was this the moment Mel had been waiting for? She told herself to appear not too single minded, to start with generalities, let the coffee flow, talk about yourself. But when it came to it, Mel couldn't always stick to a plan.

'So how *was* Stratford?' she asked.

'Loved it. Better late than never for an RSC debut! Hard work, and when I wasn't on stage, I went roaming the town with a cine camera.'

'Anything spooky happen with the Scottish play?'

'Tried my best!' Maria replied, flashing a ghoulish grin. 'I played Witch One and doubled as Lady MacDuff.'

'All the witches were tall, weren't they?'

'If I'm honest that's how I got the part. They'd been drying up a while.'

Mel decided there was no way around the next question. She took a deep breath.

'How d'you get on with Royce?'

'So, agents don't know everything!' Maria said, provocatively. 'See if I can remember. It's two years now.' She was into teasing mode and the Espresso bar suddenly felt warmer. Mel could feel her face flushing and tried to pass it off as 'hormones'.

'You want to know if we hooked up, don't you?'

'That obvious?'

'That *was* the script. What a voice, what eyes! I wanted it to be this slow-burning thing—it's a long season! We were getting on just fine when one day he was somewhere else, *with* somebody else.'

'Who?'

'Nobody knew. Then it got around he was seeing this journalist, maybe theatre critic who'd just flown in from the States. Why it had to be so secretive no one knew. The best source said her name was Laura, but that was all anyone ever knew.'

'As you said: agents don't know everything,' Mel managed to get out. But why she should hurt about that now went beyond reason. Maybe she felt a certain sympathy for the Mel coming to terms with the end of a marriage while trying to find her feet in a strange city. And was she just a little touched that Royce had tried to spare her some heartache? It hadn't worked, of course. Maria was asking after him.

'They're back in the studios, wrapping a movie. They've been shooting in New Mexico. He'll be home soon.'

'Does he own you—I mean the agency,' she asked, correcting herself.

'It's about 50/50.'

'So, what's his next project?'

'Back with the RSC. Prospero.'

Maria said she looked forward to seeing the play. She was shortly returning to Southern California to sort a few things—her move back to LA, and the ever-on search for someone to invest in her film-making.

'I'll be back though, tying up Mum's estate, following any leads I get on my sister. I'll give you my cellphone number in case my UK one doesn't work there. It would be great to hear from you even if you don't get anything on Jo-ju.'

Mel agreed to do just that. It seemed they'd become friends. Did that mean she could ask about the other reason for tracing her sister?

'Don't answer if it's too personal,' Mel began, 'but I'm curious about this cell business.'

'Are you superstitious, Mel?'

'Aren't we all in this business?'

'Okay, so after that long season at Stratford I was getting very tired. It didn't improve with a vacation. So I had a blood test and found I'd got leukaemia, myeloid leukaemia.'

'I'm so sorry. I shouldn't have asked,' Mel said, hating herself.

'No way. Thanks to the Marsden I'm in complete remission and fit as a flea! One day my sister's bone marrow cells may come in handy, though I might never need them. There's other treatments coming along all the time.'

'You're amazing, Maria.'

'Not me, the hospital. They said, when I asked, it had nothing to do with, you know, the play,' Maria said, then she mouthed the title and adopted a ditzy expression. She laughed so invitingly, it gave Mel the cue to laugh too. She could just imagine the doctors shaking their heads and wondering why a perfectly adjusted person should ask such a question. They wouldn't understand. Underneath the camouflage of humour, she was thinking of Royce and the weird and tragic figure he'd encountered on Venice Beach. His own 'curse' seemed to have come rather late in the day—if that's what it was.

'Remind me how the weird sisters were dressed,' Mel asked, having never seen any of the production.

Maria's description fitted Royce's sketches.

All the way back to Hammersmith Mel was trying to get a picture of Royce's mystery lover, Laura. How could she have pushed aside such a siren as Maria? Did height come into it? Royce was such an impressive figure on stage but, in bare feet, he only tipped her by an inch or two. Even in elevator shoes he'd be looking up to Maria, which may have been just what the play's director had in mind. Off stage he might have felt at a disadvantage.

Over a late lunch Mel gave Holly a pared down version of her coffee talk with Maria. It was still enough to pique her assistant's keen sense of conspiracy theory.

'It's just come to me... the tall fiend on the beach. It was her... Maria! She was at Universal at about that period, wasn't she? Probably had time on her hands... wanted some payback for being passed over by his sirship.'

'And knew he'd be on Venice Beach after sunset on that particular day?' Mel countered, not wishing to disclose Maria's San Fernando Valley alibi.

'She had a tip off.'

'An accomplice?' Mel replied, entering into the spirit of Holly's narrative.

'Probably.' Holly gave no sign other than total belief in her story.

 Mel had often marvelled at Holly's ability to paint a ridiculous story with utter conviction. It had become something of a signature act and, but for the tragic ending to this particular story, would have had Mel in fits. One day, her assistant, she predicted, would break out of their one-and-a-half room office, follow her nose and do stand-up at the nearby Apollo.

After lunch Mel produced her paints, and in her sweetest adult-to-child voice, asked Holly what character she wanted to be.

'A witch, of course. The kids'll love it.'

After Mel had transformed Holly's face to their mutual satisfaction, her assistant began to act out her new persona, regretting there was no hat or broom to work with.

'Mustn't go scaring anyone,' Mel warned.

As they walked to the local primary school, Holly, deciding to be a white witch, went casting 'good' spells in everybody's direction. Her boyfriend's sister taught at the school and face painting was just one of many fund-raising events taking place. Parents, teachers and pupils were doing sponsored runs, gymnastics, not to mention pledges, fancy food and cakes. To everyone's relief the April sun shone true to its forecast.

Mel was soon busy with her brush, sponge and glitter gel in front of a line of excited children who, if they were girls, wanted to be *Frozen* characters, Elsa or Anna, a cat or a fairy; boys asked for Batman, Spiderman, various animals or a zombie. Sometimes, if a character eluded her, she'd engage the parent or look up the image on her phone. When she'd finished painting, it was fun watching them all turn unselfconsciously into their new characters. A few parents stepped forward, not quite knowing who or what they wanted to be and Mel was free to exercise a little more creativity. She would never forget being painted herself, not just her face, but her whole body, all in the name of Art. Of course, she had no say in the content of the artwork. It took all day—and then a photographer came and took dozens of shots. Royce had entitled the work, *The Porcelain Pictures*.

'Anything on this weekend?' Holly asked as they were leaving the school.

'The gym,' Mel replied, grimacing. 'Might check out a volleyball game.' She needed something to do to stop her dreaming up nightmare scenarios—top of the list a tidal wave blitzing the Sussex coast. Holly and her partner would be attending a big-league soccer match and on Monday—translating as she went—she'd faithfully reprise the crowd's earthy language and songs over coffee.

How much easier Mel found it to get off her butt on a Saturday morning and head for the gym. There were kids and families about and while Mel went through her routines, she was able to tune into some of their domestic chatter. Another plus was the better air quality in the equipment room. In the week the atmosphere bordered on sour—hardly ideal for an asthmatic gasping and pumping in all that stale air. The demographics differed too. After work the musclemen predominated and she'd feel the pressure of their eyes on her, and occasionally the necessity to respond to their coded language.

She dutifully 'burned' on the cross trainer, then set the treadmill to dispose of the maximum number of calories. Her lungs were soon snatching at elusive air, her muscles creaking and aching, her heart pounding. It had become so much part of Saturdays as to practically define them. She tolerated the self-inflicted pain knowing how it was taking care of her health, her weight. Sometimes, coming away from a church didn't feel a whole lot different. A few generations back she'd have been an ace at self-flagellation. Nowadays there were endorphins and dopamine to explain the highs that followed self-torture and denial. After her session she scrutinized herself in the mirrors, convincing herself the bump of flesh beneath her chin had ever so slightly receded. She swore when she saw a tiny lump of blood on her face. Earlier she'd absentmindedly scratched a zit.

There was a text from Jess with a photo of her and Billy flashing salty smiles by the sea. Were their expressions intended for Mel or Jess's mum, a.k.a. Granny? Mel was pleased she'd not ended up with such an elderly label. She was still afraid that Billy, eccentricities apart, would so melt his grandmother's heart she'd start claiming kinship rights and become more involved.

After lunch, Mel slipped on a baseball cap then bookended her journey with two spells of speed walking. In between she caught a train that took her across the sprawling incognita of outer London suburbia. The vast sports centre was milling with scores of teams, some on court already playing matches, others warming up. After checking out all the men's courts she failed to identify anyone resembling Billy's psychologist, Lou. She tried again, this time searching all team personnel, including the subs' benches—still no Lou. She pinned her hopes on him turning up in one of the later scheduled matches and went to watch the women play.

Closely fought, the match was fast and thrilling and she could smell the excitement, share the adrenaline in the final set. It was years since she'd played, yet it seemed like yesterday—the shouts, the screech of trainers on the floor, the huddles. After the match she felt a keen physical emptiness like hunger and went to the bar to restore herself with a double espresso. Her emotions had been spiked from every direction and were now in disarray. Watching those young women's excitement and camaraderie had been uplifting and damning at the same time. For one insane moment she toyed with a notion to harangue the players: *never stop playing, this is much more than a game.*

The next women's match was nothing like as intense, the standard lower. It brought her some perverse relief and afterwards there was no plummeting off a cliff. She began to look for Lou again, but half-heartedly. It came as some consolation not to find him as she hustled out of the sports centre.

By the time she reached home she'd brokered a reconciliation between the young Mel and her older counterpart. The unique odour of women's volleyball had sent her tracking back through time. She was ambivalent about repeating the process. Tomorrow had quiet catch-up written all over it.

She opened a can of lager, snacked on some chips, put a pizza in the microwave and relived the volleyball matches as if she was about to write them up. It was an old habit; after taking part, she used to send match reports in to the college magazine.

Jess's text, an hour later, caused all the adrenaline to come rushing back.

So sorry to hear on local TV news about your friend, Lady Helena. Did you know? Riding accident, taken by air ambulance to hospital. Recognised the name of the estate so it must be her but wish it wasn't.

We love you, xxx

Chapter 9

Monday morning, at her desk, Mel was barely any wiser. The countess had fallen from her horse while riding in the grounds of the estate and been hospitalised with a head injury and a double fracture. What Mel *had* learned, after searching social media and BBC South online, was that local news channels produced rather less content at weekends. The accident had not made the main news so that Holly was somewhat encouraged by the lack of information.

'They usually say life-changing injuries if it's really bad. Then, I expect it would have been in the national news,' she said, returning, after more reassurances, to her task for the day—the agency newsletter.

On Saturday Mel had sent Helena a text as soon as she'd heard from Jess. She hoped her friend would soon be recovered enough to be able to read it. Recalling that at their last meeting Helena was forgetful and inconsistent, Mel was led to wonder whether there was a connection between Helena's mind and her accident. Sleep that night was elusive, her dreaming wild and dark.

On the Sunday morning—two weeks on from their last meeting—she'd retraced her steps to St Paul's, taken part in the Eucharist and said prayers for Helena. The day was dull and humid; this time it was refreshing to cross the Thames on foot. She bought coffee, sandwiches and provisions from the Borough Market then headed west along the river. She kept adding PSs to her prayers, her mind split-screening between Helena and Jess and Billy. And then an escape route offered itself. She crossed the river and made her way to the National Gallery.

Mel busied herself at her desk until 9.30 am before making the call.

'Pemberley Weddings.' The voice was posh and professional. Helena had never said much about this aspect of the house. Was she being tactful? Perhaps not— she'd not mentioned the gardens either. Over the weekend Mel had more than once clicked on the photo gallery and audio, the first time half-expecting to hear a familiar voice extol the virtues of the family, the house, the cherished gardens. Instead, a slick female accent set the scene: a huge marquee on the croquet lawn, the services of a designer, Italianate gardens, all amounting to *the perfect romantic summer wedding in the heart of Jane Austen country*. Couples exchanged vows in the *East Wing* then repaired to the *any-theme-under-the-sun* marquee. The gallery closed with shots of bridal couples in various garden locations with only hazy views of the honey-coloured mansion.

'I was hoping to speak with Lady Helena's secretary. About the accident.'

'You need to speak to Fliss, the house manager. She'll know if you're Press, by the way.'

'No, I'm just a friend.'

The woman took down Mel's details—full name, email and agency website and told her to expect a call 'sometime'.

For the next hour or so she fired off a barrage of texts, emails and tweets while Holly, busy with shorthand, conducted a phone interview for the newsletter. At coffee they exchanged notes, adding appointments and memos to the day book. Afterwards Mel read Royce's latest email again. It gave her an approximate date for his return and thereby a chance to arrange something special for his return. It was otherwise full of film crew bitching, which had got worse since returning to the relative claustrophobia of Burbank. He *never* wanted to do another lousy movie. The phone call came while Holly was out getting sandwiches for lunch.

'Hello, am I speaking to Mel Giammetti?'

'That's me.'

'I'm Fliss Ephgrave. I'm returning your call to Hambledean Hall. Sorry I couldn't get back to you sooner.'

It was another posh English voice and it had Mel wondering if this and the Pemberley woman weren't one and the same. It also made her think of thoroughbred horses and ball gowns.

'You must be very busy right now,' Mel offered.

'We don't seem to have you on our lists.'

'That doesn't surprise me. We only go back a couple of months. We meet up occasionally in town.'

'That's all right; the lists aren't exhaustive.'

'Is Helena—sorry, Lady Helena—in a coma?'

'Lightening, we're all pleased to say. What I'll do is make your name official so you'll receive the bulletin I'm going to send out twice weekly, or whenever there's a change.'

'Thanks, I'm so grateful. I've texted but… please send my love when that's possible.'

'I will, and thank you for your concern. Goodbye.'

The call had lasted barely a minute and Mel wished now she'd asked more questions but had not wanted to take up the woman's time. She was evidently super busy *and* super-efficient.

It touched Mel to learn she'd not been pigeonholed under any old official list. Didn't that mean friendship rather than acquaintanceship? She could imagine the Fliss woman obsessing over her lists and being slightly pissed at finding an undeclared, informal relationship.

Over lunch Mel thought back to her own wedding. They'd decided on the Faculty House at Columbia. It was low-rise and close to the Hudson, but there was a late, unexpected hitch and the other strong contender, an elegant Fifth Avenue penthouse, part of a brownstone block, became available due to a cancellation. There was only one problem—Henry got panic attacks just thinking about going up the seventeen floors. Never quite certain he'd make it, her prenuptial nerves had gone off the scale.

Before they were quite done with lunch, some flowers arrived with a 'massive' apology from Maria. She'd suddenly clicked, or strongly suspected, the reason Mel had pumped her about Royce. Holly hovered, admiring the bouquet, but when she was told from whom it came, did a little sidestep and said, 'Don't ever cross that woman.'

Mel still hadn't the heart to tell her assistant the weird woman's fate.

The following Saturday morning they were shooting down the motorway in the sense that Anto's car, a vortex of noise and vibration, was hitting speeds it was clearly unused to. When they did occasionally pass another vehicle, it seemed to demand a collective gritting of teeth—Anto, Mel and some demented component under the hood. Distraction by light conversation had become the order of the day but Mel's had only garnered monosyllables from the driver. She'd responded by retreating into silence.

Billy had been ill on her watch and it had rattled her. After Tuesday preschool he just wanted to sleep. His temperature was up, and after checking and re-checking the dose, she'd sweated over giving him Calpol from a syringe. She was a bag of nerves by the time Jess got home and had waited anxiously for texts on Wednesday while Jess stayed home to look after him. It wasn't until Friday that Billy was well enough to eat and Mel sufficiently relaxed to think about the Saturday trip. When Anto first brought up the idea of visiting the gardens at Hambledean Hall, she'd declined—it felt like snooping on Helena. The accident had somehow changed all that.

'How green everything looks,' she said, trying once more to get a response.

Anto swivelled his head her way then back towards the road ahead as if he'd just heard Mel at her most banal. His eventual response was anything but.

'*…and summer's green all girded up in sheaves,*' he recited.

'Go on…'

'Can't remember anymore,' he replied, unconvincingly.

'D'you think Shakespeare ever came this way?' Mel asked.

'More than likely. His company, the King's Men, played in Winchester.'

They took the Winchester turn-off. Soon they were going east on a sunny ridge, then by rolling hills and woods until, in a valley, they took a left onto a narrow road and the car responded by pottering contentedly through a couple of villages. After making more turns they ended up in a car park under tall trees and evidently downwind of a herd of cattle. On foot they joined others making for the entrance—a down-at-heel wooden hut beside an uninhabited-looking lodge house. Mel paid for the tickets and a map, and after passing a shrubbery, they followed a high wall, which led them to a jumble of rustic buildings. Close by was a low stone wall with railings, behind which stood the mellow stone pile of Hambledean Hall.

They entered a gateway guarded by two bronze eagles, but instead of proceeding through a parterre towards the main entrance, they were directed by the sign *This Way to the Gardens* which took them to the right of the building and by a gate to the largest croquet lawn Anto had ever seen. In the middle of it stood an imposing rosé-coloured marquee.

'Pemberley weddings!' Mel exclaimed.

While staff bustled in and out of the structure, the visitors came across another sign pointing the way, by a circular path, to a small loggia in the opposite corner. Mel longed instead to take a peek inside the marquee to see how the current wedding theme was turning out. From the loggia a brick path descended by steps to an old orangery overlooking the Italian garden. Once inside the ornate structure, and out of the wind, they felt the dry heat of the sun. It was full of fig trees and vines; Mel sat on a metal bench and sent a text to Helena. During the week she'd heard from Fliss and, reading between the lines, gathered that the full return of Helena's memory had still some way to go. Was it a coincidence that it was this that had worried Mel at their last meeting? The upshot was a decision, for the time being, to allow Lady Helena only a few visitors to her hospital bed. Mel looked up at the house now half-hidden by trees and wondered whether she still formed any part of Helena's consciousness.

In a concentric fashion they descended the shallow terraces, Anto leading and identifying most of the plants—low boxwood hedges, bay trees, herbs and oleanders not yet in flower. The scattering of slender cypresses imposed a deep green verticality on the garden. Some were disproportionately tall and swayed in the breeze. They walked the length and breadth of the watercourse which rippled with every gust, taking in the dolphin and cherub fountains and other classical statues that had all seen better days. 'A sense of ruin is always a nice touch whether intended or not,' Anto slipped in between naming plants. For a moment Mel stood admiring a tropical looking plant while Anto, going on ahead, called out that he'd discovered a lemon tree in a pot and was in raptures about the scent of the flowers. He was in Kew mode—expansive and masterful. She ought to take notes just in case he asked questions later.

Trespassing onto the croquet lawn on their way back towards the café, Mel attempted to get the attention of some of the wedding staff but was irked by their lack of reaction. She grumbled to Anto about it, her antennae suddenly busy telling her all sorts of negatives about the place. The gardens, Anto had remarked earlier, seemed a little neglected, even unloved.

Over lunch, Mel was content to listen to Anto bounce around his ideas for transforming her roof terrace.

'… decking and pebbles,' he said, indicating something rather larger than golf balls, 'and a small water feature with subtle lighting.'

She began to realise he'd 'laid out' the terrace garden some time ago—the plans made zero reference to the garden they'd just seen. The visit was beginning to feel like a waste of time.

'What is it, Mel?'

'Just thought I'd get all the right vibes here. I got this feeling Helena doesn't know me anymore. I sure as hell don't belong here.'

'These head injuries take time. I'm sure when you meet…'

'But supposing she doesn't.'

On the return journey Mel was subdued. Finally, Anto broke the silence.

'Didn't want to bring it up while we were there, but a year or two back there was a more serious accident on the estate. Did you know?'

'No. What happened?'

'A workman was killed. It went to court. The estate lost out—mega money and reputation. I think you sort of intuited something there. If you click on the Hall there's loads of links. I'm sorry.'

'I shan't be reading any of that. Just wonder whether that explains the charity work.'

As they drew close to Chiswick the mood lightened. They'd booked a table at the bistro to which Anto promised to bring his coloured computer plans for Mel's roof garden. She'd heard from Jess—Billy was back to normal and his mum had given her blessing to Mel's idea of a treat for him: a boat trip on the river. The plan had come to her while the pair were away in Sussex. It was a welcome and prevailing distraction—for a while Mel could put aside not only her forebodings about Helena, but the narrative of an avenging curse on the Hambledean estate.

By the time her doorbell rang, Mel had become quite familiar with Shakespeare's sonnet number 12, in particular the final couplet:

And nothing 'gainst Time's scythe can make defence
Save breed, to brave him when he takes thee hence.

On their way to the bistro, she wondered whether it would be possible, wise even, to work the sonnet's theme into their after-dinner conversation. But the meal was taken up with planning Wednesday's boat trip, safety issues, and the weather. Anto's boat handling abilities and knowledge of the river, she'd ascertained, were not in question.

'Not as if we're going very far,' he said.

'Far enough for Billy. And far enough to get me one over Granny. Awful aren't I.'

'Yes,' he said, laughing.

'I'm afraid she might butt in one day.'

'Come on, she's very part-time. Nobody's gonna trump you over that little man.'

When the table had been cleared away, Anto got out his plans. They were in brilliant primary colours, which only served to confirm their claim to permanence—a fait accompli. But what did Mel know about garden design anyway?

'You've done this before,' Mel speculated.

'First the hardware. You'll need power, plumbing and this perimeter wire fence,' he said, pointing to the metal feature. 'You can't rely solely on bay trees in pots, especially in the dark. Remember Floyd's near accident?'

Mel drained the last of the wine from her glass.

'What did you ever see in that show pony? Sorry.'

They were swiftly back to the subject of the roof garden. Anto already had someone lined up, 'an artist to his fingertips. He'll probably improve on these plans. Some scaffolding's required. I'm thinking under a week to complete.'

'How exciting! Until I get the quote.'

Leaving the bistro, Mel was grateful for what had been achieved. It was too late in the evening to start on another topic, especially the one she'd had in mind. By the house they parted with a kiss and then both stood back and looked up at the roof, Anto's parting shot, 'he might want to put a tree up there.'

Chapter 10

The headache gone, it felt good to be getting out of the office, even better that Mel was en route to collect her special little man, now fully recovered. Monday had been one crazy day—the sound booth in use throughout. While Holly dealt with the technical side, Mel, having close-read all the books on the list—English novels in the main—took care of editing. She listened, chapter by chapter, to the actors' narrations, checking against the text for voicing, pauses, dialogue and all the factor Xs. The intense concentration resulting in a blinding headache.

She'd brought a whole pack of cookies—he needed feeding up after his illness. As she waited in the cloakroom listening to the murmur of tiny voices, she felt her throat go tight and fought against it, trying to compose herself with deep breaths. Billy would understand neither tears nor the question, 'Did you miss me?' At last, he was there, this time with Rahni, and Mel could hug him, pick him up and whirl him around. He was happy—he'd seen the pack of cookies.

Rahni said how well he'd got over the virus. There was something else to report—his singing. Once only a mime show, now he was becoming audible.

'Does Jess sing to him?' she asked.

'Not sure. We sing together, don't we, Billy?' Mel said, taking his hand, placing it on her nose and ascending and descending a major scale, Billy achieving some accuracy with the intervals.

By the time they were back at the flat she was breathless from pushing the buggy faster than normal while trying to sing *Do-Re-Mi* at the same time. She was looking forward to lunch, hers because she was always ravenous after a migraine, his because she wanted to see how many treats he could get down.

The final tally was one each—she'd loved the choccy confection as a kid—it summoned, in some Proustian way, something of her early years. Later, after Billy had slept, they went to the play park. She strapped him into his 'new' hand-me-down trike, which she found wobbly to steer and he tricky to pedal over the uneven pavements. There was another discovery—when planes flew over, instead of putting cotton wool in his ears, she hunkered down, placed his hand on her nose and sang *Do-Re-Mi* loudly.

When Jess got home Billy was tiring, so supper and the bath time rituals were rushed through. He soon settled and went fast asleep, looking like an angel. Over a pizza and wine, Jess and Mel could relax and talk.

'Something's puzzling me about Dad,' Jess began. 'You know how he walks up from the British Museum. And if it's fine, meets me in the square with coffee and a sandwich?'

'Uh-huh,' Mel said, not entirely sure where Soho Square stood in the capital's warp and weft of streets. All she knew—in case of emergencies—was the phone number of the high-end fashion shop.

'So today we meet in the gardens; it was good to be out in the sun. Then he's off again and I'm getting just a bit more sun when I notice he's left his paper and reading glasses. So I'm running up to the corner, turning right and then I see him by all that building work that's been going on for ever. That's when he disappears.'

'In the crowd?'

'It wasn't that busy. Anyway, I know his route, so I run down New Oxford Street fast as I can. He's nowhere to be seen.'

'He doubled back to retrieve his paper and glasses?'

Jess shook her head, opened her bag and produced the mislaid articles, explaining that when she finally got him at home, all he said was he'd been shopping.

'What's with this building site?' Mel asked.

'Big, big make-over for Centre Point, new piazza, shops, eateries.'

'What's Centre Point?'

'They say it was the tallest building in London in the 70s, thirty floors or so.' Jess replied.

'Think I got it, Jess! Your dad's practising heights again like he did after the Twin Towers. How he gets access to a place like that I don't know. One thing I am sure of— he's still got incredible determination. What I'm saying is: don't worry. Just don't let on you know. He's secretive and proud. Didn't tell me anything until he showed up for our vows.'

Why couldn't she have just said wedding? She'd brought attention to herself—the breaking of her promise of fidelity to Jess's dad—but, tactfully Jess had not responded and the subject was dropped.

'You still okay about tomorrow? We'll take every care with him,' Mel said.

The taxi was waiting as they emerged from the nursery, Mel with a backpack, Billy looking a little uncertain, which probably meant he was excited and therefore unlikely to need any sleep. All the way to Chiswick pier she chatted away to him, from time to time bringing the taxi driver into the conversation. Billy was convinced they were going to London and Mel, loathe to disappoint him, gave it the name, 'Little London'.

Anto, sporting a blue nautical cap and holding a blanket was waiting there on the steps by the pier. He posed in an official sort of way and introduced himself as 'their captain for the day', announcing that the weather and tide were both favourable. With that he left them to picnic on the steps while he checked out the boat. Billy looked lost and remained mute. Mel spread the blanket and out came his familiar lunch fare to which he did some justice. They shared a cookie.

After Billy performed a cautious wee into the river, Mel holding him tight for the purpose, Anto helped them aboard the small motor cruiser. It rocked gently against the pontoon, its hull throbbing impatiently, the motor gurgling. Next, it was time to don the rather cumbersome life jackets. Billy's was too big for him, he kept sniffing the material but seemed to accept Mel's explanation that it would keep him warm. Snuggled up together behind the skipper, her arm around him, she said a silent prayer as the boat bumped its way out of the berth then pottered calmly upstream. Mel chattered non-stop to calm herself and reassure Billy, pointing out the sights, other boats and any birds she could name.

It wasn't until they approached Barnes Bridge that Billy began to get excited. Gliding beneath its ironwork he was fascinated by the structure and kept pointing to it. He was too awestruck to speak and kept swivelling his head this way and that to get a better view. Then Mel drew his attention upstream to Chiswick Bridge and Billy's excitement grew again. They went as far as Kew, by which time the skipper had become adept at slowing down the boat then winding it in and out of the arches of every bridge so that Billy could marvel and Mel had time to capture his amazement on her phone. The highlight came when a train sped across Kew Railway Bridge. On the way back Mel hummed the famous boat song from *The Tales of Hoffman* but when Anto joined in, Billy looked puzzled.

'Everyone knows *that* song, Billy. Just like the ones at nursery. It's not like one of our secret songs, is it?' They hummed it together every time Billy played on the pirate ship in the park. One day she'd have to explain to him that songs don't belong to any one person. She wasn't quite sure how she was going to go about it. As soon as they landed safely back at the pier Mel texted Jess with photos and a video.

As if by magic, Anto, after he'd secured the boat, produced two fishing nets and a towel, explaining that the tide was now just right for some 'dipping'. Mel had visions of their skipper going for a deep paddle, even a swim and declined to join him.

'No, no. The kids paddle and *dip* their nets in the shallows to see what wildlife there is in Old Mother Thames, not to mention finding the occasional Neolithic or Iron-age shard.'

He admitted he sometimes took a net himself and joined local kids in the shallows near the eyot. It was where he intended taking them now.

'Sounds fun. Okay, Billy? Let's do some dipping with the captain,' Mel enthused.

As soon as they'd braved the shallow water between the bank and the tiny island, Billy piped up, 'It's like the sea!' It wasn't long before they'd caught some tiny shrimps and crabs, leastways Anto had. Neither Mel nor Billy could net anything of much interest. It was evidently a practiced art and Anto, still wearing his seaman's cap and bending low, was a mean hand with a net. He showed Billy his 'exhibits' before letting them go. Next thing the two were working the same net and getting excited about an elusive crab, which they finally landed. Anto held it out in the palm of his hand for Billy to see, delivering some kindergarten biology, his pupil's face a study in wonderment.

All the way back in the taxi Billy talked excitedly, his words tumbling off his tongue, getting stuck, then racing on while he struggled to put his narrative together in the right order. When they were back at the flat Mel suggested he draw pictures of his favourite bits of the trip. She flopped with a mug of tea, they shared a cookie and then Billy began to draw the river, the boat and then the bridges. She texted Anto, returning the compliment he'd paid after seeing her show—pitch perfect. She'd met with a different Anto today. It made her wonder again about his take on Sonnet No. 12.

'I counted fourteen bridges!' Billy boasted.

'Did you, darling?' Jess replied, Mel indicating a back-and-forth itinerary. Billy was still tiring easily and before his account had got as far as dipping by the eyot he was closing his eyes. He was quickly undressed then put to bed. Mel was tired too and declined Jess's hospitality, but not before she'd imparted some hot news.

'Hey, listen to this,' she began as she scrolled her phone and related the message she'd received only that day from a French woman who thought she might have met the missing sister.

'How recent?' Jess asked.

'In 2014, at a Goth festival. I assumed it was in France until I read Whitby. Doesn't sound very French, does it?'

'It's up North, by the sea where *Dracula* was written,' Jess said. 'You know—all that cosplay in black lace, velvet, bombazine, whatever.'

Mel knew almost nothing of Goth culture and so Jess gave a brief tutorial. 'I'd love to create something for one of those festivals, maybe even go up there and wear it,' she sighed.

They talked a little of Maria whom Mel had already contacted with the news. It was morning in LA and she was busy moving her base. Before Mel left, there was time to take Jess through every splosh and splash of the boat ride, the paddle and the dipping. She wanted to know how Billy got on with Anto.

'Captain Anto, if you please. They totally ignored one another for the first hour. Ended up catching a crab together, both very excited!'

When Mel left, Jess was still red-eyed. 'It's what he needs,' she said. 'I must send thanks to Anto,'

'Captain Anto.' Mel reminded her, and they laughed.

By Thursday morning Mel was able to put the possible sighting of Jo-ju into some sort of perspective. A lot can happen in two years. Was it a one-off visit? Was it even her? How quickly might the trail go cold. The one positive to come out of her research was that all recent Whitby festivals were accompanied by extensive photo-montages which Maria was already scanning, paying particular attention to the year 2014. They were held twice-yearly she'd discovered, and had asked the French woman to specify—April or October.

As soon as Holly arrived, she was loudly into her midweek soccer match report, proselytising to Mel the benefits of an interest in the game—better understanding of British ways, stronger bond with Billy. As it was, Mel was even more than usually inattentive, not to say preoccupied.

'You okay, Mel?'

'Mustn't get too excited but we've had a sighting.'

All soccer talk was swiftly terminated while Holly retuned to Mel's update on the possible meeting now understood to have taken place in April 2014. Holly began a discourse on Goths, most of which Mel had already assimilated but it was hard to stop her assistant when she was in full flow.

At their break it was obvious Holly was in deep thought about something, her brow furrowing above her coffee mug. Either for dramatic effect or out of politeness she was waiting for Mel to give her her cue.

'Go on, then.'

'Well… there's two missing women, both with a penchant for dressing up in a certain alternative way. Couldn't they be one and the same person? In other words, it was this sister of Maria on Venice Beach that night, not Maria after all.'

'What was she doing out there?' Mel asked.

'On the trail of her sister, of course,'

Mel nodded as if enthralled by this feat of sleuthing. There wasn't a hint of humour in her assistant's delivery. Now was hardly the best time to put her right on the beach woman's untimely fate. Would there ever be such a time? It was all nonsense, of course. Maria, an actor in the public domain, would have presented the sister with little difficulty in running to earth. There was no question though, that Holly's gothic twist to the story had unnerved her. The woman's body lying in a Santa Monica morgue was, according to Royce, still unclaimed, still unidentified. And then there was the curious tie-up between the sighting and the RSC's Scottish play—both in 2014. That it was entirely random made not a whit of difference to Mel's imagination, which was already feverishly adding new twists to the tale. They all began: suppose, just suppose…

Mel walked north from Leicester Square Tube station, thinking of Billy at the Centre all day on a Thursday. He was probably still describing in minute detail all the bridges of 'Little London'. It made her laugh out loud. She carried a lightweight case and when she arrived at the square, found a bench in the sun, sat down and waited for Jess. Henry, though not due to show today, might turn up anyway, she'd been warned. All Mel needed was five to ten minutes of her stepdaughter's time, hoping she'd also managed to squeeze in some 'research'.

They hugged when Jess appeared. It was strange to be meeting without Billy. Mel had to keep telling herself he was safe. He was probably in the safest place on earth.

'You got the story, bit garbled, I guess,' Mel began, opening the case, and handing over some of the contents. Jess had been unable to do any searches. 'These are all the shots I could get off the RSC's Scottish play. I've cropped some for convenience.'

Jess handled and viewed them all in turn with what seemed like a professional eye.

'Now look at these,' Mel said, handing over what remained in the case. They showed, in a variety of poses, the Weird Sisters in their costumes, which matched, more or less, Maria's description and Royce's sketches. 'Is there any connection between what they're wearing and Goth-style costumes?'

'No,' Jess said emphatically, 'they're Mummers' costumes.'

'What the fuck's that?'

'Goes back to the Middle Ages, I think. Troupes of actors going round the houses, putting on plays, singing and dancing—all for some nosh and booze. The costume's a sort of disguise.'

'It has nothing to do with Goths?' Mel asked, hardly able to get her words out.

'No, it's a much older tradition.'

'Thanks, Jess, you've just saved me from my insane imagination,' Mel blurted out, holding her head in her hands, still hyperventilating. The dark abyss she'd been staring at for the last three hours—Maria having to identify her lost sister in a Santa Monica morgue—had receded, Mel's kamikaze imagination safely grounded.

This time it was Jess's turn to have a theory. She wondered whether the imminent return of Royce was adding to Mel's stress levels.

'Won't he be difficult to handle coming out of that movie bubble?'

In a way Jess was right, but not for the reason she'd proposed. It was much easier talking about Captain Anto, which they did at some length.

Chapter 11

Mel couldn't decide: spray-on tan or the lace top hold-ups? She had a hunch Royce might have seen enough of California tans, and wouldn't there be a demarcation line somewhere unless she sprayed it rather generously? At the start of their relationship, he'd set great store by her 'Celtic' skin and how well it would take primary colours. While she was thinking clothes, he was already thinking acrylic paint and *The Porcelain Pictures*.

After showering and moisturising, her skin felt silky under the bathrobe while she went around pulling out drawers and thinking about underwear. By the mirror, in her hold-ups, she tried on various bras and briefs then settled for the black and peach set. Back in her comfy bathrobe she dried her hair and widened her wavy ponytail with a clasp. Still with time to kill she went up to take the cooler air on the roof terrace, now half-shaded. A gentle wind, barely ruffling her hair, fluttered the leaves of the trees in the street. There was something calming about it, wistful too. She thought once more of Helena, wondering if they would ever meet again. Although she was out of hospital and becoming mobile, the bulletins regarding her mental progress had become rather static.

The scaffolders had turned up a day early, their power tools puncturing the peace of a bright May morning. The roof garden was still work in progress; the raw materials—paving slabs, decking, bags of pebbles and compost—lay randomly about on the dull grey surface. The bay trees had all been taken away for repotting in larger, glazed containers with individual art nouveau motifs Anto helped choose. Without their green enclosing effect, the terrace felt foreign, even slightly precarious. Mel longed for the return of its intimacy, and, of course, the completion of the garden. In preparation, electrical and plumbing terminals had been created to one side of the terrace.

After her makeup she slipped on the strappy maxi dress then wasted an age searching for green shoes that even half matched the woodblock print. At least her eyes co-ordinated. She settled in the end for an old pair of black Latin dance shoes. They gave her height—enough to make her dizzy. The pearl necklace and earrings completed her outfit. Even self-doubting Mel had to admit she looked hot.

'Local Italian not good enough?' her taxi driver joked when, rather diffidently, she bid him take her to *Daphne's*.

'He wants to impress,' she replied.

'Not the only one!'

Mel, after blushing, calculated she'd be just nicely late.

If her stage career had stressed the importance of anything, it was how to make an entrance. She'd watched Helena carry it off to perfection at the Ritz. Outside the restaurant she did a quick run through in her head, took a deep breath then made her entry, the old bullet points just keeping her panic under wraps. A moment later, as if from nowhere, Royce appeared and took her in his arms and they briefly became the centre of attention. He wore an old suit. Hollywood seemed to have taken it out of him—he'd lost some weight, making his high cheek bones more prominent. His eyes and mouth were as expressive as ever.

'How goes Prospero?' she asked once the effusive greeting was over.

'So glad to be back, especially now,' he said, taking her hand. 'It *feels* like twelve years. Don't exile me again, will you?'

'But what could be a better preparation for the role?' Their laughter turned to bemusement when they discovered they were both avoiding alcohol. They ordered the same romantic-sounding mocktail, and clinked glasses, declaiming in unison, '*O brave new world*'.

Royce was enjoying himself mock-surreptitiously spooning Mel a little of his wild boar ragu. He showed no interest in her focaccia.

'Mmm,' she murmured appreciatively.

'Louder, louder.'

'Stop it, Royce, you'll get us thrown out. Tell me… about the play. I understand the colonial trope doesn't cut it anymore.'

'No, it's all existential. Flawed Prospero, burdened with guilt, finally assuages it with these incredible reserves of forgiveness. Exit the magic spell. Talking of magic,' he went on enthusiastically, 'the production's going to be a complete box of tricks—motion capture technology, holograms, avatars. Ariel really *will* fly.'

'*Where the bee sucks, there suck I*,' Mel began a little uncertainly, '*In the cowslip's bell I lie*, something about… *owls do cry, On the bat's back I do fly*.'

'*That's my dainty Ariel*,' Prospero replied. 'You haven't asked about the movie.'

'Because I don't think you're happy about it.'

'Dead right I'm not. Oh, it'll gross a hundred and fifty. Just not Fellini, is it?'

To Mel's relief the subject was dropped and there was

no mention of the drowned woman. She steered him back to the stage and he responded with a host of anecdotes, some, she was sure, pure invention. But Royce's gifts had been lying fallow for just this chance to shine again, to challenge, if not totally suspend, disbelief. It reminded her of something Maria had said, *He never stops—acting I mean*. Now he was joshing in Italian with the waiter and she could understand only a little of their conversation. Her Italian had never gotten beyond embarrassing.

The waiter disappeared then returned with the next course—veal for Royce, lamb for Mel, assorted contorni for both. These heartier dishes seemed to require a period of near silence for their better appreciation. It was broken at last by Royce who wanted to know what Mel had been up to. She updated him concerning the agency—names, dates and future productions, drawing his attention to the increasing demand for audiobooks.

'Flourishing side line, Giammetti,' he said archly.

'So's the competition. Some of our actors want to go freelance. Watch this space.'

He nodded while he chewed and then swallowed. 'I really meant you personally, Mel.'

It was rare for him to address her by her proper name—she'd gotten so used to being *Irish*. *Mel* sounded awkward and Royce had probably never sounded awkward in his life. She spoke about Billy: the sometimes-terrifying role as his carer two afternoons a week and her worries about how long the honeymoon might last.

'You look amazing on it. Serene I'd say.'

'Thank you,' she mumbled. 'How's the family?' she asked, then regretted it.

'Fine. You know Milan: fashion, football and The Last Supper.'

For once the anodyne appeared before her with perfect timing—she began to twitter about her roof top garden project until his responses took on a purely mechanical character. Changing tack to Elizabethan theatre she brought the conversation full circle. When they first met it was Shakespeare, in particular memories of learning speeches in their teens, that had helped them click. Royce was doing a short season at the Players Theatre in the Village. She was there in some official capacity at the premiere but, helplessly magnetized by his voice, his stage presence, she couldn't keep away. Soon they were spending her lunch break in his hotel room. *If you ever get to London, give me a call* were his parting words.

In the taxi Royce had found—discreetly through her dress—the lacy stocking tops while he nibbled her earring. Now, kneeling on the thick-pile bedroom carpet, he held up her dress and repeated the discovery, this time with his lips which were soon moving north. She parted her legs and his tongue moved hotly between them. Then, as he got to his feet, he raised her dress further and, her arms raised, relieved her of it entirely. As he rained kisses on her neck and cupped her breasts, Mel's breathing came quickly and her body surged with the familiar chemistry of desire.

But there was something almost mechanical and staged about Royce's foreplay and where she'd expected to feel his hardness there was only a doughy mound. Had she lost the trick somehow? She'd not had sex with anyone for at least four months. Her Adonis stagehand had turned up again and she'd ignored the loud cynic in her ear. Within no time it was needling her: *told you so*.

Royce seemed relieved when she hunkered down on her heels and unzipped him. His non-erection pointed disconsolately groundwards. Was this major malfunction his or hers? Assiduously she worked it with her hand, lips and tongue but could conjure no magic. She took him in her mouth, hummed, made eye contact and even faked a gag or two. While his vocal responses were loud and hot-blooded there was no match from where it mattered most. In the past, round about this point he'd have begged to be inside her while she'd tease and stall him with bogus pretences. There'd be no games tonight, no sex and just as surely, no 'outcome'. The chances of getting herself pregnant had just gone from longshot to zero.

Mel was grateful for the anonymity of the taxi. She couldn't bear even the thought of anyone looking at her and somehow guessing the downward spiral of her evening. The spasms—half sob, half shiver—had yet to work their way out of her. She tried to concentrate on anything and everything that passed by.

As he'd lain in a heap on the bed swearing about the curse of a woman, Mel had mistakenly thought of his ex-wife, the opera singer, and gathered there'd been an awkward family re-union in Milan. She replaced her dress, got on the bed and tried to console him.

'Not her. The woman on the beach. That hag's cursing me from the grave.'

'How?' was all Mel could muster.

'I was fine before that. Okay, once in a while it didn't happen. After that night, zilch. So I end up seeing Madam Ruth.'

Mel could remember two occasions when it didn't happen. 'What about you try the little blue tablets?' she suggested.

'Sure, they worked a treat. Then one morning I woke up with this blurring in one eye. Saw a specialist same day. He said I'd been lucky. Lucky!'

'What…?'

'Said it could have been the macula. So, no more blue tabs for Roycey boy. The curse, you see.'

'What about the blurring?'

'Oh, that's gone.'

'And Madam Ruth?'

'She dressed like a lawyer. Has a place on Sunset Boulevard. Tarot cards and the like. She gave me a hint that *you* were in the cards, that *you* were the one to help me. So much riding on tonight.' *He could say that again.*

A kind of calmness, really numbness, had settled over her, cocooned in the taxi and distant from everything outside. They were passing a large area of parkland and it occurred to her she had no idea where she was. It was oddly comforting—in the dark void of the taxi her mind was a perfect match, her imagination, for once, stalled. In theory it could remain so indefinitely. But once she got out and paid her fare, she knew there'd be a reckoning.

There was some hold-up on the main road and at the next turn the taxi swung sharp left. All the side streets looked much the same to Mel at night, the trees obscuring the houses and the solid lines of parked cars narrowing the gap to one lane. Sensing they were nearing the end of her taxi ride, she still felt lost. The larger houses gave way to rows of terraces; there were shops then a pub, and, as if her vision had suddenly acquired 20/20, she recognised the street as Anto's and asked the cabbie to stop.

Second thoughts gnawed as soon as she rang the doorbell. No one answered and, relieved she wasn't about to invade his privacy, she turned towards home at some pace, her Latin heels loud and resentful.

'Yo, Mel, come back,' Anto shouted after her. She slowed then turned, feeling like a child who had to face the music after some misdemeanour. She walked slowly back to the house, where Anto stood sentinel in bathrobe and pants.

'Sorry, it's late. I'm imposing on you,'

'Allow me to disagree.'

'I hope we're not going to start arguing in the street.'

He ignored the half-hearted gruffness and led her into the familiar hall then to a longish lounge she'd not set foot in before. Excusing herself, she slipped into the downstairs loo to check her mascara. On her return her host offered a range of food and drink but all she could face was tea. While he went to the kitchen, she peered about the room from the antique armchair she'd settled into. There were oils, acrylics and delicate Japanese prints on the walls and little Giacometti-like figures on tables and shelves. A stone buddha meditated on a rug.

Anto served tea with a formality Helena would have approved. Mel hadn't the nerve to ask whether the cups were bone china in case it made her nervous.

'Lovely to see you in your finery, Mel. What goes?'

'The food was great, can't say the same for what happened later.'

'You weren't… *please* tell me if you were… forced…'

Mel burst out laughing, shaking her head. It suddenly cast her evening in a whole new comedic light. Seconds later she went silent and dabbed her eyes. For once Anto was struggling for words as well.

'Thank you for your concern,' she said, recovering at last. 'The answer's no. I'll tell you more, only… first I want to know your take on Sonnet Number 12.'

'Okay,' he said after a long pause, 'cards on the table. Last summer I met with a surrogate. Got on well. Agreed terms. Tested okay. Of course, it all came to nothing.' He avoided eye contact.

'How did you know that I…?' she got out, her heart hammering.

'I guessed. And then you and Billy are a bit of a clincher. I thought maybe Henry—older—didn't want kids. Does Billy make it any easier? I mean easier to cope with…'

'Worse, if you must know. About tonight… my boyfriend couldn't get…' she said, indicating with her elbow Royce's failure to produce an erection. 'Never happened before. So, no baby juice and tonight's the big one. Comprendo?'

'Think so.'

'Been taking this fertility drug, Clomid. Then there's these injections I get from this rip-off clinic. I inject myself. In theory I'm all ready to roll.'

'Mind me asking how old your guy is?'

'50s.'

'And I take it he's unaware of your intentions?'

'You got it in one.'

Despite the gentle thrum of a pendulum clock, the

silence of the room only seemed to have grown. It cast its spell over Anto and Mel. They were both looking at the same piece of art for inspiration—the stone buddha.

Under the trees the street-lights cast mottled shadows as the two walked towards Mel's house, her Latin dance shoes beginning to sound irreparable. Neither said a word until they'd reached the house. Mel dived into the kitchen, recovered two sterile syringes, changed her shoes for a more comfortable pair, grabbed a few toiletries and exchanged her silk wrap for a warmer top for the walk back to Anto's.

Anto was worried his pleading had offended her. It wasn't that at all. She didn't want to put anyone else through those false hopes and daydreams that, in her case, always ended the same way. Why drag anyone else into what she'd almost learned to live with? With Henry, the repeated IVF cycles had worn them down to the point of destroying their marriage.

'I'm 44, legs are getting veiny. Keep saying it's my last chance. Most of my eggs, I'm told, have unviable mutations. But, because there's still a tiny chance, I go on with this fantasy life and every time,' she paused to get her breath back, 'I get this buzz. Like drugs it never lasts—you come crashing down until the next time. You want to be like that, Ant?'

Nothing she said had any effect. She gave up—the signal for Anto to go online and revisit the little how-tos he'd read up on last summer on artificial insemination. Then he became didactic—sperm from anyone over 50 was a no-no. Mutation risks. He was 41. And then he nervously produced two official A4 size papers. 'Please read—before we go any further.'

It felt like snooping but he was adamant. The documents were concerned with the usual police checks teachers and others who work with vulnerable persons have to submit to. She was surprised by the date.

'2015?'

'I was thinking about getting back into teaching.' It came out almost like a confession.

While he disappeared upstairs with the small sterilised cup, Mel dropped her briefs and lay on her back on the lounge floor. Straightaway she was taken with a fit of giggling and knew at once that from then on the procedure would play out like a pantomime.

Anto's off-stage cough as he approached with 'the goods' was almost too much for Mel. But when he told her to raise her knees and go all floppy, she had cramp trying to control her giggles. By staring hard at the buddha she was able slowly to bring mind and body under some control. Only then had she enough cool about her to withdraw the precious fluid into the syringe, find her cervix with the fingers of one hand and inject with the other. If she'd expected the moment of calm to last, it was trashed by Anto's impersonation of a night nurse. 'It's time for your orgasm now, Miss Giammetti.'

After he'd left the room, she got to work. 'Getting off' was considered essential to the process of sperm-meets-egg and Mel, no slouch in that department, was done and dusted in no time. She replaced her underwear and waited for the return of some semblance of normality, which arrived in the shape of Anto bearing a pillow, a blanket and more tea.

After he turned out the light she settled down to sleep,

first slipping the pillow under her butt. Would gravity help? It was all guesswork, of course. Life, at every turn was so much guesswork. She was soon asleep and dreamed of Mt. Sinai Hospital and the O.R. Large with Lennie's child, she lay on a gurney being wheeled down an endless corridor. It was the end of their relationship but she'd got what she most wanted. Then her dream cut to her on the table undergoing surgery and, at the same time, observing from above. She felt no pain, then heard someone say, 'They have to remove the baby to save the woman's life'.

Mel woke early, bursting for a pee. Having relieved herself, she went to the kitchen and drank half a pint of water then left a note for Anto. It was only then she noticed his to her.

Mel, I should have told you this last night. I don't carry any faulty genes that I know of. That includes the recessive gene for cystic fibrosis. My sister died of it in her teens.

Anthony.

He'd never spoken of a sister. What was her name? Was she younger? One day she'd get him to talk about her, and maybe his 'broken' career in teaching too.

It was Friday 13th—the reason Royce, more superstitious now than ever, had changed the restaurant reservation to the 12th. As she walked home the sun went flashing off the cars in the street and every tree she passed was loud with birdsong.

Her curtailed nightmare was not so far removed from how things had turned out. Lennie, married with a kid, was furious she'd got pregnant and instantly dumped her. She had a miscarriage in the hospital. A memorable year, 2001.

Chapter 12

'My head's a fucking crime scene,' Royce groaned down the phone.

Mel had been putting off speaking to him all morning. 'Gimme a minute,' he barked.

She made sympathetic noises and waited for the relevant parts of his brain to cohere. He crashed about, went to the kitchen, poured water then slurped. Next, he deserted the phone, swore, retrieved it then sat down.

'Royce, thank you for the lovely dinner last night… and the stimulating conversation.'

'Hmmm… and afterwards?'

'I'm sorry I failed you.'

'I'm not buying that. You did all you could. I'm the one that's cursed.'

'Royce, I heard about something that could help you.'

Walking home that morning it had suddenly come to her—an article in The New York Times about a diabetic who couldn't take Viagra. He'd found a safe, medically approved alternative, which worked well with no side-effects. But after searching while she travelled in to work, she'd failed to unearth it. She wouldn't dream something like that, would she?'

'While we're on the subject,' she said, after describing all she could remember of the article, 'why don't you get a blood test done—just in case you're pre-diabetic. So, go see your doctor.'

There was silence while Royce gave the impression of digesting Mel's advice and half-remembered news item. Either that or it was alcoholic inertia. And then she heard the phone being put down, possibly dropped, followed by the distinct sound of retching. Poor Royce! She told him to take care; she'd phone later, and ended the call.

The next call followed without much of a break. It was Fliss, the house manager at Hambledean Hall, her tone perhaps a shade softer than last time. After pleasantries she laid out her pitch—the yearly summer fair in the grounds of the house, lots of stalls, local crafts and food. All happening May 21st. Charity the main beneficiary.

'Her ladyship will be out and about on the croquet lawn with her crutches to meet friends and well-wishers. We'd be delighted if you were able to join us.'

'Does she remember me?' Mel asked.

'She still has lapses, I'm afraid. Especially for more recent events.'

It was clear Mel belonged to this 'recent event' category and felt little desire to travel to Hampshire just to engage in a one-sided conversation that might prove upsetting to both parties. Fliss 'understood' Mel's ambivalence and countered it with an easy charm and a tone that said she usually got her way.

'You might just jog her memory. Isn't it worth a try?'

Mel gave in, but how was she to make her way from the station to the estate? She could hardly ask Anto again, they needed a break from one another right now.

'Taxi's the best,' Fliss advised, 'I'll get someone to run you back after the fair.'

Mel could almost feel the soft leather of the barouche, see the coachman, hear the jingle of the harness.

Much later Royce called back. He was well into recovery mode, even sounding perky and made no reference to the earlier phone call. He was revisiting a favourite subject. Mel gave a barely audible sigh.

'Soon I'll be sending you the best twenty-four of *The Porcelain Pictures*… by special courier or in person. Which has the stronger safe? Home or office?' he asked.

Twenty-four of the body paintings—her body, his painting—sounded obsessional. He'd gone on about how the Chinese had learnt to paint porcelain in the 9th, or was it the 10th century, and this was his way of paying homage. As recently as last night he'd made a painterly reference to her skin, recalling the day he'd painstakingly mapped out her body in block colours, runes and Chinese characters. She'd reminded him he wasn't the only who'd taken pains.

'Home's best,' she replied. She could just see it, Holly going to the office safe, being confronted by the images and freaking out. The pictures were 'available' on Royce's web pages but the images purposely small and of low resolution so that anyone trying to enlarge them would see only grainy pictures—just how Mel preferred them to be!

'They're from the master file and they'll all be printed matte. Sorry it's taken so long. It was one, long day's hard work and you well deserve to be one of the custodians of the project,' he declared in a rush of flummery.

Did she? Just how many 'custodians' were there? She preferred not to be involved but now was not the time to go upsetting the maestro, who insisted on calling it her highest artistic moment. He was already working on including some of the images in a small private exhibition. How was she going to get out of that invite?

The following Tuesday afternoon Mel's honeymoon with Billy came to an abrupt end. They had ambled home as normal from the nursery where he'd spent a routine morning. And so she was shaken when it happened.

She'd gone to the kitchen to prepare lunch while Billy played with his bricks. At some stage of assembly, a small piece went missing and neither he nor Mel could put their hand to it. His loud shouting and tears shredded every layer of Mel's composure, exposing it for the sham it was. Bitterly, he railed against *Mister Bugger* whom he accused of stealing the piece as if the bogeyman was there in the room. She'd often wondered how she'd cope in this sort of situation and tried hugging and plying him with soothing words but he kept pushing her away and trying to self-harm. *You're not Mummy. I want my Mummy. You go away.* The energy in his lungs and voice made her eardrums rattle. If that wasn't bad enough, he'd started to hiccup badly.

The absence of a tiny object had brought his ordered world crashing down. He'd have to learn that the world could be like that, and you had to accept things were rarely ideal. At least that's what she tried to tell him, leavening the medicine with a spoonful of sugar: sometimes, just sometimes everything turns out right. And then you sang *Hallelujah*. Billy, even at the best of times, was a stranger to any show of gratitude. One day she would gift him a Mason jar so that he might, just might, come to appreciate a connection between himself and other things, other people.

The eye of the storm had stretched to thirty minutes, a period when it was as if her presence made no difference to Billy, who acted as if he was quite alone. But after a few false starts, she was allowed to cuddle him, and although he pretended otherwise, he was beginning to hear, if not listen to her. His hiccups were now replaced by a succession of loud farts.

'What is hallelujah?'

'When things turn out just right. When you're just so happy... and grateful, it makes you want to sing.' It was, she thought, best not to burden him with God right now, his mind had already constructed a perfectly convincing devil in the guise of *Mr Bugger*. One thing at a time. As she began to sing the Leonard Cohen song, *Hallelujah*, his fingers gently sought her face then came to rest on the bony part of her nose. Their 'chemistry' had a sound scientific base. Singing—and listening to—a favourite piece of music produced the same 'cuddle' hormone in the brain of the singer and the listener alike.

Lunchtime had come and gone and neither Mel nor Billy had touched a crumb. Her instinct was to forget about it altogether, the risk of a relapse too high. She'd sneak out a few of the chocolate cookies as they set out for the park—just in case. When they got back, they'd do lots of drawings of boats and bridges. She'd play it by ear whether to make lunch.

Chapter 13

As the train pulled away from Waterloo Station Mel half stood up and tugged her dress down. In no time it was riding up again. She hadn't known what to wear; the dress code for a country fair at a posh venue was some way off her radar. She consulted Holly.

'Not a wedding is it, Mel. You can't go wrong in a summer dress, and best to take a cardy, just in case.' Meeting Helena was always a dress conundrum and sometimes Mel felt she'd not got it quite right. She loosened the matching belt, relaxed and scanned the photo file of her completed roof garden.

The party was already planned, Anto looking forward to cooking with a brand-new gas barbecue and planning the wines. This time there'd be a dozen or so instead of the old foursome on whom the sun always shone. She was excited, nervous too.

There were two announcers on the train: one recorded, sounding almost as refined as Helena; the other, live and determined to inject a slice of humour into his patter. Mel ordered a coffee and thought of how often her titled friend, sitting in First Class, must have ridden this train.

On arrival she had to ask someone if this really was Winchester, the station, she thought, impossibly small to serve a city. As the taxi took off at speed she twisted and turned for views of ancient monuments and buildings but in no time, they were batting along open country roads.

While the car park was filling up, a crowd—locals she assumed—was drifting in on foot. At the lodge it was a surprise to find that all visitors, children excepted, were charged an entrance fee. How different from the US where, after parking and going in for free, you were parted from your money by a whole shebang of hard-to-resist products and pitches.

There were stalls for different meats, specialised cheeses, ciders, gins and all manner of plants and flowers, not to mention a tack cum garden machinery shop. Insurance and tourist agents were banking on footfall and offering discounts. The fresh cooked food stalls were tempting but Mel didn't plan on touching a crumb until she'd spoken with Helena. She was becoming nervous again about the meeting and distracted herself by watching kids on a bouncy castle and trampolines. The stalls were set out in a ring outside of the tall trees framing the croquet lawn and here and there were raised speakers reverberating to the sound of classic pop and a DJ doubling as the announcer. At the centre of everything, as before, stood the pink marquee.

Once again, she was unable to resist her curiosity. Someone told her there was to be a wedding the next day. So, what was the theme? She passed under the thick guy lines and tried to peep through the netting material that made up the windows. There were only dark shapes visible, no detail. And then she became aware of another person who seemed to be pursuing the same quest by another window. In New York or London, he would have been invisible, but here in an otherwise one hundred percent white crowd his Middle-East appearance made him stand out like a sore thumb. He looked puzzled then turned towards her.

'What happens here, please?'

'They get married in the house. Then they party in

here,' she explained.

He still looked puzzled, 'They party…?'

'Yes. In here they have a party.'

'Ah yes,' he said, smiling.

She tried once again to view the marquee's interior, this time by cupping her hands and blocking out the sunlight, but her ploy was no more successful. Admitting defeat, she came away expecting to encounter the man again, but he was nowhere in sight. Checking her phone, she had such a neat idea and couldn't think why it hadn't occurred to her before. She kept the text short but included a few aide-memoires that might direct Helena's brain back to early Spring and a certain Harley Street Clinic. She'd concluded with *See you very soon.*

Her instructions were to wait by the loggia at the edge of the croquet lawn where she took the weight off her legs on a park bench. A small entourage had already emerged from the house and was making its way slowly in her direction. At its centre a woman propelled herself with the aid of elbow crutches. Helena seemed to have shrunk a little. People were coming up to her and either shaking her by the hand or giving her a polite hug. Their conversations were all quite brief and appeared to follow a pattern, which made Mel wonder about Helena's amnesia—until her text arrived! But before she could even read it, she was distracted by a stir of laughter from the advancing group. She stood up to get a better view, her mind wrestling with the word order of speeches A and B.

What had scarcely bothered Mel when she first spotted the group was now the cause of some concern as she began to revive her memories of Helena, which were becoming, as the crutches approached, more at odds with what was unfolding in front of her eyes. Two explanations filtered through the fog swirling inside her head: Helena's injuries had been far more serious than the official bulletins had made out—or Mel's brain was headed the same way as Henry's.

For no good reason she looked about her. The Middle East man she'd met by the marquee was standing just a little way off and to her right. He held a bunch of flowers. As she turned back to focus on Helena, Mel was seized with such a potent sense of the surreal, it put her in mind of the scene in *Alice in Wonderland* where Alice is challenged to a game of croquet by the Queen of Hearts. A maverick giggle threatened until her nerves kicked in again.

The group stopped in front of her and a stick-thin woman with a mass of red hair—factotum Fliss, she guessed—turned to cue her boss as to Mel's place within this august company of women. Mel came forward to greet Helena who wore a frowsty grey skirt and top and the chunkiest pearl necklace she'd ever set eyes on. They both smiled politely and, it seemed to Mel, strove as hard as the other to discover a state of mutual recognition. It was no use—they'd clearly never met before. Suddenly, Lady Helena raised her stately voice,

'Quick, somebody, she's going to….'

It was only later, when she was back on the train that Mel was able to piece together more detail to the build-up to meeting the *real* countess. She remembered the wind getting up in the trees around the croquet lawn, the leaves making a whooshing, watery sound when, suddenly, they went silent. A second or two later, the countess's voice went the same way.

She came to, smelling the grass, her head between her knees, butt against something hard. Somebody was calling her by her name and squeezing her arm. Bit by bit she became aware of a uniform and a woman's voice repeating something that sounded important. Finally, she got it: the ambulancewoman had another call to make but would return as soon as possible. Meanwhile Mel was ordered to remain sitting on the park bench while her 'friend' kept an eye on her. Her 'friend' introduced himself as Hassan. He said her bag was in safe-keeping with 'one of the ladies'. *How did she feel?* Apart from acute embarrassment she was 'just fine'. She was sorry to cause so much trouble. As she pulled her dress down her hand made contact with her phone. It had been nestling in her crotch.

'The ambulance lady said you should keep your phone on you,' Hassan explained, looking a little uncomfortable. Closer now, his face suggested a pock mark or two and a receding hairline.

Without replying she went straight to the last text message. After a second reading, her voice exploded, 'Oh, Nooooo! What a *fool* I've been! I can't *believe* it,' she repeated to herself over and over, her voice beginning to crack while she held her head and stamped her feet. Her appointed watchman, she now realised, had witnessed every excruciating detail of her mad scene. After Mel's profuse apologies he had little choice but to listen to the story of Helena, the *fake* countess. She figured the uniform could not return a second sooner for him.

'Did she take money off you,' he asked politely.

'No, never.'

He nodded, then said, as if he understood everything,

'She must be leading a fantasy life.'

Mel, still close to boiling point, was needled by this softer interpretation of her nemesis and started to hyperventilate, even wheeze a little. Only now she had no access to her inhaler—it was in her bag, which someone had 'kindly' taken care of. To calm herself she took deep, slow breaths, which caused Hassan to express concern.

I'll be okay, don't worry was more for her own benefit than his. It stalled any further conversation and gave her the opportunity to examine the flowers on the bench, intended, she presumed, for Helena, the real countess. They were the same sort she'd bought at the Tube station: alstroemerias. Hassan sat like Rodin's *Thinker* in a dark suit that had seen better times. He had a longish nose, prominent lips and large brown eyes. He looked a long way from home.

At last, they were going to be relieved of one another's company. Fliss, the first responder and three other smart looking women—but no Lady Helena—were returning together from the direction of the formal gardens. The house manager was carrying Mel's shoulder bag. Hassan picked up the flowers, stood up and waited for the women.

'Please give these to Lady Helena. A sincere thank-you on behalf of Refuge UK,' he said, a little awkwardly to Fliss while the uniformed woman came over to check Mel out. Given the all-clear she was swiftly on her feet and anxious to apologise to Fliss.

'I skipped a meal, went a bit hypo… and then the heat. Sorry.'

Fliss was gracious and mentioned neither Lady Helena nor her 'amnesia'. Cradling the flowers, she turned to

Hassan and expressed a long-held concern for the plight of the Syrian refugees, using the pronoun 'we' several times. Hassan assured her the money from the fair would make a real difference. It all seemed a bit staged, and then she noticed one of the women taking notes—a reporter perhaps.

'Did you really swim from Turkey to Greece?' Fliss asked.

'Many do, you know. It's only a mile. I hope this is what you wanted,' Hassan replied, handing over an unsealed A4 brown envelope from which Fliss recovered a file.

'Hassan's Story,' she said, again a little stagily, reading to herself from the first page of the file. 'This is just what we wanted. Of course, we won't send it anywhere without your permission.'

The group was on the point of breaking up when Mel caught Fliss's eye. Of course, she'd promised to find her some transport to the station, but just as she took her phone out for the purpose, Hassan butted in,

'I've got a car—if that's any help.'

Everyone gave Mel the same quizzical expression. To decline the offer would be rude but it made her uncomfortable and Hassan, or more precisely what he'd evidently been through, made her feel more uncomfortable, especially after her outburst. It was the same when he suggested they check out the food stalls. Choosing her words carefully she accepted both offers. *She* would pay.

Eaten al fresco the tortellini, they agreed, was perfection. Mel sat in the only chair available, Hassan on the grass. He could probably see all the way up her wayward dress and she wondered about his sex life, guessing it was plentiful. He wore no ring and was likely younger than he looked in the old suit—maybe he was still in his thirties. To her relief he made light conversation, his English colloquial and fluent.

Walking back to the car park he had a question for her but came to it in a roundabout way. By now she'd learnt he was studying—an MA in Conflict and War—and worked as a waiter at the weekends.

'They'd like me to work here in the gardens. Would it offend if I said "no"? I really like the restaurant. It's near where I live. Full of happy people. Good tips too. Why do they want me here?'

Mel suggested he should politely refuse. 'I guess it has something to do with publicity—casting the estate in a more favourable light. Surprising with all the negatives now about refugees.'

'I'm not a refugee! I've got ILR! Of course, I could still be a terrorist,' he cried out, haranguing some invisible third party but at the same time seeming to reserve a portion of his anger for her.

She froze as he turned his gaze towards her. They eyeballed one another until her nerve failed and she looked away; only then did he make an apology. Still scared, she tried to concentrate on him working as a waiter. *Happy people, good tips.* It would make the car trip easier. If she made it safely to the railway station, she'd do all sorts of good deeds.

The car belonged to someone else. 'A nice person,' he said. It was small and tidy, which could only mean he'd borrowed it from a girlfriend. She relaxed a little in the car and attempted a placatory offering.

'I can understand your country making you very angry.'

'It doesn't do anyone any good, does it?'

'What about your family?'

His expression darkened. There was the briefest headshake as if to say, *Don't ask me that question*. Instead, she prattled on about the pretty countryside, apologising once more for her—in the grand scheme of things—overreaction to her setback. At the railway station he insisted on waiting until her train arrived but the silence got to her, and still curious about the background to *Hassan's Story*, she waded in. This time he answered without restraint.

'This was the deal: write an epic story and we'll make a donation to the charity. I think they wanted something like Homer,' he said, laughing.

'You doctored it?'

'I left out stuff, smoothed the rough edges, gave them what they asked. But I don't want it going public, not yet. You think I made a mistake?'

She warned him not to underestimate Fliss. Didn't the charity have a legal officer?

As the train approached, Mel found herself digging out a card from her bag and handing it over. 'If you need help or advice…' She was about to claim kinship as an immigrant, then thought better of it.

As they shook hands, Hassan had some advice for her.

'Please give your ghost lady another chance. Everyone has at least one true story worth listening to.' It sounded like the voice of hard-won experience. Maybe it was just a quote. After she took her seat Mel texted Jess but got no reply.

On the return journey there was a more orthodox announcer, who introduced himself as their manager. An economist with words, he reduced all railroad passenger information to a minimum. The briefest update informed her the train was running six minutes late. Mel told herself, for the umpteenth time, she'd pick up the pieces without so much as a wobble when she got to Waterloo. It became her mantra as the summer meadows of Hampshire flashed by. She would shut out of her life forever the creature calling herself Helena. There was no reason to reply to her rather pathetic texts, but to satisfy the wish of a stranger she'd promised to run it past friends. Somewhere between Clapham and the end of the line Mel reconstructed the real Lady Helena's face from their ultra-brief meeting. She was younger, more delicate than her impersonator whose face job suddenly made sense. And, although there was a discrepancy in height and build, there was, now she thought about it, a certain likeness too.

She saw him coming down the platform, wading through the tide of alighting passengers. How did Anto know which train? Why had he come to meet her? It was that awful, surreal feeling again. As they approached one another, she tried to read his expression. It was completely flat and as the distance between them shrank it hardly altered. She was struggling to breathe, to stand. *Please God, not Jess or Billy*. He caught her but she wouldn't have fainted, not this time.

'What?' she gasped.

'It's Henry. He's fallen from a height. Tall building. Nothing anyone could do'.

Chapter 14

As soon as she'd learned of the accident, Mel began to construct a charge sheet against herself: she should have arranged a follow-up meeting to check on her ex-husband's state of mind; she shouldn't have been so reassuring to Jess about his renewed obsession with tall buildings; it was wrong to have fostered such bitterness between herself and Davina. If it ever turned out it wasn't an accident, then the first charge would be even more damning.

She was puzzled at first as to why Anto had driven into town, the explanation: he'd been visiting with his parents in Sevenoaks. On their way back they stopped at a supermarket and he got into an argument with another customer over Brexit. 'Isn't it obvious that to go it alone when the Chinese economy is shrinking is financial suicide?' he harangued. His 'opponent' only wanted to talk about immigration. It jolted her to hear the word 'suicide'. Henry had apparently left no note, but she, and evidently his GP had thought him depressed.

On the Sunday, after a long hug at the door, Mel let Jess talk at random until the tears got to her.

'I shoulda done more,' Mel insisted.'

Jess was shaking her head. Meanwhile, Billy was playing calmly with his Lego. Even more bizarre was his reaction when his mom had given him the news of his granddad's death: *by the time he comes back, I'll be at school.*

Mel warned Jess against viewing her father's body, and then wondered if she'd done the right thing. She remembered being told that those who leapt to their death from the North Tower ended up with grossly disfiguring injuries.

On Tuesday—Jess insisting on going to work—it was as if nothing had happened when Mel went to pick up Billy. The two spent such an entirely routine afternoon together that Mel, fighting back tears, wanted, at times, to scream. In the evening she and Jess typed up from memory a chronology of Henry's life, promising to firm up dates and finer details later. His trajectory had been steep and prosperous—from merchant bank to fund manager to trader, to broker at the World Trade Centre. Mel stayed over and discovered Wednesday's Billy was not much different from Tuesday's. In the evening, returning early, she called on Anto who listened for two hours to her Mel and Henry monologue. They drank nothing stronger than tea from bone china cups.

Holly was visibly relieved when Mel—giving way to her assistant—agreed to take a short break from the office, her powers of concentration having for once deserted her. She kept cutting off into long reveries of the good times in New York. She owed that much at least to Henry's memory, but the other times—discords over the IVF failures and later, her pursuit and 'conquest' of Royce, were not so cheaply paid off.

The only time she felt useful to anyone was talking—more often listening—to Jess or looking after Billy. She was caught between opposing theories of coping and, just when she was muddling through in the middle ground, Davina's edict arrived—Mel would be *persona non grata* at Henry's funeral. His widow even talked of hiring security staff to stop her 'polluting' the service. In the absence of any suicide note, neither Mel nor Jess could bring themselves to speculate as to the cause of Henry's fall from the building in Canary Wharf where he'd once worked. That would be for the inquest to decide. There was already an unspoken consensus: they'd never know.

Saturday, two weeks on, Mel was waiting for her guests to arrive. The shock and subsequent rawness of Henry's death had shifted into a morbid fascination with the manner of it. High buildings had somehow marked out their story together and now his grim fall had brought back its beginning—the desperate plight of those caught above the fireballs, some of whom she'd seen jump from the North Tower before it collapsed. It still sent visceral shockwaves through her. She couldn't get out of her mind what had gone through Henry's during those final seconds—a similar and equally fruitless question had haunted her since 9/11. They always said you had as long as ten second's thinking time.

Another shock, but hardly a surprise, was the dawning reality that her egg and Anto's sperm had either failed to meet or failed to make friends. She'd called on him and waited for his reaction; he just nodded and she was uncomfortably reminded of the way Billy had handled the news of his granddad's death. Anto had almost as much right as Mel to cancel the party but insisted they go ahead.

She opened a red, and left the white and the Prosecco on ice. The party food, side salads and poppadums were out on trays. Anto would cook—steaks, burgers and spicy chicken.

Maria, who had only been back in London a couple of days, messaged to say she'd be late. So, when everyone else had arrived and been introduced, they went up to the terrace, each carrying a dish, a tray or a bottle. It was a sultry day with high, thin cloud; no threat of rain.

Georgie and Mick had been the first to arrive and were barely through the door when the two women broke out into a few bars from the musical they'd performed together, Mick harmonising on air guitar. It soused Mel's smouldering thoughts and put a smile on her face.

'Oh, that city-slicker voice, that accent,' Georgie gushed.

'Straight outa 42nd street,' Mel responded in something closer to Bronx than Brooklyn.

Her guests aped her voice, crazily tweaking their accents, in the middle of which Anto arrived with a cool box. Mel introduced her music theatre friends, who immediately feted him with kisses and hugs, reminding him of his review of their show, 'high octane performers and a rock band on raw adrenaline'.

It was what the terrace had always cried out for—a real party. Before the make-over it had been an underused, 'spare room' with few features or furniture. Now there was decking, Indian limestone, a statuary water feature, various plants in decorated pots and planters, and stylish garden furniture. Mel was still thrilled by the 'new room' and well-pleased by the way her guests set it off to perfection. *You wait, the lights are somethin' else*, she announced loudly, before telling herself to go easy on the wine. A little later she was intrigued to hear the word 'Italianate' and, turning round, found Holly discussing design with her partner.

Maria phoned from the street and Mel called down to her over the barrier. She'd been in Yorkshire checking out possible leads on her sister. She was still 'hustling the suits' for loans. It was the first time Mel had detected in her friend anything less than total effervescence. By her own standards Maria had dressed down—jeans and a denim shirt—in contrast to Mel's strappy top. She picked up the house key Mel had thrown down and by the time she'd reached the terrace Maria was wearing her party face. Once she'd picked up a drink, Maria looked about her and began to mix. Mel learned later that the trail in Yorkshire had gone cold.

Una, the short film auteur, was holding forth on the genre to the group of actors Mel had invited. Her next film would be a '15-minute epic' with drone shots 'before they become me-too routine'. It had to be in the can in time for the next London Festival.

Mel went over to Georgie and Mick, who were entertaining Maria with their 'magic five nights' at the Tabard Theatre and, not wanting to steal any of the glory, steered away in the direction of the drinks for a re-fill. En route she picked up a snippet from Fran, explaining something about her life in TV to Anto.

'... a real quick turnaround, hardly any time to re-hearse.'

Mel worried about Fran without fully knowing why. She was doing alright but how much close social support could she count on? Maria might get more out of her. She didn't want Maria and Una to hog one another too early in the evening.

As soon as Anto deserted Fran for the barbecue, Mel

introduced her to Maria then went round with top-ups, tuning in. It was a relief to hear nothing so far about the most toxic word on the planet: *Brexit*. The issue didn't concern her directly but one of her guests, an Anglo-Indian actor, had been threatened and manhandled on the Tube. Tuning in again she was staggered by Maria's openness. Did Fran really need to know every which way there was about porn? Whatever, she was getting a tour of the industry.

'That's why I did it,' Maria went on, 'so's I'd know exactly what to avoid to make erotic movies.'

Anto was soon prodding away with his meat thermometer, cooking to order and serving to the appreciative gathering. It was from about this point he and Maria got their heads together and nothing Mel could contrive was successful in splitting them up for long. Their soft conversing frustrated and intrigued her. They would no doubt be giving their two cents' worth on the fake countess and Mel's gullibility.

The party, into its second wind, became louder, more laid back. Stories of auditions and casting waiting rooms from hell were dusted off to great effect, during which Mel became the recipient of a second round of bear hugs and tender words, and for a while went round nursing moist eyes.

Then Georgie said, 'Are we singing?'

Mel assented, and the trio sang from *Cats* and *Phantom* to a backing track. They'd hoped to present a song from *Hamilton* but there'd been no time to rehearse. Everyone was talking about the new hit musical. Later, an unlikely sunset peeped briefly over the terrace and, when Mel couldn't wait a moment longer, she operated the remote to bring the various combinations of white lights into play. Her favourites were the stick lights that enhanced the water feature and the ornamental grasses. They were already in her Gratitude jar. Two weeks ago, she'd opened it to rid herself of the slip bearing the name *Helena*, then changed her mind. *Past* gratitude might still be worthy of the jar.

The party finally began to gravitate downstairs when someone, discovering the piano, extended it for a while until their repertoire was exhausted—cue a general exodus, apart from Anto and Maria who were soon busy tidying up, loading the dishwasher and stashing away food until they and their hostess ran out of energy.

'Bit wankered, hun. Could I crash here for the night?' Maria asked.

"Course. Have the spare bed,' Mel replied, trying to remember when it was last occupied. It deserved some sort of medal, having served the cause of countless sofa-hopping actors.

Anto picked up his cool box and, after hugs from Mel and a kiss from Maria, went home.

Mel woke to percussive sounds in the kitchen and a little later Maria appeared at her bedroom door with an offer of coffee.

'Mmm, please,' Mel said, then jumping out of bed, threw on clothes and joined Maria, who preferred her coffee strong. She'd been busy putting to rights last night's mess, the result: a kitchen cleaner and tidier than for some while. Mel was taken aback by the scale of her own embarrassment and issued profuse thanks.

'No trouble. I still owe you. Nice to meet your friends.

You've a great crowd around you, Mel. They came through for you last night.'

'I'm lucky. Mustn't go round moping though. As of tomorrow, I'm starting over', Mel said with forced determination.

'About your dilemma. We—Anto and I—looked at every angle…'

'Thought so, *and*…?'

Maria cleared her throat. 'We think you ought to meet her, and soon. Anto and I can be as close as the next table. Then again, we don't want to crowd anyone.'

Everyone thought they knew what was best for Mel. They were probably right; she'd been slowly coming round to the case for a meeting. A fantasist, they said. But harmless? She was trying to figure who of the two of them would be more on edge and only a one-to-one would settle the matter. After a tight hug, Maria went on her way leaving Mel to send a text to the fake countess, committing herself to a one-off meeting. No way was she going to go without back-up.

Hadn't she been a fantasist too? For the first time perhaps, she was beginning to grasp the futility of her own obsession. She would have to heap all her love on Jess and Billy instead, though his responses, so far, came some way short of what she longed for. The clinic was working on social responses—smiles and gratitude. Maybe one day a Mason jar really would come in handy. On top of everything, her body, behaving with treachery, was into irony too. At times of stress, she reacted with twitching of the muscles around her eyes. Right now, it was in her lower abs, but not so much twitchy as fluttering.

The following week was easier, Mel more focused after her break, the sound booth busy. The demand for audiobooks was showing a modest rise but still lagged the US pattern. For the moment the agency was just ahead of the curve. She'd heard from Hassan. It was more images than text—a series of post card shots from in and around Winchester. There was something about being a tourist guide. She couldn't decide if that was supposed to be a joke or an encouragement to visit. He mentioned a contact in Shepherd's Bush. She had reasons to be on edge about meeting him again; reasons to be curious too. What would they talk about? She'd need to update herself on the conflict in Syria—grim reading.

Chapter 15

The day before Henry's funeral Mel went straight from work to Willesden with flowers for the service and a puzzle book for Billy. Jess, like her dad, tended to tie her feelings up inside but this time there were tears and self-doubt.

'How will I cope tomorrow?'

Mel did her best to reassure her.

'I mean how will I cope without *you*?' Jess said, before losing control again.

Mel floated the idea of Jess sending short texts from the funeral service. That way *she* would cope better too. Jess agreed, adding that she might try—tasteless as it sounded—a few discreet photos.

Just before 9.00 am the following day, having lit a candle, Mel took her place in a pew at the parish church and waited for Morning Prayers. She left before mass and in the churchyard fell into conversation with a sprightly, white-haired woman, who sang in a local choir. By the time they parted—near the eyot where Mel and co. had dipped their nets—the woman, Catherine, a kind of elderly version of Helena before the unmasking, had listened stoically to the ups and downs of Mel—before, during and after Henry. If she hadn't already thought Mel crazy then she must have done so when she heard her say, 'I'm going to put you in my jar'.

Mel pressed on towards Hammersmith as if there were deadlines to meet but Holly, with the best of intentions, had factored in a preoccupied Mel rather too well. The result: little to do apart from drinking coffee and chatting.

Mel might have preferred cajoling some high and mighty in casting or working on her blog.

When the occasion demanded, Holly could talk for England—about her Northern roots, her partner, their vacations, his odd relatives. She had an ear—or was it a nose?—for the toe-curling and amusing that evidently passed for routine among his and her relations, who all seemed to be variously jinxed. Nearly every family venture, it seemed, ended up 'tits up' at some juncture. Maybe, Mel mused, all families—divorce and death allowing—behave a bit like that with time.

Holly's lively reportage and Jess's texts meant the period of the funeral passed more quickly than Mel had dared hope. When they were all done there was a lightness, a feeling of release that forced her to place her ten-year marriage into perhaps a softer, truer perspective. Had Davina done her a favour after all? Her thoughts turned to Jess and Billy and the pure necessity, not to mention yearning, for ever closer ties. If she had wondered how she was going to recycle this empty child-free space in her life she might have reasoned that the bonds between her and Jess and Billy would only grow wider and stronger with time.

About two weeks after the funeral Mel had a text from Maria with 'news'. There were no details or exclamation marks. Could they meet tomorrow night at a local pub and might she borrow the spare bed again? Mel's gut tightened—the caginess carried a gloomy feel about it. If she'd heard anything about her lost sister it was not, on the face of it, a cause for crazy celebration.

It was a mild evening when they caught up with one another in the local pub garden, Maria on time, Mel late. The former wore a grey pantsuit, and a matching tote bag stood by her feet. As they came close, Maria's scent came over like jasmine followed by earthier tones.

'Been to the Royal Marsden today. They're so clever and kind I always make an effort,' Maria began, indicating her outfit. 'Then I can seriously look the part going round Harrods. Just fantasy shopping, mind.' It wasn't all frivolity, she explained. She'd taken the opportunity to check out the latest exhibition at the V&A. Now she was exhausted and in need of something long and cool.

Mel went to the bar, returning with two lagers and low-salt chips, or crisps as she'd almost learned to call them.

'They couldn't be happier with me, Mel. Don't need to go back for a whole year. Cheers!'

'Cheers!'

'Ready for news item number two?' Maria's voice was flatter this time and Mel's heart gave a skip. She could barely get out 'Go on'.

'Are you cold, hun?'

Mel denied it but could hardly conceal the onset of a shiver. They moved indoors and occupied themselves with the food and drink before their conversation went any further.

'Enough of me,' Maria blurted, 'I've seen the video of *Murder Ballad* at the Tabard Theatre. You were a sensation, you little hottie, you. That costume! You held the tension throughout. Anto watched every performance.'

'Thank you. I hear you two have gotten quite close

since the party.'

'I'll say. I've shown him some of my scripts; he gives me a whole new perspective. A critic after all. But the real big news is…' Maria said, pausing for effect and making strong eye contact across the table, '…he's gonna bank roll me, my darling!'

'No kidding! That's amazing,' Mel responded, wondering how Anto had described the genre of the movies to the folks in Sevenoaks. She knew he received a regular allowance from them but this had to be big bucks.

Was it her imagination, Mel wondered, as they ambled down the High Road smiling vaguely at one another? Or was Maria saving something that would trump all her other news, something special for the ambience of the terrace? It was turning into a perfect summer evening. Apart from a few wispy gold-fringed clouds the sky had cleared and the light seemed to come all the way from Southern California.

It was sheer nerves, Mel reckoned, that caused her to start singing *Maria* from *West Side Story*. And then Maria joined in and it was as if the frisson of tension between them—if it had existed at all—had evaporated.

'Wish I had your voice,' Maria said at last.

They sat out on the sunny side of the terrace, drinking their coffee, looking out on a row of suburban trees that shone and quivered in the gentle breeze, trees Mel claimed for her own from the perspective of her private 'belvedere' as Anto loved to call the terrace. She was faintly amused to think that, for once, Maria might be lost for words. Where were her gags now? She had even repeated herself and then enthused again about the body stocking Mel had squeezed into for her part in the Off-Broadway musical. What was she getting at? Had she been just a little turned on? It seemed to Mel her friend could use a cue, and being Maria only outrageous would do.

'So, you wanna seduce me, right?' Mel ventured as coolly as she could.

Maria smiled slyly. 'Oh, if we had world enough and time, my darling! Something a little nobler is what I had in mind, still relies on sex though.'

Mel had not the faintest idea what her friend was trying to say and the blank expression she knew she wore was in sharp contrast to her friend's contorted features. Maria's hands were fidgeting more than usual.

'I want to be your surrogate, Mel. Only "want" is no way the right word. I *desire* it with a great passion. If you'll only let me. Please say "yes". There—I got all the words out.' She crossed her hands and placed them over her heart.

Mel was dumbstruck. Then it dawned: Anto. And not just kind, persuasive Anto but the small matter of serious money. Perhaps there'd already been a down payment. She told herself to keep calm and stick to practicalities.

'It's impossible, Maria, you have a medical condition, which...'

'Let me stop you right there,' Maria interrupted, 'Guess what they said at the hospital today when I specifically asked. *Go ahead.* Which was no surprise because I'd been reading these blogs from women with my sort of leukaemia who'd had normal pregnancies and normal babies.'

Mel nodded in a sort of daze, then said, 'Fertility?'

'Sure, it's not a given but all my tests are okay.'

'How can you work and…'

'Mel! It's the 21st century, remember. Anything else?'

'Does money figure in this somewhere?'

Maria's face darkened with bewilderment. 'My dear, lovely Mel, please get this straight. Money plays *no* part in this. I would never, never ask for any payment. It's illegal anyway.'

Maria held her head in her hands and seemed on the verge of tears. Mel launched into a grovelling apology and the misunderstanding was awkwardly unravelled. There had never been any discussion with Anto on the subject. What had it got to do with him anyway? All Maria's researches and hunches were private and had come to a head in Mel's kitchen the morning after the party.

'Looking for the coffee things I came across a certain blue product. That, and all the baby and toddler photos added up to a lightbulb moment,' Maria explained. The mask Mel had worn so long was off and she was now and forever free to talk about her long quest for motherhood and how recent events had caused her to put some distance between herself and her obsession. She explained how Anto had quite accidentally become involved and about their doomed attempt at conception.

'After the funeral I went into "appreciate-all-you've-got mode". I told myself I'm so over it—the obsession, I mean. I know I've got to talk to Anto, which will be hard. I've been disappointing myself for so long. Now I'm gonna have to do it to somebody else.'

Maria stood and walked in little circles trying to compose herself. 'He's not the only one that'll be disappointed. Wish we'd all met sooner.'

'I know he still wants to be a dad. Maybe he'll find someone,' Mel said, trying to be easy on herself. In just a few days she'd gone from obsession to reconciliation to guilt.

'O my God, I could be so good for you guys,' Maria said, then sat down and cleared her throat, 'Like the doctors today. They've got the gift of life. This was *my* big chance to help you out too.'

Mel's mood and self-esteem were in freefall. How was it that not so long ago, Maria's offer would have sent her crazy with joy? Now she was spiting her friends. How had it come to this? Henry's passing and then the funeral had triggered something it would take time to explain, to work through. The expression *drawn a line in the sand* kept coming to mind. Deep down she carried this mental furniture—had for years—the shape of a triangle: herself, the child she hoped to have, and God, more exactly, *belief* in God. If only *He'd* give her that child, what wouldn't she do, what wouldn't she become?

In bed Mel felt no better, her mind shifting crazily from one scene to another. She felt quite alone and began to cry, softly then uncontrollably louder. Knowing it was all about loss and catharsis didn't help much. And now she could hear Maria moving about; the next thing her guest was suddenly at her bedside and full of anguished apologies. They were so undeserved, it put an abrupt stop to Mel's tears.

'Really sorry. I wanted so much to give, it was painful,' Maria said.

'It's not you. Me, I'm all mixed up.'

'You really loved Henry, didn't you?'

How could Mel tell her she was mourning the loss of not just one life, but two? How could she tell anyone? She cried again but softly.

Maria eased onto the bed, lay down, dug her long arms under the duvet and cuddled Mel.

'Don't worry about me. I've been through worse than this. I'll survive,' Mel said, knowing it would give comfort to Maria. She took something from her own words too.

A little while later, Maria slipped under the duvet.

'Mel, I want to tell you something.'

Chapter 16

Riding the tube together, Anto seemed to have decided silence was something to be avoided and with that in mind he was trying to distract Mel by paying Maria various tributes. She could only take in half of what he was saying, her mind swinging from one re-imagined fake countess to another.

'Underneath all that rock 'n' roll she's really quite savvy. Writes a tight script; her humour's all the way from laugh-out-loud to caustic,' he said.

'Not those awful vagina jokes.'

'Well, not so far. More romcom… with a twist. She knows who she is, where's she's going.'

Unlike me, Mel almost said aloud.

Anto prattled on for a while but at some point, must have seen the look that told him she was trying to prepare herself for a confrontation with the woman X—identity and intentions unknown. That this person was not a complete unknown made it just a little scarier, which finally persuaded her to give up all attempts at second-guessing the outcome of the meeting. Instead, she listed to herself Maria's good points. They were in evidence the night she'd stayed over when neither could sleep for the unhappiness they'd unintentionally caused one another. It was then, in those sleep-starved hours, Maria talked of a play that had cost her something precious—her mind.

'I played *Yerma* once. *Lorca*, comprendo,' she'd begun to explain.

Mel was familiar with the story of the barren Spanish wife and nodded.

'We toured the North. Someone said they understood Lorca better up there—more primitive, more superstitious. Well, she wasn't me at all. More my ex—he *wanted* kids, but that's another story. I read around the part, researched, got inside this woman and she got right inside of me. In the play it sends her crazy, so crazy she kills her husband. You say you're over it. I'm not so sure. Either way, don't let it send you loony, hun.'

Maria hedged for a while then admitted the part had sent her to a therapist—but not until the tour was over.

'When I stopped inhabiting this woman, I thought I'd be free. But she was still there. I needed help to persuade Yerma to finally leave me in peace. Still think about her.'

This was not at all what Mel wanted to hear. She thanked Maria all the same and promised there'd be no mad scenes—at the same time uttering a silent prayer. As much as Mel appreciated and admired her friend's qualities, Maria had only seemed to highlight her own inadequacies. She hardly dared admit that it might bring some relief to see her friend leave for this new life of movie-making in Southern California. Wasn't she just a tiny bit envious, too? She'd still miss her.

At Waterloo they separated, Anto dropping twenty yards or so behind Mel. Minutes later, halfway between The Eye and Hungerford Bridge, she clocked the tall figure of Maria gazing across a grey expanse of river. Maria and Anto—the unabashed authors of this dorky game of cloaks-and-daggers—were to *almost* meet up with her outside the Espresso Bar. Inside the bar they would rush to her aid at a pre-arranged signal. Sometimes the pair were deadpan; other times they exchanged suppressed smiles.

Mel waited for their approach then, half giggly, half scared, went in. Before she'd even scanned the tables, a woman was rising from her seat looking only slightly less the aristocrat. She wore a half buttoned expensive-looking trench coat, and an unfamiliar synthetic smile. As Mel approached, neither side made any move towards physical contact.

'Mel, how good of you to meet me after I behaved so badly. It's wonderful, if rather daunting, to see you.'

The familiar alto voice brought back their meetings, the locations, the earnest conversations. A designer handbag hung from her chair.

Let her do all the talking, Mel told herself, keeping her distance and determined not to let the occasion dissolve into a teary line-under-the-past reconciliation. Her minders were just taking their seats at a nearby table.

Between sitting down and ordering drinks the fake Helena introduced herself as *plain* Helena and explained, 'As I said in my texts I was always going to open up. I just wanted you to catch me out first. Last time we met I gave clues, made deliberate errors. It was the truth, I swear, when I said I was going to tell you something next time. I meant my imposture.'

'I thought you were losing your memory, even began to believe you had the same condition as my ex-husband.'

'That was clumsy of me, sorry. Isn't he—have I got this right—part of the Renegade Economy Movement? Writing a book?'

'Something like that,' Mel replied, regretting having mentioned Henry.

'I always wanted to be someone else,' Helena began to explain. 'Mel, you'd never guess I wasted a whole year at drama school, the least talented of my group. I found finance so much easier it became my forte.'

Mel was nodding automatically at each revelation, trying to understand the complex character unfolding in front of her, vaguely aware of the café noise, the smell of fresh coffee and her friends' now irrelevant presence.

Helena continued, 'My background is stockbroking and wealth management. Our clients were A-listers. That's how I met the earl and countess.'

'And you became obsessed, wanted to be her. No?' Mel suggested.

'In a way. I wanted to be a *better* her. With that title and influence she could *do* so much more than just being the patroness of some horsey charity. At the time I was going through something like a religious conversion. Chucked in my highly paid position and went to work for two charities.'

'Sounds kind of religious.'

'Anyway, I'd been head of research at the firm so I went to town on the countess, got to know her inside out. Studied her, sort of incognito, in the flesh.'

'She didn't recognise you then?'

Helena's smile seemed genuine. She gave a quick laugh. Mel imagined some elaborate disguise.

'I got a wardrobe together,' Helena continued, 'changed my email address to hers minus one character, rehearsed, did dummy runs. I'm familiar with the structure of companies, the workings of charities.'

'Isn't it illegal to impersonate someone?'

'Only if it's a police officer or you stand to gain by the deceit. Once, to sound more plausible, I told you I took a small commission. In fact, I never have.'

'What about Hambledean Hall? Have they a fat file on you?'

'Not sure. Probably. But what do you do with someone who keeps polishing your image without ever sending you the bill?' Helena said, raising the pitch of the last word then tittering contentedly. The stranger—for that was how Mel still saw her—seemed to have an answer for everything. But Mel was struck by this cute way of raising funds for charity. Sure, it was by deception but nobody was getting really hurt. Could she believe all of it?

'So who are you? And what do you do when you're *not* being Lady Helena?' Mel asked with a touch of sarcasm.

'Good question. I have to admit I've missed her dreadfully. Got very low about it. Lost confidence. My doctor gives me pills but it all takes forever. Who am I? What am I?'

Helena had begun to grip the table to lessen the tremor that had just started to take hold of her hands, and her face, despite heroic efforts, was beginning to twitch. The mask of the confident, rational stranger was slipping, but instead of feeling triumphant, Mel felt only shame— her desire to take the woman to task entirely spent. In the midst of this hazy turnaround an epiphany had just announced itself.

'I'm sorry. I've not been very kind,' Mel said, seeing a different persona to the one she'd always attributed to the aristocracy in general and Lady Helena in particular—a mask *behind* the mask.

Helena produced an embroidered handkerchief from her bag and was dabbing her eyes with it. She shook her head. 'No, you've been very fair. I know I'm a freak. A fake countess and… you must have guessed… a fake woman.'

'Don't say that, Helena. It's not the truth as far as I, or anyone else, are concerned.'

'Thank you.'

It was time to steer the conversation to a place of relative safety. Mel began to describe how in the aftermath of the Twin Towers she'd got started on her Gratitude jar and how, among the slips of paper there was still one bearing the name *Helena*.

'Touch and go for a while,' Mel teased, which made them both laugh. Their friendship—from the start—had relied on overlapping comedic temperaments. There was nothing fake, though, about Helena's sense of the ridiculous.

'Enough of me. Let's talk about you, Mel.'

'You know all about me!'

'There's always something more to tell. Why, for instance, the cosmetic... adjustment?' Helena said, touching her face. 'Did it have anything to do with appearing in that musical and I wondered... were you planning a return to the stage? But no. Affairs of the heart? I wasn't entirely convinced but then I remembered you describing a much younger boyfriend. Another time I saw you look so intently at a mother talking to her child, I thought that must be it.

'*You can't always get what you want,*' Mel almost sang, a picture in her head of a warm summer's evening in Hyde Park, she and Royce at The Rolling Stones concert. Was it really three years ago?

'But what had that to do with this?' Helena probed, stroking her face again.

Mel shrugged. She had no wish to embark on precise explanations right now.

Helena smiled, nodded and, as if it was her turn to change the subject, delved into her bag and retrieved an A4 file, then laid it out on the table in front of Mel. The printed columns on the left contained the names of charitable sounding organizations and, to the right, of companies and retail outlets. Mel knew the names of only two of the businesses and none of the charities.

'Turn over. Look at the last entry, Mel. Found it?'

'The one you dug out of me! Never thought you'd actually… and all in the name of Lady Helena,' Mel said. Their laughter was only a little restrained.

Helena's returning confidence gave Mel the green light to an idea she'd been wrestling with for some minutes. Would it be so crazy to introduce everybody? How would it go down with Helena? After only a moment's deliberation, she said it would be 'quite okay' for Anto and Maria to come over and join them. Mel went to their table and gave them a speed-briefing before making the introductions.

Helena appeared to revel in the attention, fielding easy, polite questions. Then Anto asked her where she lived and, without missing a beat, she replied 'in the country', treating her small audience to a Lady Helena masterclass. How the sunlight came 'streaming in through the east wing in the morning'. And when she'd quite done with Hambledean Hall, the gardens and a dubious connection with Jane Austen, she exhaled deeply and gave a diffident smile, the performance—or was it therapy?—over.

'Should have stuck to drama school,' Anto responded.

'The money, dear, the money,' came Helena's reply. She picked up her papers and was about to put them away when Mel asked if her friends could see the 'accounts'.

She was feeling proud of Helena and wished a little more recognition for her. Again, there was a moment's hesitation, then, 'Of course, but please, this mustn't go any further.'

Anto scanned the papers while Mel beamed at Helena. The ensuing silence seemed to be a good time to prattle on about her own accounts and how Holly took care of them; she was never any use at math.

'Over half a million...' Anto announced.

'...and counting, with the sponsorship,' Helena replied, 'drop in the ocean to the major charities, which is why I select only those of meagre means. That way I can make a difference. The annual budget of the biggest charity is now close to a billion so you see I'm very small beer.'

There was a chorus of disagreement followed by jokes about the real Lady Helena receiving an MBE for 'her' services. After Maria had made a brief inspection, the papers were put away amid more business-like noises from Helena instancing someone with a 'forensic approach' who might want to check the entries with Companies House and the Charity Commission.

Shortly after, Anto and Maria made their excuses and, after fond goodbyes, left Mel and Helena alone together.

'I like your friends, Mel. They didn't make me feel uncomfortable.'

'Why should they? So, what will you do now?'

'I'll have to wait a bit for madam's fetlock to get a little stronger. I worry about her memory. She wasn't wearing a *proper* riding hat, you know. I need to invest in a posh walking stick, practise the walk. I'm always researching. Hope to hustle again soon.'

'You are obsessed, aren't you? I mean in the nicest way.'

'I suppose I am. Think you are too, still.'

'No, I'm cured—thanks to pollution and climate change,' Mel said.

'I'm not convinced these are *your* reasons, Mel.'

'They're reasons enough.'

'Come on, let's walk. I've a brolly if it rains.'

They could still hear Billy babbling away to his monkey, Wolfgang, while Jess poured more wine. Mel had no idea how her 'confession' might go down with her stepdaughter or whether it would lighten her own darkness—a condition that had settled over her since the heart-to-heart with Maria.

'I drove your dad crazy with my obsession,' she began.

'He never said.'

'He wouldn't though. And all those IVF cycles drained us. If I'd not been so totally fixated, we'd still be together. He'd still…'

'Save it for the priest, Mel! You've done nothing wrong in my book. Who wouldn't be obsessed—and the clock ticking. Must *be* like a kind of madness. Only… please tell me you weren't doing stuff at the time.'

'No way! That was how we coped with the failures. Like afterwards, you know.'

There was silence for a while—almost. Billy had gone to sleep but the plumbing in the apartments above was still some way off going into quiet mode. Mel plucked at the sleeve of her top as if that might help summon the reserves she was searching for.

'I feel like this character in a Spanish play. She's desperate for a child but her husband isn't all that sympathetic. Everyone else are having babies. They blame *her*. The people are steeped in folklore and superstition. In desperation she seeks some religious intercession. In the process of losing her mind she kills her husband.'

'Mel, you *know* your life with my dad wasn't like that.'

'But the coincidence really haunts me'

'You have this imagination whereas I prefer to stick to the facts. Like I put pressure on Dad to come home when you guys were doing all right in NYC. And then there's the dementia and how that ties up with him marrying Davina and what a bad call that turned out to be. I wasn't going to tell you, but she's making noises about the will,' Jess said.

'What!' Think I *could* be homicidal after all!'

'Sorry. Didn't mean to upset you. Dad *was* sympathetic, wasn't he?'

'Of course he was. Just wish I'd known when to say no more IVF. Just wish he hadn't…'

By mutual consent a respectful silence followed, Jess pointing to the wine bottle which Mel declined. There was something else Mel, out of shame, would never admit to, especially to her stepdaughter. Jess wasn't the only one to put pressure on Henry to make a move to London. Royce was still starring in all her daydreams. Eventually, picking up a different thread, Jess said, 'That terrible day, the day you met the proper countess, you also met someone nice.'

'I don't know about nice. Impressive, yes,' Mel replied.

'You said he had beautiful eyes.'

'Did I? S'pose I did. You really don't mind him coming on the boat trip? He's never been to London.'

"Course not. It'll be good for Billy. The clinic are

working hard on his smiles; he can practise them on the guy,' Jess said, adding slyly, 'Where's he staying?'

'Shepherd's Bush. Don't you give me that look, Jess. I think he has all the women he wants.'

Chapter 17

Jess's face said it all: she'd had a fight with Billy, and the north side of Westminster Bridge was clearly not where she most wanted to be right now, *and* they'd arrived only just in time to catch the boat. She barely acknowledged Mel's visitor, taking out and checking instead her phone after handing Billy over. Overawed by the crowd and 'Big London', he clung tightly to Mel. In the press and chaos, she went through the motions of introducing Hassan as a newly qualified tourist guide who doubled as a waiter. She'd clean forgot to mention he was a student or what he was studying. It hardly mattered—Jess still had half an eye on her phone. Mel and Hassan had just come away from Westminster Abbey where, in about one hour flat, Hassan had quietly finessed her weak grasp of English history.

The river sparkled invitingly in the sun and there was a noisy buzz of excitement as the crowd went forward to board the vessel. The moment they found their places, Hassan—ending up next to Billy—looked away, rubbing his eye as if there was dust in it. As soon as Mel saw through the subterfuge, she realised her gaffe, imagining overcrowded boats sinking or breaking down, scenes of panic and tragedy. She'd not gone into any detail about the sightseeing trip.

'Sorry. Crowded boats. I should have known.'

Still avoiding eye contact, he shook his head, 'It's the boy,' he said.

Had he read something sinister into Billy's gauche efforts at smiling? She tried to explain, adding that he was only four years old and crazy about boats and bridges.

Hassan shook his head again. 'He reminds me…'

Was he trying to let her off the hook? Did he mean a dead child? That was the downside to making an effort to research the war in Syria—her attempts at comprehension were no match for its horror and depravity. Hassan had reasons aplenty to explode with anger as at Hambledean Hall when he more than seemed to take pleasure in making her feel small and scared. If there was any repeat of that in front of Billy, she would make it her business to match his anger. But as watery London slipped by, Hassan and Billy started a conversation about bridges. To be sure, it was mainly Hassan; he seemed to know the names of all the Thames crossings and spent time getting Billy to repeat them as they passed beneath every bridge. Then he'd take a picture and let Billy hold his phone. In between bridges Mel trotted out the usual tourist landmarks and again Hassan seemed to have done the relevant homework.

The buzz on the boat went up a few notches as they approached Tower Bridge. Billy, beside himself with excitement, failed to take in Hassan's two–handed demonstration of how it worked. No matter, a high point was reached when man and delighted boy combined to photograph the famous structure. At least *some* of Billy's smiles, Mel reckoned, were genuine. Meanwhile Jess was quiet and remote. She looked cool in her sleeveless, polka dot top and linen shorts. Mel also wore shorts, the difference being in her generous use of fake tan so that their legs matched as far as skin tone went, otherwise Mel's were longer by two or three inches.

Henry's death had begun to pose questions of their easy sisterly relationship and there were times when Mel felt the need to act more like a parent towards her stepdaughter. There'd been sympathy and invitations to stay in West Sussex but so far, no visit by Jess's mum was planned. Putting an arm around Jess, Mel offered to look after Billy more often, maybe for a full weekend. Jess nodded, smiling briefly. It had been hard work just getting him out the door today—he'd wanted so much to go to 'Little London' and see Captain Anto again.

At Greenwich they looked around the Cutty Sark but didn't venture inside. Jess, recovering her manners, explained to Hassan the experience would be 'a bit too much' for Billy.

'He'd get so blown away, he'd never want to leave. When he's older we'll do a project on it.'

They bought a ball and a few goodies for the picnic and made for the park, climbing the grassy hill until they reached an unoccupied viewpoint. And there, staring Mel in the face was her worst gaffe of all.

'Looks like New York!' Hassan exclaimed, gazing at the high-rise cluster across the river—Canary Wharf.

'That's where Mel comes from,' Billy informed Hassan. But Mel wasn't listening, she turned to Jess and gave her a hug.

'Please, *please* forgive,' Mel blurted, horrified, 'I had no idea…'

'It's okay. I'm as much… didn't occur to me when you said Greenwich.'

It was exactly six weeks to the day Henry's body was found close to one of the towers in the financial district now in plain sight.

Hassan and Billy had already begun to kick the ball about, unconcerned as to any possible delay to the picnic.

After Jess had opened her shoulder bag and rolled out the mat, the two women sat on their knees and pretended to watch the ball game. They talked of Henry—their own precious memories of him. Then Billy called out to Mel to join in the game.

'Go on,' you're still his favourite footballer—just,' Jess said, watching Hassan dribble and do keep-ups.

Once the picnic was set out, the food was rapidly consumed with the exception of Billy's meal. He needed bribery—the offer of a cookie and the promise of more football—to empty his plate. Hassan showed no reaction to Billy's unusual eating habits. Afterwards the women watched as he and Billy kicked off another game and Mel unconsciously compared the scene with that of Anto—trousers rolled up—dipping with Billy in the Thames. Both men had been schoolteachers and handled her step-grandson confidently. Hassan, though, possessed a warmer touch.

On their return they stopped by Bankside, crossed and re-crossed the Millennium Bridge before taking in a fleeting glance at the Globe Theatre. Mel had once tried to explain to Billy what plays were: stories you could see and hear. To her surprise he'd retained this catechistic scrap, proudly repeating it almost word for word. It brought about a round of applause—and then a prize. Hassan dug inside his jacket pocket, produced a small book and presented it to Billy. It was all about the Cutty Sark. For a few seconds Mel was flustered as she came to terms with the coincidence of Helena giving her a book for Billy only a few yards from where they were standing. Several thank-yous, goodbyes and smiles later their ways parted. Mel and Hassan going off to Bloomsbury to spot blue plaques, Jess and Billy to get the Tube.

Later they found a cool place to sit near the fountains in Russell Square, Mel exhausted and, once again outmatched. Apart from the Pre-Raphaelites and Charles Laughton, the actor, she recognised none of the names. Hassan was ahead by a couple of plaques when, recognising her irritation, he suddenly called a stop to the 'game' and said he wanted to go to nearby Great Ormond Street to see the world-famous children's hospital.

They glugged on bottled water no longer cool, then Hassan went quiet, turned toward her with an uneasy smile she imitated and returned, adding a *what next* expression. Within his large brown eyes something had replaced the anger she'd witnessed before. She thought she could detect a determination, even coldness. But wasn't it that quality that had served him well enough to escape Syria and begin his 'odyssey'? This time, to her surprise, he was the one to turn away, as if he felt awkward after acting the geeky tourist guide. Turning back to her again, he enquired about Billy's difficulties and nodded while Mel skated around her step-grandson's 'communication and locomotor problems'. He promised to send her the photos he took on the Thames.

'You were good with him today. Thank you,' she said.

Hassan's response was to take out his phone and say, 'My son is a little older than Billy. This is he,' he said, scrolling the photos for her.

A shaven-headed boy of 4 or 5 years smiled sweetly at the camera. In some shots he wore short trousers and a sporty top, in others he had a woollen hat and a winter jacket too big for him. There was a video too. The boy waddled up to a ball and kicked it with some force. There was shouting and cheers from an unseen crowd and a confusion of voices.

'He has beautiful eyes. What's his name?' Mel asked.

'Mohammed.'

Then it hit—none of the photos was recent. Mohammed looked about Billy's size.

'When did you last…?' but Mel got no further. The poignancy of her question stopped her in her tracks.

'It's nearly a year,' Hassan replied, and at once his face was on the move and he struggled to contain the restlessness that had captured the rest of his body. Mel tried to look away but a feeling of responsibility made her watch him fight the sad genie her question had unwittingly released. Six weeks on, the healing breach in Mel's emotional defences was being blown wide open a second time. Hassan slowly regained his composure while Mel twittered her apologies and tried to take the conversation elsewhere. But he'd already intuited what would have been her follow up question.

'One, only one,' he said, adding, 'kids are not kids for very long in Syria.'

Desperately looking for distraction, Mel sprang up and suggested they go to a nearby pizzeria she'd been to before.

'Come on, with your professional eye you can rate the service out of ten.'

She'd get him to talk about being a waiter in Winchester and maybe resurrect some of her stories of when she was a waitress at Ellen's Stardust Diner. She could do with a drink too.

Next day, Mel was sat on the steps outside St Paul's, listening to the long peal of bells that followed the Eucharist service, which she hadn't quite been able to bring herself to attend. It was all Anto's fault—he told her the bells would do her more good, offer her more Zen than going in and attending a service. Perhaps he was right. The guilt she still felt about Henry's death was complex and in part had all the makings of *doing penance*, a phrase much used by her mother at the height of her religious fervour. It would therefore last just as long as it was supposed to, and nothing she did or didn't do would wipe it away any sooner. Yesterday Hassan had been a welcome distraction. Today, Maria would be her distractor.

The penance, or the idea of a penance, was losing some of its sharp edges amongst the hefty reverberations of the bells. They freed her mind enough to imagine a period— early in her marriage—when she'd slip down to Trinity Church in Lower Manhattan and sit and listen to the bells or a concert being given by the choir. It was close to where she'd met, more exactly, found Henry. He was in shock while others, fleeing the dust from the collapsing towers, sought sanctuary in the church.

For several minutes a happy balance held between those early days, the dwarfed church and the twelve bells of St Paul's. She opened her eyes and recognised Maria in a bright summery combination sitting lower down. She must have seen Mel but didn't want to invade her space.

It wasn't until the peal went silent that Maria mounted the steps and joined her. Mel stood up and they hugged.

'Hiya, babe!'

'Hi there,' Mel replied.

'How did yesterday go?' Maria asked after their usual exchanges.

'Mostly okay. It was a long day. Billy took a shine to our visitor. Here—take a look,' Mel said, handing over her phone.

'Hey, I could *use* this guy, and your stepdaughter is pure class.'

'Screen tests for two then,' Mel responded.

'Is she anything like Henry?'

'Funny you should ask. Since he passed, I see more of him in her. Spooky.'

They followed the familiar route and once more the skateboarders were out in force on the slopes as they took the steps towards the river. Maria was animated, talking about her upcoming movie making, outlining plots and locations.

'You must come over. Be my Best Boy,' she joked.

'Love to.'

They walked to the Borough Market, enjoyed a coffee and bought provisions before visiting the recently opened extension to Tate Modern where they split up—Maria to the photography rooms, Mel to the art. Mel had a sense that Maria wanted to discuss something before she finally left for California. They were both thankful to be neutrals where Brexit was concerned but deplored the way it had divided and brought out the worst in people. And now, out of that, the tragic murder of a young Labour MP.

'There's two cultures here now. Remind you of anywhere?' Maria observed.

They met up for lunch in the cafeteria.

'Let me drool over that guy again, will you,' Maria pleaded.

After some teasing Mel handed over her phone. 'Sorry to disappoint you but he's in love… with Winchester. And I think Winchester's in love with him.'

'You just want him for yourself, Mel,' Maria joked, and they both laughed.

'He's gotten quite close to the house manager at Hambledean Hall. They've practically adopted him, plus he has girlfriends in the town.'

'Lucky guy!'

'Not so. He pines for his son in Syria. Hasn't seen him for a year.'

The conversation stalled, Maria handed back the phone and they scrambled to find lighter material to trade. It seemed Maria was going to wait for their walk along the South Bank to broach whatever it was that was distracting her. Was it about her sister? They were both coming to the unspoken conclusion she'd never be found. It seemed to have entered that vast repository of life's unknowns, such as did Henry fall or did he jump?

Chapter 18

Trying not to touch anything, Mel strode about the house wearing surgical gloves. Her method was high on an impression of serious intent, low on logic. Clasping her hands together for the purpose, there was more than a hint of prayer about it too. She guessed that Anto, whose 'package' she anxiously awaited, was way better prepared, although he was taking his time about it. The compulsion to imagine him jerking off then dropping the 'goods' down a drain was straight out of last night's dream.

The doorbell duly rang. She rushed to the door to be confronted by Anto's unshaven face which gave little away. He held the plastic container in both hands and without saying anything, released it into Mel's gloved hand then left, believing, she reasoned, that mere words would add little to his vital donation to the enterprise. At his instigation all three of them had made wills and signed a legal document.

In the kitchen, holding her breath, Mel withdrew as much of the 'goo' as possible into the syringe—air bubbles and all, and as she headed upstairs her breathing seemed to get out of sync with the rest of her body.

She half expected to find Maria naked but she still had on her leopard skin dress, her briefs by her feet. She lay on the lounger by the fountain and swore as Mel approached. It was either relief, excitement or both. To hand on Anto's sperm—and all their hopes—Mel, rushing in, brushed against a whole row of lavenders in bloom. They were scenting strongly and had become a magnet for honey bees, some of which she disturbed into flight and had to dodge.

'Thought you was never gonna come, babe,' Maria said, in a mock-weary East End voice.

'Glad *someone* came,' Mel said, and they both laughed. The 'pantomime' had begun and, all of a sudden, Mel could take more air into her lungs. Without any prompting, the 'patient' flexed her hips, flopped into lithotomy and began to reprise her stock of vagina jokes, to which Mel had become somewhat immune. Gently, almost reverently, she began by parting the labia, and then a wave of panic seized her as her fingers flailed about in a void. Maria, unable to keep a lid on her instinct for irony, gasped,

'Get it right, girl. Don't fuck up on me now.'

Mel would never have guessed she could panic and laugh at the same time. And the more she panicked, the more desperately she pressed and searched for Maria's cervix. At last, her fingers tipped the landmark and, holding her breath, she squeezed the plunger. For a while all she could think of was the shape and consistency of what she'd made contact with, how closely it matched the tip of a firm penis.

'Okay?' Maria asked.

'Right over the target. Up to you now,' came the reply.

'Y-e-a-h,' cried Maria, with genuine relief. She'd already started dosing on vitamins. Now she reminded Mel of their joint pledge to forgo alcohol if things went 'according to a certain plan'.

'Let's seal it now,' she commanded, indicating an embrace.

Steadying herself on her wrists, Mel bent down and angled her head. It gave Maria the advantage and, with her hands free, she turned Mel's head and pressed her lips against her friend's. Mel offered no resistance. She was neither offended nor surprised; she was learning to read her rambunctious friend better these days. As it was, their relationship had travelled 180 degrees. Once, Maria was the beholden one; from now on it was Mel who would owe the favours. Maria was the latest to be given a place in the Mason jar 'Hall of Gratitude'.

They released one another and as Mel slowly got to her feet they fist-bumped.

'This feels weird, Mel. After all this time I'm back with Yerma, but this time there's no stage. *This* is for real.' Mel searched her brain for something fitting to say but could only come up with a mere practicality.

'You know what you've got to do now?' she said in a neutral voice.

'It's the only part I was able to re-hearse,' Maria said, and they smiled conspiratorially at one another.

Camden High Street was heaving with shoppers and tourists so that Mel had to pick slowly through the crowd on her way to the gastro pub, which gave her time to take in the colourful street art, the wannabes and the clothes. She could smell incense and the tang of leather. Either she'd been too busy before to notice any of this plethora of sensuous delights or she'd arrived late at night. Despite typically running late, she was in no hurry to learn the identity of the strange woman Royce had briefly encountered on a Los Angeles beach.

Although his letter was headed 'A Revelation', what followed was anything but. A single reference to the

'Weird Sister of Venice Beach' was followed by a list of unlikely explanations: she was an hallucination; she came from outer space; she was the woman in Ibsen's *The Lady from the Sea.* The elliptical style was pure Royce, with a touch of the schoolkid—he'd sketched an erect penis, adding the caption 'not actual size'. Did that mean he'd gone ahead with medical treatment for his unfortunate problem?

Mel had been quite relaxed about the Breton T-shirt, cropped jeans and white trainers—until now. Here, with just a few variations, it seemed to be the badge of the majority of tourists over a certain age striving to look hip. What nod to fashion would Royce be wearing, she wondered? He'd recently been back to Milan to lavish his Hollywood largesse, no doubt in the lost cause of patching up family relationships.

He was sat at a small table with a glass and a bottle of wine, reading a newspaper. Wearing white chinos, he sported an expensive blue shirt and skinny cravat. As soon as Mel tapped him on the shoulder, he shot up out of his chair and made a big fuss of her. She was pleased to see him in such high spirits. He'd gained a few pounds and lost the haunted look. After the pleasantries he bustled off to the bar with their food and drink order. Returning, he showered her with gratitude and compliments.

'I've you to thank for my restoration,' Royce said, pouring himself more wine.

Mel was no wiser, until his clarifying charade.

'That! You'd have found out sooner or later. I just read it somewhere in a newspaper.'

'And I don't have diabetes, at least not yet. So, the other

business is sorted. You didn't tell me I'd have to *inject* myself,' he said, laughing and illustrating with another charade, his voice booming across the tables, turning heads.

'That would've put you right off,' she said in a hushed voice then turned the conversation to business, the theatre and *The Tempest* in particular, during which their order arrived—two identical paninis, a salad and a St Clement's. Royce had opted for the healthy option too. Between mouthfuls and hasty sips of wine he treated her to an essay on *Milano*, often slipping into perfect Italian to showcase its culture and cuisine. It gave her an idea: Royce on Radio 4 on Italian cities, and if that went well...

Now he was back to the minutiae of self-injection and Mel felt all the way from squeamish, through fascinated to entertained.

'And then, before you can say *Cosi fan tutti*, it has the kind of effect you only read about in erotic fiction—two hours rock hard, no kidding,' he said, lasering her with his blue eyes.

'You must be overdosing, Royce. Please check it out with the medics.'

'Me*dics*! Geddit? Never felt better,' he responded, roaring with laughter.

There was no stopping him now. Dropping his voice only slightly and switching to voice-over mode he began to talk of the 'endless possibilities', about parties and 'choreography'. Why was he doing this to her? She'd felt sorry for him and this was how he repaid her. She did not want to hear about threesomes, still less participate. She sprang up, expressing a sudden need for 'fresh air'. He'd talked about a walk by the canal. With a head start she wove at speed through the crowd before becoming aware of his laboured breathing.

Neither uttered a word until they reached the towpath. She preferred to think his silence contrition rather than lack of oxygen. Hers was pure fury. Beside the canal, whose still waters seemed to calm things down, Mel listened to a sombre Royce.

'There's been a development. Been in touch with the good lieutenant.'

Mel could only wonder what style of communication he adopted with her. He still had this thing about her— the Spanish looks, her holstered gun. But in the letters and sketches he'd sent via the agency, she'd formed an impression he was also a little wary of her. Was it a kind of reverse macho thing?

'Our mystery lady was a journalist, freelance, writing a book on crystal meth. She got hopelessly hooked. Also, she was obsessed with the Scottish play. We know she was in Stratford that time because she reviewed it for a magazine.'

'Poor woman. But please don't tell me her name, Royce. I'll only start to imagine her, construct some sort of elaborate bio.' Mel was speaking from the heart but there was this cynical area in her brain—to be sure a rather underused facility—that coldly informed her the woman's name was Laura, and that he was covering up some vital part of the story.

'She must have recognised you? Didn't she say anything?'

'She was stoned. And yeah, some crazy incantation.'

'Did she have family?'

'Don't know. Bit of a loner, I think.'

While they drank tea at a floating café, Royce, in marked contrast to his earlier ebullience, retold the beach story. His nightmares about entering the morgue alone and finding the woman still breathing were less frequent and he hoped now for some kind of closure. Back on the towpath neither spoke until they reached the Tube station. Mel's thoughts were going every which way and travelling at great speed. And everywhere they went they threw up more questions. The big one: if Royce *still* couldn't admit to an affair with Laura, what else might he be concealing? Did he hide stuff from the 'good lieutenant'? And if so, why? The touchpaper had been lit on her incendiary imagination and she knew she was in for sleepless nights. Surely it was unthinkable he was in any way responsible for the woman's death. Logic was one thing: imagination another.

'Don't judge me too harshly, Mel. I know I'm a *picaro*. It's what I take on stage. It's what gives me the pure effrontery to lie and cheat my way into a role. There's too much of him off stage, I know. Once I thought you might cure me of him. But I'm much too weak, you see.'

They were waiting for her train and, not for the first time, Royce was attempting the trick of distancing himself from his 'great character flaw', even hinting that if only other lesser talents had tried to understand him a little more…

She wasn't quite sure of the meaning of *picaro*, she guessed rogue or scoundrel. Mel was hard put to explain how the same man could have her in tears one minute then infuriate her the next. It wasn't just *what* he was saying at their parting, it was *how*. It was the picaro talking for sure, but how beautiful it sounded—until he named the cure: a few days away together at some palazzo in *La Serenissima*. Her business mind kicked in again—his voice on radio paired with the sound of bells and vaporettos up and down the Grand Canal.

But as far as words went, she was lost—her mind a blank—and as a result, unable to come up with an appropriate version of *thanks, but no thanks, let's keep it entirely professional*. Instead, she panicked, blurting out, 'I'm pregnant' just as she stepped onto the train.

Chapter 19

'W h e e e e,' went Mel as Billy's monkey, Wolfgang, shot down the slide on his own. 'Now you two together,' she said encouragingly. But Billy was having none of it—it would somehow kick against his world order if his arms weren't free on the slide. Not even watching Mel going down with Wolfgang would do the trick. Another time maybe. With prompting, the monkey had slowly begun to replace the go-to pack of cards without which no journey was previously possible.

On their way home they played I-spy. Billy's phonetic grasp of the alphabet was coming along, even ahead of the curve, she'd heard. Once indoors, they killed time with cards, dominoes and slapstick mime until Jess came home, when Mel could relax and take a back seat. But Mum was tired and Mel offered to take a turn in the kitchen. After the meal it was Mel who got Billy ready for his bath.

'I'm surprised you've not been back to Winchester yet,' Jess said with a touch of sarcasm as soon as the bedtime rituals were over.

'Don't know what you mean,' Mel replied disingenuously.

'You fancy him, don't you?'

Failing to smile quite as enigmatically as she'd intended, Mel replied, 'I'd fancy him more if he lived up here in town. It's complicated; he has a young son in Syria who needs hip surgery.'

'You believe all that? Isn't he too good to be true? And he knows you were taken in by that fake Lady Helena.'

'What! Of course I believe him! He showed me photos

of his son, a video—the boy waddles.'

'Sure the boy's *his* son?' Jess probed.

'He has his father's eyes. What are you getting at, Jess?' Money? Sex?'

'Worse than that.'

'No. He abhors violence. He's too his own person to be radicalised.'

'Okay, okay. Just don't always see only the good in people,' Jess cautioned.

'You sound just like my old mom. God! I could use a drink except I made a pledge with Maria.'

While Jess was out of the room making tea, Mel went through all she could remember of Hassan's visit. The only time he'd said anything really personal was when he talked about his son. Otherwise, he'd gone into raptures about writers—English and American, and he was pretty hot on English history too. He came over—Mel remembered the scene at Russell Square—like any other father desperate to secure treatment for a disabled son. Okay, so he might have melted a few hearts with pictures of his son, then turned them to his advantage. That wasn't to say they weren't genuine. Saying goodbye at the Tube station they'd touched each other rather stiffly then engaged in a hug, Mel's thoughts almost entirely, but not quite, dominated by the boy.

'You know I voted leave, don't you?' Jess said after returning with the mugs.

'Sure I do. That's democracy.'

'I never said why.'

'I can figure it out.'

'I'm *not* racist, Mel. Listen, everyone I know has trouble with social services, the NHS, housing, jobs. Yet the authorities have to bend over backwards for these people. We've got to care for our own ahead of anyone else. Fuck austerity—we're one of the richest nations on earth.' Jess's voice had sharpened a few half tones

Mel made concurring noises. She'd witnessed the rise from nowhere of food banks, the proliferation of charity shops, street begging and other claims on her purse. She was well aware that even in rich countries people could fall on hard times—a nowhere land between official and charitable assistance.

'And some of them mean us harm. I get frightened going to work thinking about it. I think a lot about bad things. What would happen to Billy?' Jess lamented.

Mel stood up and hugged her seated step-daughter awkwardly. Since her father's death it was noticeable how Jess had become more convinced that something terrible was going to happen. Mel voiced reassurances she hardly believed herself.

'There's another reason to go easy with this guy. All to do with you being American. Know where I'm coming from?'

'Nope. Not a clue.'

'If he marries a Brit he gets his British passport that much quicker,' Jess said with obvious distaste.

'So, if I get a marriage proposal, I know he's not foolin' around,' Mel responded. But the joke bombed, leaving her embarrassed and anxious to apologise. Not so long ago, Jess would have come out with something raunchy and laughed. Now she looked tired, had got herself bogged down with 'piddling' alteration work and she was behind with the wedding dress.

That night neither of them slept well. Jess got up early

to work on the dress and barely acknowledged Billy or Mel. These Wednesday mornings Mel had begun to take over Billy's care, making sure they hit all the time targets before getting him to nursery. This time, after kissing him goodbye, she walked to the centre and asked to speak with Lou. Twenty or so minutes later the sporty hunk emerged and the talk began with news of next season's volleyball before moving on to Jess.

'She's losing it with everything and everybody. Not sleeping well. I'm sure she's lost weight. All this since her dad's awful death,' Mel said.

'Thank you, Mel. We should have seen this coming. It's going to impact Billy in a big way—*could* do is what I mean. I'll get my wife to call. She knows her better than me. Poor Jess. You're in for a hard time with her too.'

Mel, can I talk to you in person. I've just spent time at the home office. I realise it's not much notice and you'll be busy with all kinds of stuff. So maybe it's not possible. And I've just worked out where you work—a long way from trafalgar square.

So hello and goodbye. I'll be in touch, Hassan

Mel had got a little lost again in Theatreland and had her phone out for directions when she found the half-hour old text. It was Friday, 5.30 pm, the traffic was nose-to-tail and commuters bore down from every direction. She texted back saying she was only ten minutes away. It would be about Hassan's son, Mohammed. Maybe they'd been given the green light—the okay for his surgery at Great Ormond Street. She was excited for them and tried upping her pace through the crowds. It was going to be a long ten minutes, added to which Hassan would be at the station by now and maybe already on the train.

Mel had just come out of a meeting with 'Mr Musicals'. At the outset it was like turning up for an audition, adrenaline levels and the like, but they settled soon enough when he began to talk Broadway and the shows he'd been involved in. 'Like Hotel California, you can never really leave, can you?' she responded. He seemed to like the metaphor.

Mr Musicals was hefty—around 250 pounds—but brisk and precise, his immaculate office was at one end of a long room, and at the other stood a grand piano. He spoke mid-Atlantic, a little out of fashion these days, and she wondered how twangy she came across.

'New Yorker—am I right?' he asked.

'Thereabouts. Came over in 2012'.

'Before that?'

She explained about working for the agency.

'And before that?'

'You could say West 42nd street was my second home.'

He nodded and smiled and the talk turned to Off Broadway shows in the 90s. He recalled 'heady days' when, as a lowly production assistant he'd had a hand, a *very* small hand, in a few well-known Broadway shows. Then it was down to business. They sat on swivel chairs—close but not too close—while they viewed Spotlight files, resumés and video clips. It had been a long shot on her part—casting directors rarely gave audiences.

'Haven't we met?'

He said it with such seriousness she tried her best to summon him from the past—with no success. He must have meant back in 90s New York. 'I don't think so,' she replied, awkwardly.

'It doesn't matter,' he said, shifting in his chair and then recapping some of the video material they'd discussed earlier. 'You've no idea what I sometimes end up with,' he said, laughing, 'self-taped auditions, bits and bobs from someone's iPhone is no way to showcase your skillsets. What do you think?' he added, shooting her a glance, as if she'd so much as even toyed with the idea.

'No… quite. They're on such tight budgets. They don't do themselves any justice, do they?' came her meek reply.

And then he perpetrated such a ghost of a smile as if there was a funny side to his gripe, but try as she might she could find no humour in it. Was the joke on her? If so, she'd missed it by a mile. She thanked him politely for his time and made a move to leave when, in a sudden turnaround, he became courteous and professional again.

Somewhere down the Strand her mood began to slip away. By the time she'd mounted the steps to the National Gallery it was extinct. Hassan was nowhere in sight. She walked in circles, scanning the square, willing a text to arrive. Arching her head backwards in frustration she took notice for the first time of the bluer than blue sky and the grand buildings that framed it. The sun had painted the taller ones in gold leaf and, just for a second or two, she was back in the Big Apple watching the evening light fade over the Hudson.

Hassan's out-of-breath arrival was hardly the perfect start to a flowing conversation. In its place Mel cut the formalities and went for bullet points:

Looks like you could do with a meal.
I know a place.
Stay close.

'Same again, please,' Hassan said as he reached the meals counter of the underground cafeteria. After Mel paid at the check-out, they emerged with identical trays—burger, fries and tea.

Something didn't feel right and the suspense of not knowing spoilt her appetite. But not his—he finished off her uneaten fries and only when his plate was empty, did he begin to explain.

'Somebody put the finger on me. That's what today was all about,' he said with a minute gesture in the direction, she presumed, of the Home Office.

'Who? How?'

He smiled as if she was having trouble keeping up. 'You don't like the look of some foreign bastard? No problem. Just dial the hotline.'

'Surely they can tell when some screwball... someone with a grudge...' Mel reasoned.

'They have to follow everything up—even anonymous calls. Otherwise...'

'How did they justify today?'

'They didn't. They talk of alleged document irregularities, inconsistent statements, blah blah.'

'And you checked out okay?'

'They only say, "That's all for now, you'll receive a letter."'

Her face felt hot. Was her step-daughter in her grief capable of such an act? She'd sounded more vulnerable on the phone yesterday when Mel had expected a row for talking to the clinic. Jess's mood could turn on a dime. Mel prayed: *let it not be her*.

Hassan said he wasn't entirely surprised by the summons—he'd been subjected to verbal abuse, threatened and spat at. But it had got worse, he said, since the referendum.

'It's only a small minority. Winchester has been good to me.'

'I'm so sorry. I was hoping you'd had news of your son.'

His deep eyes caught hers and he shook his head. 'I'm sorry to waste your time. I just had to talk to someone before I went off my head.'

Mel slightly resented being 'someone,' as if a total stranger might have done the job as well. They *were* virtual strangers but had Hassan lived in London with no ties, she guessed they might have gotten closer by now. He aroused her curiosity… and more besides.

'I meant you, *not* someone,' he said, correcting himself. 'You look fantastic, by the way.' It sounded clumsy for someone with his command of English.

'Thank you. My early fall look,' Mel joked to hide her embarrassment.

'Should I have said that? I mean… you're married, aren't you?'

What he was trying to ask—again none too subtly—was whether she had a partner and, if not, the significance of the wedding ring she was wearing. Maybe curiosity was killing him too. She plumped for mystery, telling him she was in a *slightly* unconventional relationship.

Her ring acted like a talisman when she needed confidence; she'd worn it more since Henry's passing. She'd also come to rely on it to deter unwanted male attention. Had it been of any use with Mr Musicals? She couldn't quite work him or his humour out. Some would look at her outfit—claret microskirt and black leggings—and say she wanted it both ways. It was time to ask about

Mohammed.

'Would it be any good if I wrote UNHCR?' she asked.

'Please do. I'll send you the link. The refugee charity is sending letters, also Lady Helena.'

'Illustrious company! Do they still want to publicize your story?'

'Fliss keeps on about it. I'd prefer to write it in the third person—that way I won't be a target for right-wing extremists.'

Mel nodded, acknowledging that the referendum and related issues had released such a barrage of poison and division.

There was still a trickle of emails from Fliss, and Mel often wondered what the woman wanted off of her. But it served a purpose; reports on the countess's progress were like gold dust to Helena and perhaps that was it—Mel the go-between. Helena had at last revealed where she lived—Uxbridge, but Mel had yet to be invited. They'd met a couple of times in town as if—and Mel clung to the theory—the woman worked her best magic in the bubble of London. Helena would slip in and out of her Lady H persona just to 'keep her hand in' and Mel did her best to act her foil. On one such occasion, her 'ladyship' spoke with regret about the fatal accident at the hall and how that had led the way to hiring major-domo, Fliss.

And now Hassan looked around as if he was mustering himself for the journey home. He was grateful for the meal and her time. She'd been determined, before he left, to enquire about his home city, how it was before the war, but half-checked herself, thinking that might be too sensitive a question. He responded, but with few facts: his son lived in the relative safety of the government-held area of Aleppo. His parents were alive, eking out a living near the Kurdish quarter which so far had largely escaped the air raids.

As they walked towards Waterloo Station, Hassan sang the praises of his adopted city, its history and architecture. Winchester, he told her, had voted by a sizeable majority to remain in the EU.

'You must come sometime. I'll give you a tour. I know the perfect B&B,' he said as they stood looking up at the departures board waiting for the platform number to show.

Mel was careful with her response; she didn't want to sound too enthusiastic. What would go against visiting wasn't Winchester or Hassan. It had to do with Mohammed. She no longer watched the nightly news coverage of the children of Aleppo being maimed and killed by the shells and bombs. To have a connection, however tenuous, with a particular child in that city would send her crazy.

Alone on the escalator, Mel was still thinking of the moment Hassan's mask seemed to slip a little as they'd said goodbye near the barriers. She glimpsed a weariness that while he was describing his ordeal at the Home Office had never shown. She guessed that Mohammed's deliverance had become a little less certain.

Travelling home on the train did nothing for her restless mood; she coped by texting Hassan—the first of many efforts. Trying to work up her earlier buzz and send messages of hope, the words refused to knit. The result sounded false or childish and she gave up, almost in tears.

Later, she binged on comfort food, an anonymous non-alcoholic drink and *West Side Story*. In another life she was the Puerto Rican heroine voicing the songs and the part almost word-perfectly. It always left her questing for—and finding—a softer denouement. Tonight was no exception, and in the afterglow of her revised narrative she sent her text:

It must break your heart that your son's future has been in any way compromised. It breaks my heart too. But I know you are strong. Please send me a photo of him. And I want to know more about him. And I want to know about his mother, which I realise might be painful for you. Perhaps I'm asking too much.

Think I'd like sometime to come to Winchester.
M x

Cindy's Puerto Rican accent was easy listening. From the way she made words sound like music, Mel guessed the woman was bilingual. She'd been called to the centre to talk about Jess.

'I've done some preliminary CBT but I'm not an adult psychologist. It's good of you to take time out.'

'My office,' Mel replied, indicating her phone.

It was Monday morning and Mel had yet to hear from Hassan; she was almost relieved. Perhaps she'd asked too many questions.

Cindy looked great in shirt and jeans; Mel felt overdressed in a skirt and blouse. The office was full of Disney characters—in pictures on the walls and cuddly 3D on the floor.

'The soonest NHS appointment I can get is three months,' she said, her mouth tightening. 'Whereas...'

'I'll pay,' Mel replied.

'You're a saint.'

'I'm a realist. If Jess goes down, I'll have my hands full.'

Cindy nodded, saying she'd liaise with Jess's doctor, who had already started her on pills. Sessions could begin almost immediately.

'We didn't go anywhere near the inquest. How did that turn out?' Cindy asked.

'Misadventure,' Mel said. 'Jess was okay with that.'

'What about you?'

'The same,' Mel replied.

'How did *you* take the news of your ex-husband's death?'

Mel hadn't bargained for this. 'Badly. I felt at least partly responsible—the divorce. I was the guilty party and got barred from attending the funeral. Which hurt bad. I felt I shoulda done something more when we found out Henry was going up high buildings again. Instead, I told Jess it was a good sign.' Mel tried to clarify by touching on early married life—Henry's fear of heights; her flashbacks to 9/11, and how IVF seemed to offer them a way out. It was only later it became the monster that informed their roller coaster of a marriage. If Cindy had set out to moisten Mel's eyes and quicken her breathing and heart, she was doing a fine job. Mel found herself cradling Olaf, the snowman, and suspected he'd been there some time.

'I give you full permission, Mel, to give yourself a break.'

A silence followed, as if Mel was being given the option to open up again. She said nothing and Cindy responded by talking about Billy and his discovery of music, in particular the 'secret songs' he refused to name or sing. They smiled at one another before chatting about

Hilary Clinton's chances of the White House, then exchanged notes on volleyball and its mind games. Cindy still played setter. She seemed to have mind-read the question gelling in Mel's head—she had no children of her own. Did that mean they'd adopted? Henry was always against adopting.

Chapter 20

One afternoon in early August, Maria stood at Mel's door with a teasing smile. In cut-offs she seemed to stand taller than ever.

'No way!' Mel gushed incredulously.

'Truly I am,' Maria replied, and there followed hugs and excited shrieks which took some time to settle before starting all over again. Maria was incapable of coming down from her dizzy height while Mel was beginning to feel the pull of a familiar force—gravity. The voice in her head was saying 'early days' and 'a long way to go'. She'd never really doubted Maria's ability to conceive first go. It was just the sort of thing her friend was destined to do well. Then Mel had played her small part too.

'Let's tell Anto the news. Will he be home?' Maria asked.

Before they left the house, Mel disappeared for a minute, returning with an ornately bound file. It seemed as good a time as any to run the porcelain pictures past the two friends.

'I've been meaning to ask both of you your opinions and now seems just about the right time, 'specially as we won't be seeing you for a while,' Mel said. Once the file was secured in a briefcase, the two set off on their happy mission.

Anto's reaction put Mel's in the shade. It was party time—the normally private man of culture whooped, danced and sang. He'd caught a bad case of baby fever and it was left to Mel to gently bring him back down to earth. It took a while.

'Mel's right,' Maria said at last, a cheesy smile on her face. 'Mustn't get carried away.'

The banter and jokes died down soon enough when Mel, opening her briefcase, set her challenge. She made no mention of 'fine art body painting', just a plea to her friends to be pure and honest critics. Art? Erotica? Porn? It didn't matter so much to her now, she was simply curious, she said almost truthfully. 'No sugar-coating, you guys. I mean it.'

Anto was banished while Maria scanned all 24 images of the file. She took her time going back and forth among the shots—acting every inch the connoisseur. When she finally said, 'I'm done,' Mel took the file next door, then returned to hear the verdict.

'It's art, and art again, my sister. I'm near welling up. There's something captured in those images which is, on the one hand, so you, and yet at the same time something alluringly other.'

'You probably guessed the artist—Royce. We hadn't known each other long at the time. I'd never met the photographer before. Can art be art by default?'

'Sure it can—they saw something. The chemistry seems more like between you and the camera. Wow! You've given me an idea!'

Mel thanked Maria then went to get Anto's feedback. She hardly dared think what he would say.

'I'm calling it Art Nouveau. Reminds me of Klimt. Great stuff, Mel.'

'It doesn't remind you of… say… Walter Sickert?'

'No way. Why d'you say that?'

'Big favourite of the artist. He has a couple of his paintings. The women are depicted… you know how.'

Anto strongly denied seeing any connection with the artist who had once lived and worked in Camden not far from Royce's place.

'It's funny,' Mel said, 'I've been into art since first grade. Never thought I'd ever be the subject of art.'

Maria came through and purred over the images again, 'Just one copy and I'll love you forever.'

'How could I deny you! For your eyes only, mind.'

Hassan's email, when it came, began with the demise of his much-travelled smartphone and the need to replace it. Then it was all Mohammed, complete with photo: 'The best son ever, a kind boy, well mannered'. Mad on football, he idolised Lionel Messi, the legend of Barcelona. Because of his hip he could play only in defence or in goal. He dreamed that a cure might one day give him the chance to score goals like his hero. He was intelligent, into everything. It struck a chord with Mel, who tended to idealise Billy in his absence. Whether the letters to UNHCR had any effect or no, there was now more optimism, and possibly urgency, about Mohammed's surgery.

But what followed shocked and angered her. It concerned the boy's permanent future—in England with his dad. Had she been so naïve as to think that after his surgery the boy would be returned to his mother in Syria? By then, the way things were going, the war would be over, at least in Aleppo. And wouldn't that serve as some sort of a victory, albeit a tiny one, among the losses and ruins of the city?

There wasn't a word about Mohammed's mother.

Surely inconvenience, not pain, had written her out of the story. Mel could see it clearly now. While reassuring the woman, Hassan was going round her back negotiating in English with UNHCR. And Mel had sent a letter voicing her support!

She was beginning to feel a warmth and an empathy towards the mother and, based on TV news and documentaries, a picture in soft focus kept emerging of a woman in a hijab and traditional dress embracing her lop-sided son, fixing his beautiful eyes with hers. For the next week or so the image haunted Mel when she was alone or riding the Tube. It burrowed into her subconscious, turning up one night in a dream in which she and a nameless woman meet in a war zone weirdly resembling London. Together they go in search of a missing child. On waking, Mel vowed never to learn the name of Mohammed's mother.

Mel was now spending more time in Willesden, fitting in around Jess's appointments and Billy's meal times. But there was a pay-off—she'd been inducted into a sorority of fun young moms among whom she was accepted as some authentic equivalent of Jess. There were visits to other kid's homes and playdates for Billy. It brought it home to Mel how far socially behind Billy was compared to his peers. She messaged then later spoke to Lou who sent her homework—rehearsing social settings and doing role play. It seemed that Jess wasn't keeping up with instructions from the centre. Although it was now the school holidays, Billy still attended pre-school.

The boy had become curious about Hassan and kept asking her the same questions, 'Where does he live? Does he do a job?' He could remember what the man had worn and a lot of their conversation. It led to Mel showing her charge a gallery of views of Winchester on her phone while trying to describe the duties of a waiter and a tour guide. Now, all the extra child care was taking its toll on Mel; she'd come home too tired to get a meal or work out in the gym.

One Wednesday after pre-school, Mel took Billy by Tube to 'Big London'—the National Gallery, where they were met by Helena and then Jess, who'd walked down from Soho Square. God only knew how her stepdaughter had hung on at work. She'd given up doing alterations and, fortuitously, the order for the wedding dress had been cancelled. She still got paid for her labour and the materials.

The sun was out and Jess looked more like her old self. Helena, who'd been angling for such a meeting, bought them all lunch while Mel provided Billy with his usual fare, plus fruit and cookies. Then it was time to proceed to their favourite paintings. En route, as usual, they passed a wealth of fine art in which Billy had shown little interest in the past. This time a nude caught his eye.

'I can see her fangina,' he said, matter-of-factly.

'Let's go and see that lovely tiger in the jungle,' Jess said, shepherding him away from the painting while Mel and Helena struggled to stifle their giggles. The rest of the visit passed without incident.

Mel was in almost daily touch with Maria, now renting an apartment in Long Beach.

'Lemme show you something,' she said, soon after moving in. Maria walked her phone around the apartment and then pointed it towards the Pacific. 'Great view, huh. Now look at this.' A few seconds later Mel was looking at a distant mountain range. Maria was in the groove; she had a shooting script and was ready to start directing her first movie. She was in good health, her haematologist confident she'd stay in remission, and she'd checked in with a gynaecologist. As she walked about the apartment her right hand was never far from her belly, her face never far from an enlightened smile.

Meanwhile Mel was thinking about what action to take over Mohammed. What could she do? Confront Hassan? That would mean a trip to Winchester and the risk of her efforts being overly construed. Then a thought—Fliss. What did the house manager of Hambledean Hall not know about Hassan's situation? Very little, Mel suspected. He in turn seemed to trust and respect her. Maybe they'd grown fond of one another. She might find an ally in Fliss, who could perhaps be persuaded to use her leverage over Hassan. That way they'd both get to be go-betweens.

'Shall I call a taxi,' Holly said as soon as she heard about Royce. But Mel had already made the decision to go by public transport. It would buy her more time to think about how she was going to handle the situation, and the noise and bustle would help to free her mind. Within a minute Holly had the route planned—three stops on the Circle Line then a short bus ride. She even knew where Mel could buy a sketch book and pencils. Until today she'd never had a good word for Royce. 'Send him my love,' she said. He'd phoned Mel late the night before from the hospital: *heart attack*, *been coming some time*. There were no circumlocutions, no dramatic pauses. He'd already traded terror for boredom, he said, asking after her own health. Side-stepping the loaded question, she said she'd turn her mind to the wording of a press release.

By the hospital elevator, Mel, a little queasy, was still wondering which Royce she was going to encounter on the 4th floor. It was naïve to want the visit to be one of pure friendship; that might serve him best but she knew business and the theatre would claim most of their attention. It would shuffle like nothing else the shifting facets of their relationship.

'How lovely to see you, Mel,' he said, reclining on his bed, a bath robe loosely, not to say raffishly, about him, his arms stretching out. They hugged, taking care not to disturb the monitor and IV. He expressed a child's delight in the sketching equipment in a voice she paired with last night's phone call. It bore traces of the North—his childhood home. 'It's not what you think. I was just pottering about yesterday morning. On my own.'

He gave a measured, but succinct enough account of 'this seizure in my chest' but it was plain there were other matters he was more anxious to discuss.

'First things first: Prospero…'

She tried to interrupt but he wagged a finger.

'He and I talked long into the night and have come to a decision to part under the most amicable of circumstances. He's in good, dare I say, better hands. Maybe I wasn't so comfortable with all that whizz-bang technology and avatars.'

Mel mumbled her assent and said something about 'a reconsideration when the play transfers' but the New

Royce hardly responded. His mind was elsewhere and he appeared to be working himself up into a speech.

'This is hard for me… and it may not be so easy for you either.'

What was he getting at? Something more serious than a heart attack? Her head felt like it was on the move and about to part from the rest of her body, which was turning to jello. Though seated, she gripped the bedframe for extra security. She'd forgotten how routinely hospital visits made her feel unwell.

'Wait till you're over this, Royce. When you're stronger…' But she could see that nothing she said was going to head him off.

'I want to come clean with you, but not the LAPD,' he started ominously. 'Stratford, the Scottish play. That's when I met Laura.'

At last, he'd admitted the liaison!

'There was no weird sister on Venice Beach, no rhinologist. The sneezing was largely self-induced. Just before I left for LA, Laura got in touch. I'd not seen her for months. Said she'd meet me at this restaurant close to the beach. She didn't show up. After a while I left, but instead of heading back to the hotel I went for a walk by the ocean.'

No, Royce. Please don't say it! You're no angel. But homicide…?

'Though I didn't know for sure, the woman I met that night turned out to be Laura. It was getting dark and crystal meth—you remember she was writing a book on it—had altered her appearance. She seemed to recognise me but she was off her head, wanting sex, at the same time trying to get herself off. I was in shock, a bit slow, tried to get away. She grabbed me, we tussled. I managed to push her off and ran.'

'Stop! Take a rest, have a drink.' Mel handed Royce a glass of water, her hands shook and she returned them smartly to the bedframe.

'Listen, Mel. I didn't *do* anything wrong,' he said. 'I just messed up. So… couple of days later a woman's body is found in the sea off Malibu. Signs of sexual assault, query homicide. My dilemma is this: Do I sit tight and hope nothing will connect me with the dead woman I'm assuming *was* Laura, or do I go to the police with another story. I go for the latter—the hooded figure, black streamers, Shakespeare, the sneezing.'

Another shock!—the sketches he'd sent of the woman were bogus. They were pure art—nothing more, nothing less! And the reason he'd sent them to the agency and wanted the correspondence filed securely? Back-up evidence. Of course, they matched Maria's description of the weird sisters' costumes, causing Mel fleetingly to believe the dead woman might have been the missing goth sister. One day she'd put Holly straight.

'They took my DNA and my passport. Then more forensic came out—the body, in sweats and joggers, was full of methamphetamine. The signs of sexual trauma were more likely, they said, to be self-inflicted—the effects of the drug. There was some leeway about the time of death and I was tempted to come clean on the assignation and the meeting. But what if it was all a ruse to flush me out? I was terrified of the US legal, not to say penal, consequences. At the morgue I was entirely truthful when I told them I didn't recognise one atom of that body on the slab. So I kept to the story and went off on location to New Mexico knowing sooner or later there'd be more questions. I began to get nightmares and panic attacks. I tried to have sex with someone. Total failure.'

Royce paused his narrative and took another drink. He was calm, even his monitor was calm. Mel couldn't resist the thought—what if she was hooked up to it right now? Would it show signs of high stress? Another thought came out of nowhere.

'*Was* there a Madame Ruth? I had a very clear mental picture of her.'

'Another of my arcane inventions. But I begin to believe in them. The hooded figure, for instance, is more real to me than the raving nympho.' He went on, 'Three weeks later I'm told of 'developments' and recalled. I assume they've identified the body, found her emails, checked out the restaurant. Maybe she kept a diary. The good lieutenant is waiting for me at the airport. I admit to once having a liaison with someone called Laura. I get such a grilling—it's like cat and mouse but I focus on the first witch in that 2014 production, or rather the tall actor who played her. Finally, Lieutenant Del Rey says, 'So you didn't recognise her on the beach *or* down at the morgue'. 'That's right' I say. It *was* the absolute truth. My passport is returned. Inside I'm weeping buckets.'

For himself or Laura? Mel wondered. She supposed it could be both. 'I guess they never quite went with your weird sister story, did they?'

'Disappointing that, because… when I'm on stage it often feels more real than real.'

'Sign of a great actor,' Mel said, but the words almost stuck in her throat, and now she had goose bumps thinking of him re-materialising Maria's witch on Venice beach. There'd been something in Holly's first 'deduction' after all!

'Or a fantasist. Look, you're wondering why I'm telling you all this now. It's a dry run. I've never been able to put all this behind me, though God knows I tried. It's mental and physical; the coronary is just the latest instalment. I need to see someone.'

Mel agreed, recalling how, after the Twin Towers, therapy had helped her. Ironic though that it was she rather than Henry who needed help. Dear Henry had sorted himself out. She'd been tempted to open up more to Cindy, but why waste her precious time?

A period of welcome silence followed. Royce glugged more water while Mel took in the view and smiled at the passing traffic of staff and relatives. But it was only a question of time before a certain subject raised its impertinent head.

'What's this about a baby, Mel? Can't you tell me?' Royce didn't believe in slips-of-the-tongue.

'I made a mistake. Forget I ever mentioned it.'

'Maybe you should have said something before,' he suggested.

'It wouldn't have made any difference. Let's leave it right there, okay?'

It came as no small relief to Mel when he changed the record and talked about the agency, how he proposed to devote more time to it. Mel's discreet cough signalled a weary scepticism. She followed by saying there were issues to be discussed but only when he was up to it. In the meantime, he'd do cardio-rehab, see a psychologist and spend time sketching and painting. He looked forward to working with acrylics again. His daughter, he thought, would come over from Milan tomorrow. Everyone else, with few exceptions, would be put off until he was allowed home when Teresa, his sister, would come down from Leeds and filter all visitors.

'So, who's gonna shade it in the US of A?' Royce asked, right out of the blue.

'That!' huffed Mel, 'America isn't ready for a woman president, so we'll get an asshole in the White House instead.'

He laughed.

'It's not funny, Royce. Just don't get me started on all of that.'

The mention of the presidential election campaign had blown a fuse, cutting their conversation dead. It seemed to be left to Royce to eventually breathe life into it again.

'I wouldn't blame you if you wanted to be out of my life, Mel.'

'You know I'd never do that.'

'The agency?'

'Not giving that up—it's what we created. What I coaxed you into... when I had some influence over you,' she said, laughing.

'You still have, Mel.'

Something told her he'd stopped calling her *Irish* for good. Towards the end of visiting, Royce smoothed down his bath robe and patted the bed several times. Then, quite abruptly, he wilted, giving way to tears and sobbing. Mel held his hand and comforted him, her throat tightening. She made no attempt to dab her cheeks. Of course, she would visit tomorrow. It would be great to meet up again with Raffaella.

Before she left, he recovered himself enough to milk the occasion. 'Our revels now are ended,' he quoted, slipping back into Prospero mode. She disagreed, and told him so.

On her way back to the agency Mel was left to wonder if she'd ever have gotten to know about the real events on Venice Beach that night if Royce hadn't suffered a coronary thrombosis. He'd kept her in the dark, and the story 'live' by pretending the woman's body was still waiting to be identified. He'd blanked it out, reasoning that was the best way to get over it. He took a risk—she might have seen something in the New York Times. But he was always a risk-taker, on and off the stage. She *was* right about the 'good lieutenant'; his infatuation was a cover up. He'd been terrified of her.

Chapter 21

On Saturday afternoon September 3, Mel fidgeted with her front door, pulled it to, then walked to Turnham Green Tube Station. She was in dress pants, a blazer and a white blouse, her small suitcase trundling behind. On the train her prim outfit made her self-conscious and she avoided her reflection. At last, there was daylight and the cooler air of Waterloo Station.

It was plan A after all. She'd never got round to breaking enough ice with Fliss, admitting to herself she was still wary of the woman, afraid she'd be subjected to an inquisition about Helena and in her confusion give out something confidential.

Royce's rehabilitation continued at a pace. He was taking daily walks in Regent's Park and frequently strode along by the canal, snapping views for his new passion—landscapes. He was finding therapy 'interesting, illuminating and painful'. He was also becoming a gym bore. She'd tried unsuccessfully to interest him in some voice work. Jess was up and down, the familiar diatribes at the drop of a hat. She was irritated by Billy's questions about Hassan. In case she asked about the weekend, Mel would invent a workshop in musical theatre.

The train chased the sun west, never catching up. Failing to cut off into her audio book, her thoughts went to Southern California, to Maria and the life inside her. She'd not taken a real vacation since setting up the agency. Would it help if she squeezed in a few days there? Might it not soften the bouts of nauseous worry and give God a rest from her prayers? She looked out and was grateful for the succession of small backyards that bordered the railroad. Their infinite variety and clutter distracted her wonderfully—until the train's abrupt panning shot of open country dotted with trees and grazing livestock.

'We need to talk,' she said as soon as Hassan came forward to kiss her, the station platform loud with whistles and slammed doors one moment, near silence the next.

'Sure. Let's get you checked in first,' he said without missing a beat.

'Talk first, then check in. I'd really appreciate somewhere quiet and private.'

He nodded as if he'd just remembered there was a mulish side to her character. She suggested a taxi at almost the very same moment he said, 'It isn't far.' She had on low heels and he seemed to have expected her to walk. He took her case and when they found a cab, he said something to the driver about a mill.

Winchester still didn't much resemble a city as they walked beside greenery and a stream. Hassan, in that encyclopaedic way he shared with Anto, explained they were still outside of the old walls. He alternated between polite chat and tourist guide patter. They stopped opposite the house where Jane Austen had spent her final days, he expecting the tourist in her to take a photo. She duly obliged.

Now they were passing through a medieval archway, which Mel assumed would lead into the city but Hassan, without a word, turned sharp left, opened a door and they were suddenly climbing an ancient staircase, which led by a door at the top to a tiny church. Her look of amazement was probably straight out of the tourist guide's manual.

'You *are* kind of religious, aren't you?' he asked.

She ignored the question and looked about her. It was the least austere church she'd ever set foot in. Finally, she sat in a pew and Hassan joined her.

She began, 'I can understand your longing to be with your son. But you're taking him away from someone who surely has a greater claim to him. The longing's so strong, I guess you'll do anything to achieve your aim. I suspect you've deceived the mother and your son into thinking that after his recovery he'll be returned to her care.' So far, so good, she thought. She hadn't fluffed any of her lines and he'd just stared at the back of the pew in front. No rage, no smile, but she had to wait an age before he said anything.

'It's good of you to have their interests at heart. You have a big heart, Mel.'

'Don't patronize me.' Getting mad felt like instant karma.

'I'm not. Believe me, Mel, no one's being deceived.'

'You find words easy, don't you? It makes you such a good… linguist,' she said, her anger perfectly maintained.

'"Liar" is what I think you meant to say,' he said, staring at her; the blinking game again, but now he was becoming agitated and got to his feet. 'Look, I never wanted to talk about this. The situation there is so bad. TV only scratches the surface. Mohammed's mother has married a widowed man with two children. The wife was killed. There's a baby on the way. They're poor. Everyone's poor. There's very little work, even less that pays.'

'I'm sure she loves him, adores him,' Mel replied.

'She does. But what is love? And what is the *greatest*

love?'

It was like a game of chess with words. What else had she expected? *The greatest love, the greatest love.* The words kept spinning around in her head. Could *she* not aspire to such lofty sentiments? Ah yes, the greatest love of all would be to give up a child for the sake of that child.

'Are you implying that I, because I've no child of my own…'

'Not in a million years did I mean that! You and Billy couldn't be closer,' he said, then pausing and changing tone, 'there's another reason Mohammed must never go back. You see… he doesn't hold back, says what he thinks. He can be quite lippy if he chooses. You know what they do to kids like that? Remember Deraa, where it all started, what they did to those boys? Look, I don't want to talk about it anymore. I've upset you enough.' He'd begun to end every sentence with loud oaths in Arabic.

Mel was unsteady going down the old staircase and Hassan supported her with his free arm.

'You're shaking,' he said.

'Not the only one, am I?' Once outside, Mel felt for her inhaler before realising she was just hyperventilating. She'd witnessed Hassan's anger again and though not its target, she still felt frightened and out of her depth. An early train home beckoned, and then he said sorry with a look of tears in his eyes. Nothing more was said until they'd reached the B&B. He asked about the agency.

'Bit flat just now,' she replied.

'It must be difficult—only so many roles.'

'There's commercials, and quite a lot of voice work. We do files for audiobooks; the demand goes up and down.'

The lady of the house was welcoming and there were

flowers in the room. She and Hassan chatted downstairs while Mel took a shower and changed into jeans and a denim shirt. It was cooler now and she was glad of the leather blazer when they went out again.

Before they'd gone any distance, Mel took a deep breath then tried teasing out the extent of the Fliss-Hassan alliance.

'It's not what you think. She's married—to the house. They've started a renovation fund, going to open part of it to the public. She wants me to give it a plug—she did help me get this job. *And* I've finally said yes to her publicity plan—but only when Mohammed is here and safely through all the red tapes.'

'She's scary. So efficient, so determined,' Mel said. 'How's the countess?'

'Who wants to know?' he asked, then chuckled.

'Okay, the fake countess *and* me. See, I took your advice and now we're good friends again.'

After a downbeat bulletin, Hassan said, 'You know, your friend should do a deal. She knows money: Fliss knows publicity.'

Mel said she would pass the message on.

Once inside the cathedral she was in awe of its age and beauty. Whenever her vestige of faith was running low, such visits were food and drink to the soul. And she'd never lost her inclination for prayer, nor the notion that petitions in 'high' places like St Paul's or Westminster Abbey—would carry more leverage.

Throughout the visit Hassan knew when to be silent, when to slip back into tour guide mode. It gave her the chance for some serious praying. Otherwise, she went around in a near-ecstasy of reverent silence, only finding her voice as they approached Jane Austen's grave. After that, the tour of the city went down a gear and they fetched up at an old pub. Neither was hungry; just as well Hassan had baulked at the idea of making a dinner reservation on a Saturday. Instead, they sat down away from the bar to light bites and lager, hers non-alcoholic. She questioned him, a Muslim, about drinking alcohol.

'On the whole I don't. Sometimes I feel the need to blend a bit more.'

By now their conversation had lost its sharp edges and they began to lance and parry with nothing more deadly than witless, anodyne jokes about one another. Hassan was trying—unconvincingly—to play the comedian. He seemed permanently on the verge of telling a funny story even a risqué one, but his evident worry about offending her held him back—a source of some amusement to Mel. Did this sideshow of levity mean Hassan's earlier narrative had won her over? Both Jess and Anto had in their different ways cast doubts about him, but they'd never heard the full story or the emotion with which it was delivered. How could Hassan have possibly rehearsed all that? Mel still felt uneasy when she thought of Mohammed's mother, now a kind of martyr in her eyes. When would she stop meeting this woman in her dreams? The self-same question cropped up with regard to another woman she would never meet in real life—Royce's Laura.

They held hands on the way back to the B&B and once through the bedroom door, began to kiss. He started with her shirt buttons and when he held her breasts the electricity chain-reacted all round her body. His kisses literally took her breath away and she swallowed noisily.

She'd known the rush of heroin but still rated sex over drugs.

'You don't think too badly of me, Mel?'

She shook her head but then he seemed to seize up. What to do? She walked to the bed, slipped out of her blazer then stagily took her wedding ring off and placed it on the bedside locker.

It was all the encouragement he needed and they were soon locked together beside the quaint four-poster, which stood as high as a hospital bed. Against its soft bulk they undressed, kissed and touched one another. She had an urge to speak, but there was nothing to explain. All she could get out was *God, yes*. At which he eased her up on top of the duvet where she climaxed seconds before him.

In the night Mel woke with a start to find no Hassan and no light in the en suite. Then she heard him moving about the room and, with the aid of a crack of light under the door, could just make out his form. She got out of bed but was scared to make physical contact. His movements were agitated; his voice, just audible, the tone pleading as if he was being threatened. Was he epileptic? Was he sleepwalking?

At last, she summoned the courage to gently touch him and his body reacted with a start, his voice with puzzlement and his posture became defensive. Rehearsing emergency phone numbers, she led him back towards the bed with the kind of soothing tones adults reserve for kids. He was strangely biddable and Mel was able to turn him around then get his butt onto the bed and heave him back to the horizontal. Soon the restlessness waned and his breathing settled into a regular pattern. She googled *sleepwalking* and found some reassurance. After checking him a few times she relaxed and went to sleep.

Morning came with a triple sally on her senses—light at the window, aromas from the kitchen, the animal warmth of Hassan's body. Mel got up, went to the bathroom then made tea. He was slow in waking though none the worse, it seemed, for his walkabout in the night. Then he shot out of bed and took refuge in the bathroom where, after rummaging, he emerged, smelling expensively of eau-de-cologne. His body, particularly his torso, was dense with dark hair.

'Sorry,' he said, indicating the theft of her scent. 'I got so hot in the night, sweated a lot.'

Mel could only raise her eyebrows as he tugged at her nightie.

'Let's take it real slow,' she said.

Hassan had never heard of tantric sex. He said that life was too short. Though he did cool a fraction and a certain languor took charge until the fever gripped them once more. He turned her onto her belly, her left side, then her right as if he couldn't decide the best way to enter her, or was this his version of spiritual sex? At last, they faced and thrusted until the fire went out of them. In no time Mel was half dreaming.

Close to the breakfast deadline they thundered down the staircase to the tiled lobby, composed themselves then proceeded calmly to the kitchen-diner. Over breakfast Hassan told Mel his son had received the final clearance to come to the UK. It only remained for the hospital to set a date for surgery.

It was such big news, why had he delayed telling her? Perhaps it was something to do with her earlier anger, which now seemed a long time ago. She expressed delight that Mohammed's hip was finally going to be put right.

'Would you come with me to the airport? Please say *yes*,' he begged.

'I'd be intruding. It's going to be all about you and your son. He won't want a strange woman hanging around. He'll be missing his mom,' Mel insisted.

'You've taken such an interest in him, I'm desperate for you to meet him. Call it a father's pride.'

Another game of word chess! She agreed to think about it. 'Where's he going to live after he leaves hospital?'

'A lovely family—through a different refugee charity. Guess who set that up?'

'Fliss, right?'

He smiled; his eyes wider than ever.

On the train Mel recalled the 'religious question' getting another airing that morning. They were on their way to an ancient alms house by the river. They'd already visited one church, Hassan making extravagant assumptions about her faith. As they entered the complex of buildings by an archway, she tried to put her religious leanings into context.

'My dad's two gods were the railroad company's timetable and his guitar. He worked as a railroad surveyor, which sounds a bit dull, but his love of music went deep. He wasn't always 'with the Lord'. Whereas Mom, born-again Catholic, was kind of fierce. I tried to please them both. Still do in a way, though they're gone now.' She didn't elaborate about her dad's periodic devotions to the whisky bottle.

As the train picked up speed, she looked out at the passing countryside; there were already some early signs of autumn in the trees. She held up her left hand, twisted it and smiled. Hassan had finally confessed that his anger at their first meeting had little to do with the devastation of Syria. It was all down to her wedding ring! Even at the telling he wasn't sure how she'd take it.

'With me, it was *coup de foudre*. Only later did I see the wedding ring. Ouch!'

Was it *coup de foudre* with her? She'd replied 'sort of', then teased him about disappearing at the marquee.

'You made me nervous and I made a fool of myself,' he explained.

'Later on, I made an even bigger fool of me,' Mel replied.

She thought again of the show-down in the little church, her anger cooling as his came to life. And then his tears. She'd touched a raw nerve, which, she guessed, came out later in the sleepwalking. Going around peaceful Winchester on a Sunday morning it was easy to talk of anything but oppression and conflict, and she learned some Arabic. Her favourite word, *Inshallah,* meant *God willing*, which was such a useful expression. There were others, harder to remember, she liked the sound of. Was that because they 'sang' or because they were happy words?

She *was* curious enough to want to be at the airport to meet Mohammed. It occurred to her it would mark a major closure for Hassan, still a prisoner, she guessed, of the past. Once united with his son he would be in a hurry to hammer the lid down tight on that Pandora's box. What little she knew about psychology told her this was a mistake and might prolong the sleepwalking.

That morning he'd caught her staring at his nakedness. She was about to blush when he said, 'Ah, the spots. Bad case of chicken pox. They had to tie my hands to stop me scratching.' There were round, white shiny scars on his chest and back. They slightly matched the fainter ones on his face she'd put down to acne.

Mel couldn't wait to get home, her first priority to induct Hassan into her great Hall of Gratitude—the Mason jar. There was no distinction there between relatives, friends and lovers. He would rub shoulders with Henry, Royce, Jess and Billy, Holly, Anto, Helena and Maria, Mick and Georgie and other special people and things. She'd thought once or twice about 'specialty' jars but no, it was one life and it seemed only right to manifest that in a single container.

As the trees by the track became a blur she went online and drafted her weekly blog then sent texts. Later she would FaceTime—US East Coast first then the West.

'It was only a teensy bit, hun. I feel fine, no pain.' Maria was lounging on a sofa, trying not to strive too hard to play down the threat to her pregnancy, *their* pregnancy. 'Soon as I saw it, I stopped doing anything.'

That was on the following Thursday when Maria had yearned to hear a reassuring voice, see something comforting in Mel's face. They were so committed in love and hope with one another, they convinced themselves it could be normal at this stage, and wouldn't a scan clear up any doubts? A conspiracy of practical optimism was uniting across an ocean and a continent. Mel's dilemma was Anto. They'd need each other this week end, which meant putting off Hassan. She'd have to act out her excuse on FaceTime.

Friday, Mel was auto-piloting at work, waiting for news. When it came there was no change. As the weekend approached, the word *Inshallah* was never far from the thoughts that spun about crazily in the dark orbit of her mind.

Mid-morning Saturday, Mel received a call. Desperately she tried to think of an inconsequential reason Maria should want to call in the middle of a California night. Nothing came but *Inshallah*.

Suddenly the picture, like the telling cut in a movie, said everything. Maria lay, washed out, gowned up on a hospital bed.

'So sorry, hun. We lost our…' Unable to get the word out, Maria began instead to cry.

A voice that didn't belong to Mel replied, 'So sorry you've had to go through all this for me. Your pain is my pain, my lovely. I'm so worried about your health.'

'I did it for me too, sweetie. Don't forget that. They say I'll be fine, no worries there. My big worry is you,' Maria said, then paused. 'Maybe it's too much to ask right now but I would sure love it if you kept to that pledge.'

'Whaddya mean, Maria? Why?' Mel's brain was reeling, incapable of taking in any more information.

'I have to spell it out for you, don't I? The night I spent at your place, after the party… when I came across those pregnancy test kits, I also found—you know what I found—the vodka, the bottles. Please, I love you too much to not worry about you.'

'Nothing to worry about, my lovely. It's ancient history. I'm in recovery, have been now for a long time.'

Chapter 22

After she let Maria go, Mel stood and screamed her lungs out. She screamed until her breath had gone, until only tears were left. There was more than an audible echo of the past—another hospital, another wound. She'd not split the air with such dissonance and volume in 15 years.

Despite her own loss and pain, Maria had still found time to comfort Mel as well as confront her with that *other* problem. *Hang in there, hun.* The only other person to come anywhere near broaching the issue was Helena.

Later, duetting with Tina Turner, Mel went from room to room, a can in her hand, trying to drink slowly. The choice boiled down to this: get out of the house as soon as the can was empty, or open another. The urgency of the words *must talk to Anto,* repeated several times out loud, saw her, minutes later, out of her door and walking up the street to call on her would-be co-parent. And break his heart.

There was the briefest moment at the door before Anto made the only possible deduction. Hard on its heels the ranking of Mel's emotions—guilt, pity and grief—kept vying with one another for supremacy. They hugged, then Anto with perfect English understatement said, 'Tea,' and scurried off to the kitchen, leaving Mel alone to study the art in the long lounge. She stared defiantly at the stone buddha, 'Fucking lot of help you and Zen were!'

Over tea and biscuits she gave her account of Maria's miscarriage. It sounded overly forensic and she gave it another shot, then another for good measure. Compensating for Anto's reserve, she talked non-stop, unable to resist reworking what she could remember of how her one-and-only pregnancy had ceased to be. Mel predicted correctly that when her words ran dry, the tears would begin again, and Anto would find a voice, if only to say, 'Let's go for a walk.'

As they approached the pier Mel stiffened. A group of kids and parents had collected on the concourse seemingly waiting for some organised activity to begin.

'Let's go,' she said, coming to an abrupt halt. But Anto, out of curiosity, carried on a little way. A white-haired woman appeared and, as she approached him, gave a wave to Mel, who swore under her breath, turned and walked in the opposite direction. It was a while before Anto caught up with her.

'Sorry. Couldn't face that Catherine woman right now.'

'It's okay. I explained. Sends her… you know. Felt weird saying 'we'. Oh, she wants you to join this choir. Knows you have a great voice.'

'How?'

'My guess is she went along one night to the Tabard Theatre. Younger than she looks.'

They reached the Meadows before anything like a conversation resumed. By the river the early signs of autumn were showing here too. The wind had picked up woodsmoke from somewhere and was carrying it down river.

'How was Winchester and the gothic house manager?' Anto asked.

'Oh, I chickened out of that. Saw Hassan alone instead. I'd only gotten half the story. UNHCR will have the boy here soon. After surgery he stays. It's good news for

Hassan—I think he has post-traumatic stress.'

'Must be epidemic in Syria.'

They walked on as far as the railway bridge, where Anto, motioning towards Barnes, proposed 'Shall we?' meaning go for a drink. Mel readily assented and they took the walkway over the river and on to the pub.

Their lagers went down in record time and, like the crisps, were soon replenished. Anto began to say something, changed his mind then tried again.

'How d'you think Maria got into porn?'

Mel concealed her surprise at the question, rationalising that at some stage he might get around to talking about their loss. She wasn't holding her breath though.

'I guess the call-backs stopped calling back. She did say something about how, by contrast, it taught her how erotic art ought to be presented.'

Anto seemed satisfied with Mel's non-explanation but showed few signs of wanting to keep the conversation going apart from affirming the lager was good. Mel nodded, took a deep breath and dived in.

'Look, Anto. I've come to the end of a long, long road,' she said, watching for his reaction, 'and I'm not gonna put myself through this malarkey anymore. It sucks like nothing else. But you've got time still to find a... I can help with my blog if you like. Nothing would please me more. Well, almost nothing,' she said with a fake laugh she never knew she had in her repertoire. Her days of dreaming of parading Chiswick High Road with a proud bump and later, a buggy had come to a very finite end.

He was nodding and exhaling deeply. 'Can't stop

thinking about…'

'I know, I know exactly…'

Anto was fighting back his tears—and coming out on top. Even on his own, Mel knew he'd be the same. She leaned across, held and squeezed his hand. She thought back to when Marty left. She'd tried a few times to make contact. He'd texted back about nothing in particular.

After more drinks they finished with double shot coffees, and then a point of honour arose—or was it bravado?—as to forgoing the call for a cab. The walk would do them more good, they agreed, as long as they took care on the walkway above the river.

Alcohol had made them over-solicitous for each other's safety and they crossed more slowly than usual, without mishap. Returning, the weather was cooler, clouds had gathered and the wind, now behind them, threatened to upset further any minor lapses in coordination. Mel's desperation to open up again was for the moment trumped by an urgent and painful need to pee. Darting behind the bandstand she snuck down out of view. Returning the other way round, she found a young child's white mitten lying on the ground. She wanted to pick it up, take it home, then a more negative reaction set in and her whole being went into stand-by. Finally, she placed the mitten on the bandstand wall, securing it with a stone. It seemed enough that she'd touched it.

Anto was sat watching the river go by, no doubt meditating on its unchanging foreverness and, by contrast, the puny, short-lived lives of insignificant human beings. He couldn't wait, it seemed, to get back to Zen.

'You know,' she began, 'I don't care so much about myself. It's the… I'll always think of her as a girl. I tried to pretend I didn't have feelings about her. Now I'm lousy with feelings for her.'

He put his arm around her and for a while they both watched the river go by. There were more people about now and louder noises from the sports fields. Even the river was busier with craft. Mel was unable to resist looking back towards the mitten as they turned to go.

'What will you do?' Anto asked as they entered Mel's street.

After a pause, as if she'd given it some thought, she said, 'More coffee, lots of bagels—got to rescue my blood sugar, long lie in the bath. Must talk with Maria—she'll be waking soon, if she got any sleep…' She was trying to remember how she'd felt that long night back in 2001.

'You'll probably disapprove,' Mel said, 'but I'm gonna send Hassan a selfie, bit of a tease, know what I mean. Tasteful though. Might make up a bit for the weekend.'

'You're in love, Mel!' Anto exclaimed.

'Maybe I am. It's very bad timing though, I know, and complicated—like it always is.' She managed to laugh almost naturally.

'Dear Mel, please be careful. There must be lots you don't know about this guy.'

'Sure. But that's half the fun. You'd get on. Ex-teacher, well-read.'

At her door they hugged then parted.

Chapter 23

As Mel's taxi neared Heathrow, her doubts about taking her place in the welcome party grew more entrenched and she quickly rehearsed plan B, this time with more conviction. There was still plenty of time to change her mind again—the Swiss flight from Geneva was due at 1.30 pm and she'd already checked it was on schedule.

It was her first visit to Terminal 2 since the make-over. The sun shone through acres of glass and there was a quiet feeling of infinite space as she made her way to the meeting place. Again, the area around the expectant crowd was uncluttered and full of light. And then her eyes came to rest on a nearby row of double bench seats. Approaching them, she sat herself down in a space that looked away from the crowd. Satisfied with her reconnaissance she went off to find a coffee, listen to her audio book and wait.

Later, checking the time, she sent her excuses to Hassan with a promise to catch up with them at the hospital. She was still stressing over the chance of bumping into him and sheer nerves made her invent some way-out, just-in-case excuse, which only threatened to bring on a panic attack. Did she give the slightest credence to Jess's suicide bomber theory? Of course not. But then why had she decided to keep her distance from the meeting place? Quite clear now in her own mind, she wanted no part in this father and son narrative, no matter how hard Hassan had pushed it. She could just imagine herself in the taxi: klutzy platitudes with the UNHCR escort while father and son rap endlessly in Arabic. Just when things were taking off with Hassan, they'd been parted by a grief she could still barely handle, let alone share with him. Perhaps she never would. And now—as from today—she had a rival.

Plan B required that she was in position in good time, her head in a magazine, baseball cap pulled down. At the critical time she swivelled into foetal mode, feet up on the seat. She wasn't surprised not to see Hassan, who must by now be stationed at the forefront of the expectant crowd with only one thing on his mind. She reflected that it was always the same at airport arrivals: you keep on scanning every person emerging through the doors as if they might morph into your friend, relative or lover.

She knew it was Hassan as soon as the shouting began; it brought a hush to the crowd and a lump to her throat. It was hard to judge the tone from where she sat. It sounded urgent, even scary but it was probably just the release of long pent-up tension and emotion. It stopped abruptly and then Mel had to wait an age before Hassan, carrying his son, broke free of the scrum of people. He ran around in circles, the two glued to one another in an ecstasy of kissing and laughter. Mohammed was no longer shaven-headed; he sported a shock of dark curly hair. Meanwhile, a smartly dressed man in charge of a wheelchair manoeuvred close by. Then, to whoops of delight, Hassan began to throw his son in the air, higher and higher, each time catching him expertly until a slight mis-catch when the boy slithered down his dad's body and both ended up on the floor where they rolled about in a moving show of tears, love and a longing that had, at last, come to an end. Finally, Mohammed was lowered into the wheelchair, Hassan acquired a backpack and the party slipped away.

Eyes burning, Mel headed in the opposite direction, her armpits damp and with more than a suggestion of nausea in her stomach. She looked for the nearest rest room. She got to thinking about her dad. Working as a surveyor for Amtrak, he sometimes had to take time away from home. He was affectionate but had never thrown her or her brother up in the air when he came home. Their mom would not have approved. They were so different— she had religion first and last; Dad had his work and his music.

Her taxi brought her to great Ormond Street Hospital where she called Hassan, then felt awkward when they hugged.

'It's the happiest day of my life,' he said, adding, 'Come and see why.'

She held back, nervous about meeting Mohammed, about her reaction to the interior of another hospital.

'And I'm the luckiest guy,' he said, piercing her with blazing eyes, then kissing her.

She played down her place in this suddenly re-created father and son universe while he looked her up and down, commenting favourably on the midi dress she'd over-discreetly chosen at the last minute. As Hassan led her to the ward, she replaced her sunglasses only removing them after they'd entered the single private room.

Mohammed's eyes were indeed large, but was that the dazzle of a new world or the effects of an undernourished body? He seemed a little short for his five years.

Another emotional reunion was then played out, Hassan scooping up his son off the bed, hugging, rocking and kissing him, their language almost song-like but this time more restrained. Before all this, Mohammed had been engrossed in a soccer video on an iPad. Still in his father's arms, he was introduced to Mel and confidently launched himself into a mash-up of English phrases, which Hassan was quick to correct in a mix of Arabic and English. Mel handed over the glossy soccer magazine she'd bought at the airport.

'Thank you… very mush,' the boy replied, grinning from ear to ear. Like Billy, Mohammed wore a striped soccer shirt, only his was blue and red, the colours of FC Barcelona.

It was worrying—and unfair—to compare his responses with Billy's. Would *his* always be rather less than what she craved? Right now, the centre was still working on all that. She'd wondered about the sort of approach they were using and it got her thinking about drama classes and stagecraft. Did they hope the sham emotions might one day make that quantum leap? She prayed they would.

While father and son babbled on in their own language Mel responded with a marathon session of smiling, Hassan translating from time to time. Then a young woman in a uniform popped her head around the door, addressed the party in Arabic and left a form listing meal choices. It led straight into a serious discussion— a.k.a. father knows best—before ticks were put in the appropriate places and the form returned when the staff member re-appeared. This was the timely cue for Mel to leave to check messages in reception where Hassan promised to join her while Mohammed ate his first meal on English soil.

There was just time for Hassan to take a few shots of 'the most beautiful person' outside the entrance to the hospital before they left together speed-walking. After turning a couple of corners, they were soon sat at the pizza place they'd fetched up at more than two months before. It seemed much longer ago that Mel was made aware of a disabled son in Syria, time and distance somehow now intersecting. Mohammed, she was told, was conceived in a period of great hope but by the time he was born the war had begun.

'I'm sorry you were upset by the hospital. Hope we didn't add to that,' he said.

'No, no. It's hospitals in general.'

She explained how it started with visiting her dad in the trauma ward after the car crash. Her mom had died instantly but her dad had hung on for a couple of weeks, seemed to get better, went back into a coma then died. She made no mention of her time in Mt Sinai hospital where the phobia really began. It was an easy decision to talk instead about Mohammed's surgery.

'Change of plan,' Hassan explained. 'He's got to put on weight, preferably 5 kilograms. He needs vitamins and supplements. Then he goes to Stanmore.'

'Stanmore? That's at the end of the Jubilee Line, North West London.'

'Is that somewhere near Wembley Stadium?' he asked.

'Yeah, think so. I ride that line to see Jess and Billy. My dad worked for the railway company, and I always feel at home on a train.'

'I want to kiss you all over, Mel,' he said, taking her hands across the table.

She teased him, calling him, *Beast*, regretting that after

the pizza they'd have to part again. 'I'm in bits about it,' she added in case there was any doubt.

'And I want it to be IRL. And I think there's a way,' he said as they kissed over the table.

The hospital, he explained, would run tests then discharge Mohammed in a day or two—a little sooner than he was expected back in Winchester. Could they come and stay in Chiswick?

She teased him again but their conspiratorial smiles matched perfectly.

Mel too was desperate for IRL. FaceTime sex had seemed the only way to conduct and advance their relationship when there was little chance of meeting for a while. It had started with her sending him that half-revealing, though tasteful, she thought, selfie. Then the mounting panic while she waited for his reply. Would he be shocked? Did it go against some religious edict? The minutes seemed like hours until her Beast appeared in all his hairy nakedness. After that, and her purchase of an adult toy, their virtual relationship developed at a pace. To Mel's surprise, it brought out the sort of feelings of empowerment and control she'd only rarely experienced with a lover before. There was an aura of transcendence about the role-playing that Royce would, no doubt, recognise. The other surprise was just how easily awkwardness would turn into laughter.

As soon as he finished his pizza, Hassan was on his feet. Halfway through hers, Mel stood up and kissed him goodbye. He took off at speed for the hospital and her appetite died. She sat a while trying to blank her thoughts, which only brought Anto to mind and the need to check him out about the chance of another boat ride. She finished her text to him as she walked towards the Tube station. Now she was quite free to visit Royce who was half-expecting her 'for tea' and a viewing of his depictions of local scenes. It was tempting to think of them as therapy, and in that vein, she'd need to respond with enthusiasm, whatever their merit. On the train she had to stifle her laughter as she ran through a few suitably arty comments. But why was that so funny? Had life taken on a more comedic turn after the discovery of FaceTime sex? Her mind was going every which way: the bounties of love, a voice—probably Royce's—was telling her.

It was a relief to slip away from Camden's noisy bustle, thread her way down the narrow street and, though she still had a key, press the bell at the old mews house. Within seconds an even leaner Royce opened the door, uttered 'my dear' and enveloped her in a bony hug.

Over tea he kept complimenting her on her appearance and dress and Mel, recognising the ruse, responded in kind: his fit and youthful appearance. She could hardly say he was looking a little reedy; there was a tacit agreement not to mention the stage. After tea he led her up to the bedroom above the garage, now his studio. It was full of light from its two windows and the work surfaces groaned under the weight of so many photos, sketches and paintings, pots and brushes. The floor was wall-to-wall vinyl.

'Watercolours! Didn't think you'd have the patience,' she said.

'Heck of a discipline. Teaches you patience. There's always acrylics when I lose it.'

'I love the colours; the light and the shade. You've caught summer just before it began to fade.'

'Thank you. Remember this room?'

'Of course. It was prophetic in a way. You painted me here, and now…'

'Didn't just paint you, did I? Did we?'

Her gut tightened and she feigned interest in a canal scene with reedy banks until the silence became unbearable.

'How's the cardio rehab going?'

'I'm ahead of the curve, they say.'

He described in some authentic detail his recovery and fitness regime. It seemed to suit his restless spirit as did the attention he gave to the artwork. How long, she wondered, before renaissance man turned his magpie mind to writing? If it ever came to it, she was well placed to win him a major audiobook deal.

She excused herself to visit the main bathroom. She'd always admired its raunchy décor—old bathtub, flamboyant floor tiles, marble walls. There was a time when she was fool enough to think she might one day call this house home, even to imagine the makeover of its rooms, but not the upstairs bathroom. In back of the house there was a small, enclosed outdoor space, hardly a yard, which, still empty, cried out for potted flowers and foliage.

Back on the train her mood was crashing. A new Royce seemed to be emerging but there were still some familiar echoes of the Royce of the past. Neither attracted her.

'I've changed for good,' he'd said. 'It's adios to the picaro. It's all behind me, thanks to therapy. It was all a front, a mask. So many masks…'

Mel's heart sank. She didn't believe him, didn't *want* to

believe him. How was he ever going to get up on stage and deliver again without his inner diabolist? The agency—her future—depended so much on the resurrection of this heartless, remorseless devil. And maybe he hadn't changed so much—he'd begged her to spend a night, *just one,* with him, 'to see me through this stage of rehab, this 'bend in the road'.

Chapter 24

Despite the fine weather, Anto was still able to hire a 25-foot launch, firmly refusing any money from Mel.

'But would you do the picnic? And I won't insist on anyone wearing life-jackets—instead I'm appointing you safety officer, first class.' he joked.

It was a deal.

Wearing shorts, a tank top *and* plenty of SPF, Mel picked Billy up early from the nursery and this time there was no lost expression when he got inside the taxi—he knew where he was going. Mel's challenge was how to calmly introduce him this time to the idea of sharing the boat trip with another boy, one who spoke little English and couldn't walk properly.

'You'll be okay. You know Captain Anto *and* Mr Hassan.'

He appeared to be sufficiently lost in his reveries of the last boat trip throughout the entire taxi ride and hardly said a word. As they approached Chiswick, Mel explained, 'First, we go to my house and pick up the picnic. You can play the piano, but not for long.'

Hassan had been busy all morning baking Syrian flatbread and—in his own words—creating a multi-ingredient salad. Squatting down, he made a big fuss of Billy and introduced the boys to one another.

'Mohammed can't walk very well so he has to use *these* legs,' he said, pointing to the pair of crutches the hospital had provided. 'He's never been on a boat before; he's a bit scared so I want you to show him how it's done. You're good at boats, aren't you, Billy?' Billy nodded with all the assurance of a seasoned mariner.

At a sign from his dad, Mohammed twisted out of the armchair onto his good leg, grabbed his crutches and began to propel himself with ease around the sitting room. Like many other aspects of his 'brave new world' it caused him so much amusement, Mel doubted he had the slightest fear of water. Billy was not a little fascinated by this curly-haired, big-eyed boy's bizarre way of getting about.

Soon they were passing Anto's house, Mel and Hassan with backpacks, Mohammed easily keeping up with his crutches and Billy holding Mel's hand, already convinced he could smell the river. 'Captain' Anto was waiting at the pier, complete with nautical cap and hamming authentically about weather and the tide, which was, for their information, falling. Introductions completed, they went to board their boat; Mel could see that Billy was registering every detail of the new, roomier vessel while Hassan hoisted his son over the side and Mel, last to board, handed him the crutches. The captain instructed Hassan how to 'watch the stern' with a fender, and the boat eased away from its berth. If it brought back any painful memories, he didn't let it show.

Mel placed herself at the front next to Anto. Turning around and kneeling on the bench seat she took pictures of the boys, their proud stripy tops contrasting with one another. Hassan sitting between the youngsters. They dutifully smiled for her, Billy quiet, but excited, Mohammed laughing and gabbling in Arabic, Hassan translating. It was hard to grasp that the boy had spent all his life in a war zone, had heard and felt the shells landing and seen so much destruction. Perhaps his effervescence was a clue, that and his heroic appetite. Mel struggled to resist making comparisons between the boys, their worlds so far apart. It amused her to learn how Mohammed—unfazed and unoffended by the sight of her flesh—had described her legs: *white like snow.* 'It's the Irish showing up in me,' she told Hassan, also in shorts. By contrast his legs were studded with forests of dark hair.

As before, Anto throttled back as they passed beneath the bridges and Hassan made efforts to convey Billy's awe and enthusiasm to his son who only showed a passing interest, reserving all his enthusiasm for waving and calling out to people on the banks of the river. In this way they chugged as far as Richmond where the barrage prevented them going any further without entering the lock. They turned around and Anto looked for a spot where the boat could nudge the bank and moor. That accomplished, Hassan jumped ashore and secured two ropes to the bank, the engine was cut and the picnic laid out. While Mel coaxed and bribed Billy, the others ate heartily.

On their return, Hassan and Mel exchanged places, Mel dividing her efforts between enthusing with Billy and trying to teach Mohammed some English. At last, the boys fell silent. She closed her eyes and was soon humming a slow crescendo—the boat song from *The Tales of Hoffman.* Gradually the whole party joined in, enthusiasm the easy winner over musicality, Billy appearing slightly put out. When the boat was safely moored, they headed off toward the eyot with nets, one of which Billy quickly commandeered and without so many words nominated the 'captain' as his fishing partner. Mel and Hassan with Mohammed in tow were no match at dipping and soon gave up. They paddled instead for a while, Mohammed limping by his father's side, until Hassan picked him up out the water and carried him to dry land. It was the first time Mel became aware that, outside of his disability, Mohammed didn't regard his life as anything but perfect. He was, for him, unusually quiet as if he'd suddenly grasped that the fun times he'd been having since his arrival were artificial and wouldn't last, that something more routine and onerous awaited in Winchester before his return to London for surgery. Mel could only guess his thoughts and emotions were winging back to his mom and she put an arm around him.

'Everything's gonna be okay, inshallah,' she said, giving him a hug.

He gave her a brief smile before retreating into himself. Hassan spoke firmly but kindly to his son, then he seemed to change subject and point to the river. The next thing she knew he'd thrown off his top and was wading back out until he was deep enough to swim. Mohammed became excited and Mel wondered how much of that was alarm. And when it was clear Hassan was striking out for the opposite bank, her twitchy heart was in her mouth. The others had stopped dipping and Anto was shouting something to the swimmer. Mel bottled her emotions and kept saying: 'it's okay, it's okay,' as if she'd watched her lover swim across the Thames countless times.

Was it possible he was re-enacting his swim to freedom off the Turkish coast? That whole chapter was a blank page she'd still not been invited to read, ditto the version he'd given Fliss at Hambledean Hall, which was, he admitted, only half the story, and doctored for 'easy consumption'. She'd thought that once he and his son were safely together on British soil, he'd begin to open up to her. There was still time, of course. But the longer she remained in the dark, the more she fretted over his silence.

By swimming into the current, he'd made it to the shallows directly opposite and was waving to the party. Mohammed got up onto his feet and waved and shouted back, steadying himself with a single crutch. Anto waded out shouting, gesturing and pointing repeatedly upstream. The message was clear: walk up against the current then use it to swim back. Mel was relieved to see Hassan take the advice and soon enough he was standing up in the nearby shallows, where Mel and Mohammed with a single crutch, went out to meet him. His face was wreathed in smiles; he picked Mohammed up and held him high like some prize he'd just won and, once again, the boy was full of laughter. The hairs on Hassan's chest were gathered and slicked down; it showed up all his chicken pox scars. Anto gave his congratulations and, turning to Billy, asked him if he'd like swimming lessons, quickly adding that they'd be in a heated, indoor pool. Mel added encouraging nods and smiles. Billy's reaction was muted but positive.

It was time for Anto to return the boat to the yard. He said he'd need some help with berthing, so asked Hassan to assist while the rest of the party went back to Mel's to clean up and shower. Later, in the sitting room they all had tea, cakes and cookies while Billy picked out songs on the piano. Hassan took out his new phone and tried to set up a video call with someone in Eastern Canada. It didn't work out, but he said he'd keep trying, explaining to Mel that a friend of Mohammed's was one of a party of adoptees now settled in Toronto.

The next morning, Wednesday, Mel, Hassan and Mohammed walked by the river a final time before father and son got in a taxi at Hammersmith and left for Waterloo. The lovers, unsure as to when they'd meet again, had been hard put to jolly one another up.

A settling-in process at Winchester awaited—micro-managed to the tiniest detail by Fliss, the Formidable, as Mel had started calling her. The woman was fast turning Hassan into a legend. The local TV station was going to film a scripted reception at Hambledean Hall in the presence of the Earl and Countess. Hassan would thank the Hall for their help in welcoming him to Winchester and providing funds for the refugee charity, his college and tourist guide courses. Mohammed had to learn to deliver a single sentence in English in front of camera, and his adoptive family would be interviewed. Follow-up programmes were in the pipeline to chart Mohammed's progress after his hip surgery. Fliss was leaving nothing to chance in her efforts to re-establish the Hall's reputation.

In the evening, after taking Billy home, Mel returned to an empty, untidy house—and the scent of exotic lilies. Ever since Hassan bought her the bouquet, its hefty musk had kept winging her back to a dingy rehab unit in Brooklyn. Somebody must have wanted to cheer that place up—the attendants too—and the flowers they were clearly stuck on were lilies. Now she might never separate that odour from the long road to stopping methadone. They said *addictive personality* like her dad, but if he was addicted to anything it was surely more his guitar than the whisky. Like a fool she'd believed Lennie when he told her *smoking* H wasn't addictive. She traced her IBS all the way back to finally coming off methadone.

Alone now, the potency of the scent was almost unbearable, and though it felt criminal, she wrapped the flowers up in a bag, dropped them in the bin, then quickly changed. Just before heading out to meet Anto at the bistro, she went round rescuing her house plants with much needed water. En route she tried to analyse her feelings: if she'd caught that scent while married to Henry it might not have meant too much. After four days of pure, crazy 'family' life, it told her she was lonely. If Mel had given it some thought, she'd have brought over some of Billy's pull-ups for Mohammed to wear at night. Now she'd have to scrub the mattress.

As they raised their glasses, Mel said, 'No alcohol for four days. I don't seem to need it when Hassan's around.'

'His religion or his culture?' Anto asked.

'Bit of both, I think. Then I have to be careful in front of Mohammed. So, what *did* you two talk about?'

'He loves Winchester. He's fluent in French.'

'I know all that. Did he say anything about how he got here, about Syria, Mohammed's selfless mom?'

'I just gathered that things are very bad there, very brutal. Got the impression he'd escaped by the skin of his teeth. No, he didn't really say anything as such.'

'A bit like you, then,' Mel said provocatively. But Anto refused to rise to the bait and their conversation turned to small talk and the menu. In four days of predominantly middle eastern, vegetarian food without so much as a gripe from her IBS she'd 'risk' a lasagne. After all this time, her theories still hovered—*diet*, *psychological*, *allergy*. Anto talked of Maria; they were heartened by how she appeared to have bounced back from the miscarriage. On the surface it seemed like they'd all found some closure, added to which, he planned to go and stay with her on a short 'business-cum-vacation'. Mel was pleased for them both and only wished she could go too. And then what would he do? He was still taking stock, he said. He asked after Helena.

'I'm going to invite her round for tea on the terrace, sorry, *belvedere*. You must come. Still haven't been over to her place and that's okay with me. I think she wants to preserve something of her mystery, her mystique. When we meet, she's almost always *Lady* Helena.'

'How wonderful,' Anton replied, chuckling in that understated English way of his. 'And how did Jess react to our latest marine adventure?'

'Fine. She's much calmer now. I thought she was going to, you know, be a bit judgemental but she even asked about Mohammed.'

'You and Hassan?'

'She's okay with that now. I think it helps she's maybe seeing someone right now. Which means she might want Billy to overnight with me sometimes. You know how quiet he was today, well, he talked non-stop about the trip to his mom. All the little details.'

'Is he still up for swimming lessons?

'Sure is. Let's do it.'

Chapter 25

On the train back to Waterloo Mel reflected on her first row with Hassan. Really it was their second, but the one in the little upstairs church had been no more than a misapprehension, the resolution of which went the way of a romantic novel ending. Only this was real life: she wanted to know more about his past, not to mention his—or was it—*their* future? When did he plan to up sticks and come and live in London? Was his love and gratitude towards Winchester so strong it overrode everything else? It was too easy to use the case of Mohammed in the cause of staying put. She did accept that the boy needed time to settle. Since his surgery he'd been getting around in an adapted wheelchair and even using his crutches to negotiate steps. 'Determined and resourceful' was how the local TV station had described him. This, despite a huge plaster cast from his belly button to both hips, then all the way down to the toes of his left foot. He'd been fortunate—he didn't need to be cut. Under the anaesthetic his hip joint was manipulated back into place, where, it was hoped, it would remain.

Shortly before Anto went to visit with Maria in Long Beach, Mel served afternoon tea for three in the terrace garden, where they sat between pots of fuchsias and agapanthus. While Helena and Mel went about reviving their Ritz encounter, Anto hammed up his rudest, stuffiest burlesque of a waiter—to everyone's delight. Her guests got on well, their English tones complementing one another nicely. Afterwards, they left together, Helena keen to see Anto's Japanese garden. It seemed to Mel that

Anto intuitively understood women, either that or he was always looking for the sister he lost in his late teens. In the long lounge there was a photo of a young Japanese woman whom he'd made reference to only once. Mel imagined the two working on gardens together: an artistic and spiritual bond. Perhaps it had been more than that.

Just when Mel had gotten used to video-calling the West Coast and seeing two familiar faces, it was a shock—Anto leaving suddenly—when it was just Maria. She denied there'd been any falling-out. Between filming and editing, she'd managed to arrange a few trips.

'Huntington was a must. He was just blown away by the cactus garden and then all those first editions in the library,' she said. 'Then maybe the art gallery topped even that—you know, all that pure white stone in the hills beyond Hollywood. We also went to the other Getty place, the villa.'

'Yeah, I know it,' Mel replied. It brought back an ugly encounter that had wiped out her self-confidence for a time. During her first assignment in Tinseltown she'd been offered a trip to the villa by some small studio honcho, and naively she accepted, thinking it was all about culture. She'd never heard of *quid pro quo* and, after the visit, had to fight off her escort in the underground car park. Her dress torn, she ran back to the villa and called a cab. It never occurred to her to make a complaint, let alone tell anyone. It would have gotten her nowhere. Worse, it might have stymied the agency's mission and put an end to the otherwise fun Hollywood trips. Of course, she kept it from Henry. Maria empathized after Mel had shared the memory with her.

'Made me so angry, I packed a small gun after that. Then I got more scared of the gun,' Mel confessed, and they both laughed. 'So what's with Anto?'

'He's got an editor after him for an overdue article. Something about Sevenoaks. He had to fly.'

'By the seat of his pants?' Mel replied, and they laughed again.

And then a certain, knowing expression fell across Maria's face. 'So… all I hear is Hassan. It sounds like the real thing, Mel. If the photos are anything to go by, no wonder. Only problem—Anto tells me—is this attachment to Winchester… and the boy. Everything else says it's just a matter of time.'

'I guess so. We had a row about it. I know I'm impatient. I feel like if I don't push, it won't happen. After they left—we had four days together—I felt lonely. And then I realised I've been lonely quite a long time. It was kind of a shock.'

'It was one of the things that drew me to you at Green Park station, my darling.'

'Oh, and what were the other things?' Mel asked, a touch of irony creeping into her words.

'It was kind of reading you like a book. I've been told I'm psychic but I don't think it's true. I could sense some trauma, but also many positives. And I just knew you'd be good for me.'

'Hate to say it. I was wary of you—only at the beginning, mind,' Mel said with a hint of humour.

'You okay now?' Maria fished, her tone altering.

What did she mean? The alcohol? The baby? Mel was quick to reassure her, adding that Jess was getting back to her old self and had taken back much of Billy's care. Life had been so full-on with him. Now that it was back to twice a week, she was missing him. The big issue now was Royce.

'Couldn't someone high up in theatre have a word, a fellow actor?' Maria suggested.

'They've tried. Professionally he's a bit of a lone wolf. And now he's got hooked on watercolours. Not sure it's his thing. He's better at acrylics.'

'I know. I look at that painting most days. Think I told you—I'm writing a script around it.'

'Looks like you did a round with a heavyweight southpaw. You okay?' Holly remarked as soon as Mel arrived at the agency on Tuesday morning.

'Fine. I was rushing on the stair. The carpet's a bit loose at the turn,' Mel replied, then added for good measure, 'I bruise real easy.'

As soon as the routine exchanges were over, Holly asked after Royce's health and, by implication, the approximate date he was planning to go back on stage. Mel wasn't ready to spell out to her assistant the true nature of the 'new Royce' or his 'epiphany', preferring to talk up his signed abstract acrylics, which he would complete over a short sabbatical, then sell for megabucks.

'Is the agency going to benefit?' a dubious Holly asked.

'I'm working on it.'

'I can cut my hours if you need.' Holly saw straight through Mel's bluff.

'No way. I need all your hours. Don't give it another thought. Unless, of course…'

The upshot, after much circumlocution, was that Holly would keep her hours as they were.

Later, Mel was sitting at the low bench in the nursery cloakroom when Billy appeared at the door. It was clear he was taken aback by the bruising on her face and wouldn't respond to her hearty greeting. The concealer hadn't fooled anyone so far.

'Hey! Clumsy me. I tripped up in the street, looking at my phone! How are *you*?'

He was 'good', but he remained fascinated by the patterning and colours on her face and inspected them closely.

'You think Mr Bugger gave me a push?' she ventured, making the sort of face she'd taught him to respond to.

Sure enough, he smiled enough to show he'd not missed the joke. The bogeyman had not been seen or heard of much recently. Her face, she assured him, would be back to normal by next week. He came closer and touched her face very gently.

'It's like paint,' he said.

She half agreed, explaining that, not being on the outside, it couldn't be washed off like ink or paint. It was *under* the surface. Unable to 'touch' the colours, he nodded in agreement. And then, as they made their way to the main door, the novelty wore away. He sat in the buggy and Mel pushed him home for lunch.

As soon as Jess arrived, Billy revived his interest in Mel's accident and spoke to his mum with some authority on the subject, even indulging in a rather ponderous re-telling of the joke. At which there was hearty laughter all round. After the meal and bedtime rituals—a tad rushed, it seemed to Mel—the women listened to Billy via the intercom. He was telling his monkey all about the accident. When, finally, he drifted into silence, Jess suggested wine which Mel declined. It seemed Jess was a little excited, had news to tell, and wouldn't pass up on a 'glass or two' of Prosecco.

'The guy I'm seeing owns a garment factory; two in fact. They cater for both ends of the market. He's been coming to the shop for ages. He wants me to design.'

'Wow, Jess! What you've always wanted. So, what's he like?'

'*Very* generous,' Jess replied, flashing a wide smile, and then slipping a sapphire ring onto the fourth finger of her left hand. 'He's *really* laid back. Okay, so he's a little older, but you know all about that. He carries a lot of guilt about his divorce. There's two teenage boys at boarding school.'

'Business *and* pleasure?'

'Didn't you, though? But he's really sweet and we've so got our heads screwed on. Same views and taste where it matters—clothes and fashion.'

Jess had just made a lightning reference to Mel's affair with Royce while still married to her dad, but thankfully it never seemed to come between them, the judgement Mel had often expected to rain down on her never materialized. Now was no exception—Jess was already at a canter through a bunch of names and minutiae pertaining to the world of *haute couture* which Mel found hard to follow, suffering, among other things, from a bad case of shell-shock. Did she still believe in miracles? Did she ever believe in miracles? She asked to see a photo.

'After the weekend. You still okay about Billy coming to you?'

'Sure. What about Billy?'

'He can't wait. Keeps talking about Captain Anto!'

'It smells different to the sea and the river,' Billy observed as Anto handed him down, complete with arm bands and goggles, to Mel, standing in the pool. She'd previously done a 'dry run' with the swimming aids and Billy hadn't objected.

'It's much cleaner,' Mel said, as if to reassure him. She could feel his little body tense up as she lowered him into the water. As she swayed and hummed the boat song, they watched Anto enter the water, swim about, duck dive and then surface in a different place.

The session lasted about twenty minutes, Billy needing to be held throughout, if only lightly sometimes. He quietly took in every nuance of the new experience, recognising that this was altogether different from dipping in the river. The introduction, Mel and Anto agreed, had gone without upset and seemed likely to be followed up by another session in the pool.

Later, the trio met Helena at Kew Gardens. This time there was no contemplative tour of the Japanese garden. Instead, the party went straight to the treetop walk where, once among the canopies, Billy, with a little help, was able to amass a collection of russet-turning leaves and study their finer detail. Before they descended, Anto put them in his backpack for safekeeping. Next, they went around the lake, admiring its vivid reflections of autumn-tinted trees. With a gentle breeze rippling its surface, it reminded Mel of Royce's acrylics, the way he made the colours run into each other to produce what he called his phantasmagoria series. Anto was familiar with the technique but less impressed with its claim to be art.

'Looks more like something out of the Hubble Telescope. I want to give them all the same title: *Where Stars are Born.*'

This proved to be the cue for Helena to reprise her haughty *alter ego*. 'The coming of photography signalled the death-knell of fine art. Give me the pre-Raphaelites *any* day,' she proclaimed in her best Lady Helena.

Sounds of appreciation and amusement followed.

They left the lake for the cherry walk, now a blaze of red, Mel stopping by the tree she'd snapped in spring for Billy's benefit. She scrolled back her photo file and showed the party the original—white blossom, blue sky *and* a bird. A bemused Billy begged Mel to take another photo of the same tree; she obliged, apologising for the lack of a bird. Anto said something about photo-shopping then reached up and pulled off a leaf and offered it to the youngster, pronouncing for the party's edification the appropriate Japanese word. It described, he explained, exactly what Billy was doing.

They returned by way of the pagoda avenue where a rich trail of red-hued leaves awaited collection. Everyone took part in the supposed ancient ritual, Mel and Helena giving their own guesses as to how it came about. On leaving the gardens there were emotional goodbyes, Helena left for home and the three returned to Chiswick.

Much later, after Mel settled Billy down to sleep, she phoned Anto and talked about Maria and his visit to California. She wondered whether his dashing off and mention of Sevenoaks meant there was a problem with 'the folks'. But it seemed Maria was right all along. He was 'overdue' with an article on Jane Austen, the Austen family in particular.

'They originated in Sevenoaks,' he explained. 'Still some Austens in the area. We've had Austens in our family a while back.'

'You're related to Jane Austen?' Mel said in astonishment.

'Very distantly, as must be hundreds of others,' he replied, laughing.

The conversation soon switched to next weekend and Hassan's long-awaited visit.

'He wants to meet with you,' Mel said, sounding a little put out.

'That would be great—if time allows.'

'Fine! You two go off to the pub while I go and watch this real hunk play volleyball.'

Mel reflected on a recurring theme—Anto's burgeoning social circle, all down to her doing. But who was she to deny him these friendships? He too, it seemed, had been lonely.

Before his bedtime, Billy had been busy gluing his leaves into a scrapbook, which Mel had bought for the purpose, when he became a little impatient waiting for the glue to set on each page, he asked, 'Can I paint a *fantagora* instead?'

'Phantasmagoria,' Mel corrected. 'Yes, I know just the place.'

'Great to see you both,' Royce exclaimed at the door, his jeans and shirt-cum-smock spattered in paint. He kissed Mel then bent down to address Billy. 'Been hearing a lot about you, young man. You want to paint?'

'Yes please, akylics and fantagora'.

Royce laughed while Mel was at pains to convince him her charge had said it right 'only a minute ago'. For once Mel was allowing Billy to skip nursery.

'Come in. I've got two washes ready and dried. One pink, the other pale blue.'

The studio was more cluttered than when Mel had last visited. There were now many completed works propped against the walls, mainly acrylics. He grabbed a few at random and laid them out for inspection on one of the empty tables.

'This is the sort of thing we'll have a go at,' Royce explained as Billy looked from one picture to another. The artist turned to Mel with a quizzical expression.

'When he goes quiet like that it means he's concentrating real hard,' she whispered. They waited for Billy's reaction. He was evidently transfixed. The canvases were covered in fantastical shapes, textures and colours.

'It's like painting the air,' Billy said, at last.

'You *could* say that. Or maybe it's the sea, or even outer space. Let's make a start,' Royce replied.

He handed his guests clean plastic overalls, Billy's literally cut to size with scissors, admitting that he usually forgot to wear any, and then began to demonstrate his technique—adding a light mix of colours in a small cup with water, then inverting it on the canvas. He encouraged his pupils to move the cup about while observing the effects. He stood back, watching their excited progress for a couple of minutes then showed them how to tip the canvas this way and that, while describing more refinements. Mel and Royce exchanged expressions as they watched Billy immerse himself in the novel activity.

'Now you do one on your own,' Royce said, when the painting had reached some sort of kaleidoscopic completion. 'You can always add stuff later.'

Later, when Billy was adding the finishing touches to the second canvas, Mel joined Royce downstairs for coffee.

'I've narrowed it down to the Barbican or the Whitechapel,' he explained, referring to his intended exhibition. 'I've posted a little of the work on the web pages to get the conversation going—and it's working. Don't give a shit what the critics say.'

'Will the agency get anything out of this?' Mel asked nervously.

'Sure we can arrange something.'

Chapter 26

Mel thought she'd get through until coffee but her concentration was deserting her so fast, she couldn't pretend to be doing anything useful any longer. And then the dam burst with sobbing and tears hitting her desk before she had time to wipe them away. She stood up to steady herself and Holly was already there, locking her boss in her surprisingly strong arms. Holly believed in a 'good cry' and 'letting it all out'. She bided her time then sat Mel down, crouched by the chair and held her hand.

'She's taking Billy away,' was all Mel could get out before there was another outburst.

Holly squeezed Mel's hand, said she'd get coffee and disappeared. In record time she was back with the jug and two mugs, Mel grimly quiet, apologising.

'Jess off her rocker?' Holly probed.

'You could say. She's fallen head-over-heels for this rich, rag trade boss, older guy, lives and manufactures near Manchester. He wants her to live up there in a big house and design to her heart's content. I'm telling her to go easy. She won't listen.'

'Oh, hell! Understandable, I suppose, after being down for so long. But not good news for Billy, I'm sorry.'

'That's what's killing me. How's he going to cope; he's made such progress. Now, I think he'll go backwards, go back inside himself.'

'You could do visits. There's a fast train. FaceTime. He could stay over in the holidays,' Holly suggested after giving the matter some thought.

'That's just what Jess was saying to soften the blow. But

what about Billy? He's going to be the big loser. Sure as hell Mr Bugger starts turning up again.'

The conversation stuttered on; optimism one minute: pessimism the next. Eventually Holly suggested Mel went for a walk by the river without her phone. She would 'hold the fort', promising—by making a joke about it—to keep her nose out of anything private. Mel thanked her assistant and decided to take her advice; she kept her phone though, satisfying Holly only when she'd turned it off.

The light off the river made the leaves on the trees glow, and gusts of wind caused them to flicker. Fallen ones scurried and swirled by her feet. There was something from the past here—images of the upstate Hudson flashed through her mind like a whirlwind, stripping away twenty-five years and more. She was once an upstate girl but the magnetic pull of New York City had been too great. Soon she was talking and dressing the Brooklyn way, singing in a different style. As the past faded, she came up with an idea—consult with Lou. He would know what was best for Billy, how she ought to play it. Such thoughts calmed her down until she drew level with the eyot where they'd all gone dipping. Now she was right back inside Billy's head again.

She found herself by the church but made no effort to go inside. Instead, she mooched about the graves and weathered headstones. There was always the compulsion, aided by flowery epitaphs and archaic script, to people the names and dates with her imagination. The grave of William Hogarth, the painter, was different—it bore an inscribed poem. He and his wife were unable to have children so they fostered foundlings instead. She liked to think the Hogarths took them dipping by the eyot.

As she was leaving the churchyard, a white-haired ghost—Catherine—appeared out of nowhere.

'How nice to see you. Mel, isn't it? How are you?'

The woman was evidently referring to Mel's 'miscarriage' when Anto had gone up to her and 'explained' their loss. The time before it was Henry's funeral. She must think Mel was jinxed, or maybe just a bad sinner.

'Fine, thank you.'

But Catherine wasn't fooled and, by her body language, was offering Mel her listening services again. They walked together towards the pier then further, beyond the eyot while Mel described her fears for Billy's future.

'I'm sorry, I've taken you out of your way,' Mel said but Catherine denied it. They stopped all of a sudden and the one-sided conversation came to an end, but not before they'd exchanged contact details. Catherine begged to be kept informed of Billy's progress. She promised to pray for him, and, after thanking her once more, Mel trudged back to Hammersmith, her pain not as sharp-edged as when she'd started out. She was ashamed not to have asked Catherine anything about herself. Although the woman was in her Gratitude jar, Mel knew next to nothing about her. She'd make amends with a phone call.

An autumn mist was settling over Regent's Park as Mel walked in what she took to be the right direction. Such daylight as there was—even as she left Camden—had become gloomy, and now she was sufficiently distant from artificial lighting and the rumble of traffic to feel adrift from the outside world. Without the odd passer-by it might have felt spooky. She was glad of her wrap wool coat and boots. She'd not had much use of the coat since coming to London. Partly it was the climate and partly, she realised, it had to do with Henry.

'I'm gonna buy you a proper coat,' he'd said, one day when her old puffer jacket could no longer maintain the pretence of keeping out the cold.

'You're always buying me stuff. I can't compete,' she said, or words to that effect. Nevertheless, they were soon making their way to Third Avenue. She walked out the store in it feeling warm and loaded. It checked all the boxes—until they arrived in London when it hung unworn and accusatory in the wardrobe. Was it progress, then, that she could at last wear the coat again? Or had she simply traded one guilt for another, Royce, the common denominator?

He'd been in poetic mood today for sure, slipping the odd pentameter into the conversation, winding up the emotional temperature with his deft choice of words. All of which turned out to be entirely fortuitous—she'd brought along a copy of T.S. Eliot's *Four Quartets*. Would he be interested in giving recitals? A short tour? It might re-kindle his lost appetite for the stage, she thought, without directly putting the idea into his head. Almost at once, tuning in to the text, he began to read aloud and a little later his body language was on the move. He was enjoying the sound of the words, the way *his* words brought the text alive. Maybe she'd found a chink in his adamantine resolution to do 'no more theatre', maybe not. He went on without a break for a good ten minutes, then slowed, and came to a stop like some musical cadence.

'Don't you just love this stuff? Beauty before beauty,' he said, looking her up and down.

Her blush surprised her. She wore the green maxi dress with a choker, her hair, now long, tied up in a low bun.

The mist had thickened a little, the park near deserted. She took out her hip flask and tipped it up between her lips. The draught hit the back of her throat like a little too much tabasco, the liquor making her insides glow as it travelled south. She'd imbibed a little more freely before 'rehabilitating' Royce. In fact, everything before, during and after went okay, if not to say rather well. Did she enjoy it? A little too obviously, it seemed.

'You know you can stay here forever,' Royce said, afterwards in bed. 'You can be the mistress of this house.' He'd said something similar four years before when she was dumb enough to believe his 'one-woman' declarations. It had allowed her briefly to fantasise about how she might go about making over the rooms. In time she got to know him better—the hard way. Now it was different— he'd changed 'for good'. But she wasn't buying any of that—she'd had to learn how to treat with the medley of his personae, all of which crystallised into a theory: to ever get back to the stage he needed not just to play, but to *be* the picaro again. She coolly predicted his return—one day. Was today a step in the right direction? She wouldn't know any time soon.

She'd forgotten how much he loved to watch her dress afterwards—and how she played to it! Indeed, he described it as pure theatre—with a sense of reverse chronology thrown in. This time it carried more than its usual *tristesse*, he said. Her final application of lippy was 'surely the perfect stab-in-the-heart'. She was adamant there would be no repeat performance.

As she was leaving, he asked after Billy and she became emotional.

'What's that girl thinking of?'

'Love. That's what she's thinking of, Royce. Makes you do crazy things,' she said.

'That boy has an unusual awareness, but he's also a rum lad. When you were out of the room, he whispered to me he'd seen your vagina at the swimming pool. Only he said *fangina*.'

At last, she was nearing the lights and noise of the city. Reality, in all its colours, calling. She'd held off thinking of Hassan for so long and now a tide of images and emotions swept through her. Thinking of all the ways their bodies interacted almost overwhelmed her. Had FaceTime sex made him as desperate as her for all those actual and intimate touches?

'This is where we nearly came that first time,' Mel admitted as they entered the burger bar. 'But how can you take a *Lady* to a place like this?'

'It's smart and functional. I'm okay with it. Not sure the *Lady* would approve,' Helena replied with a cackle from somewhere deep in her chest. She wasn't *being* Lady Helena today and Mel could only wonder why.

Before crossing the river to the South Bank, Helena had given Mel a tour of Holborn, starting with the Soane Museum. They'd walked from the Tube station to find Lincoln's Inn Fields in glorious autumn sunshine. Inside the house—an Aladdin's cave of art, antiques and curios—they negotiated the tiny passages and spaces feeling a little claustrophobic, looking in vain for any trace of a Mrs Soane. Afterwards they wandered about the ancient Inns of Court, Helena making references to Charles Dickens and Shakespeare plays.

'It'll be my first,' Helena confided, a little nervously.

'C'mon, you can do it. Remember: thumbs and pinkies below, fingers above, gentle squeeze.'

'They won't think me an awful wimp if I ask for a knife and fork?'

Mel laughed. It was the Ritz routine all over again and when the burgers arrived, Helena continued play-acting, her burger seeming to resist all her increasingly frantic attempts to detach a piece and eat it. The slapstick over, she gave in and picked up her knife and fork.

Afterwards, over coffee she said, 'See, I can still make you laugh. Even now.'

'You can always make me laugh.'

'I want to help too, Mel. I'll gladly pay for you to have residential treatment. Nothing would give me greater joy than to see you over this. Money doesn't come into this *at all*.'

'You're very kind... and don't think I'm not grateful but I need to be cut some slack right now. The Billy situation has hit hard, plus I want Hassan to say the right things without me having to drag it out of him. He's coming this weekend and if that goes well, *if*, then that would be a big help. Can I take a rain check?'

'Of course.'

'You and Maria are the only ones in the know. She stumbled on the evidence, whereas you have the most intuitive nose ever. You could have been a cop or in news media.'

'Or a student of company profiles, stocks and shares. What about Anto?'

'No. But even if he knew, he wouldn't let on. I'd have to beat it out of him.'

They laughed, concurring over their mutual friend's faults and strengths.

'Hassan?' Helena probed.

'Please God no! He's near teetotal so I don't expect he'd understand. Then it's easier to stay dry when he's around.'

'Holly?'

'I guess she suspects—the girl's nosey enough! She's also very loyal.'

The conversation turned again to Anto, who'd brought Helena up to date—in particular his failed attempts at fatherhood and how these shaped his plans for the future.

'You don't mind?' Helena probed.

'No. I told him I'm done with all that. Offered to help, but they want to do it professionally.'

'He and Maria?'

'That's right, and the best of luck to them, I say.'

'What about afterwards—assuming it's successful?'

'I daren't really go there. I'm guessing on maybe the folks from Sevenoaks.'

They walked together to Charing Cross Tube Station where, after a long, tight hug they parted, promising to keep in close touch. On the train Mel reflected what a blessing she had in Helena. Without her, she'd never have met Hassan. Equally, it was Hassan who'd persuaded her to give Helena a second chance.

Chapter 27

Anto *had* changed. When they first met, Mel was unimpressed. He was gruff and condescending. Had she not met Henry, she might have classified Anto as a typical uppity English guy. Their first meetings were characterised by spiky arguments about art, theatre and performance. She found herself taking extreme views if only to watch him bridle, while he reacted by adopting the same tactic. In retrospect, he was testing her out while making sure he didn't expose too much of himself. It seemed obvious to Mel they'd call a truce soon enough. She was the first to 'blink' and was rewarded by Anto's softer side. That side was quick to complement her on the green sequin dress she had on.

'Wow! You're looking lovely. Like a shimmering emerald, Mel.'

'Overkill?'

'No way,' he affirmed as she turned around. 'Hassan likes?'

Her expression was unmistakeable.

The three were soon turning the corner of the street on their way to an early booking at the bistro. Mel's unbelted coat flapped against her as they walked. Hassan, normally clean-shaven, sported a stylish stubble. Waiting for Anto to arrive, he had become unusually restless. Was he nervous about meeting him again? They seemed to hit it off well enough on the boat and then messing about on the river. Maybe this time he wanted to make a more cerebral impression. Did that count as a hopeful sign? It was Saturday and, although they'd spent a lovely day together, not so much as a whisper of his moving to London had been breathed.

At Anto's instigation, Hassan spoke about his MA course in War Studies. With Mel he'd always been reserved about his course—either it wasn't a suitable subject to discuss with a hyper- emotional woman, or he'd lost interest in it. The men's talk ranged from the generalities of conflict to the specific: Iraq, Afghanistan. Once again it seemed Anto was making a 'raid' on a precious relationship, but rather than getting irritated, she only saw good in it.

Anto had readily agreed to Mel's prior plea—no alcohol. He ordered lamb while the lovers decided on identical vegetarian dishes. Sitting opposite them, he launched into a string of amusing tirades against figures in the media and politics. It was entertaining fun even though she didn't recognise all the mimicked characters. The two men were apparently quite comfortable with one another, the only awkwardness came with the bill and the decision about where to have coffee, both men insisting on paying. Mel's 'why don't we split it,' only brought a loud unison of disapproval. Finally, Anto got his way, and in return asked an indulgence: could he impart the gist of his article on the Austen family over coffee, chez Mel?

While Mel made the coffee, Hassan went to check the temperature on the terrace, confirming it was too cold to sit out. Anto mooched about in the kitchen, bumbling about a chiminea then going silent. Small talk didn't feature much in his repertoire and he was soon floundering. A vivid déjà vu suddenly stormed her brain from Columbia days—two stuttering boyfriends that couldn't quite get out what they wanted—a threesome.

They drank their coffee in the living room, Mel and Hassan on the couch, Anto in an armchair. He had no notes to refer to.

'Aeons ago,' he began, 'I promised an editor an article on the Austens. I started with great gusto—the Sevenoaks connections—which then rapidly waned and I put it aside. Some weeks ago, my interest was revived by an unrelated observation in the shallows of the Thames, and as soon as I returned from the US I set out on, not one, but two investigations. They had a common area, Hampshire, more particularly, Winchester.' He paused for more coffee.

Before he began again, Hassan took Mel's hand, kissed it and continued to hold it. He neither looked at her nor Anto, staring intently ahead. For no reason she could readily identify, Mel was beginning to experience one of those dark premonitory feelings—not always reliable— that had come and gone throughout her life.

'My researches took me to Hambledean Hall where, believe it or not, there *is* an intriguing connection with Jane Austen. Yes, I met the house manager, Fliss. She runs this efficient office under the grand staircase. She was very accommodating, showed me a ledger dated 1811. I gleaned such a lot of *other* information from our meeting…'

'I don't like the way this is turning out, Anto. You've gone off script. Not sure I want to hear anything more about that woman.'

'Please trust me. This concerns you and Hassan. You've got to hear me out. I promise I have your interests at heart.'

It was the signal for Hassan to cover his face, start

rocking back and forth and muttering in Arabic.

'Please let me hold you, my love,' she implored. The rocking stopped and they hugged.

'I didn't want to tell you any bad things,' Hassan got out. 'Even now someone else has to do it for me. I'm so ashamed. You've been like a dream to me and I haven't always been straight with you.'

Mel's destiny seemed to hover somewhere between Anto's authoritative voice and Hassan's admission of deception. How bad was it going to get?

Anto cleared his throat and began again, 'Mel, you once said to me you thought Hassan had PTSD. At the time we were sharing a terrible sorrow and didn't perhaps give the situation the attention it deserved. Because you *were* dead right. Now he's getting treatment.'

'You shoulda told me, sweetheart. After that first night, I knew there was something wrong.'

'Let's cut to earlier this summer,' Anto began again quickly. 'The Home Office was casting doubt on one of Hassan's documents—whether one of them had been forged. There was a risk his ILR might be in danger of being revoked. You know what that means, Mel?'

'Think so,' she said nodding sombrely, stroking her lover's hand.

'So, desperate times: desperate means. Hassan, you tell her who came through for you.'

Hassan detached himself from Mel, stood up, cradled his chin with both hands and took a deep breath. He appeared lost, looking first at Anto and then Mel. 'I was afraid of losing everything. There was no sex, no love. It was Fliss. We got married.'

'No!' Mel screamed. 'That woman was always gonna

get one over me. How she must be laughing.'

'Not true, Mel,' Anto fired back. 'This happened before you were on the scene. And the heat came off so maybe she did right. No one knows for sure. Now Mohammed's here, his dad's almost certainly safe. It all gets a bit technical.'

'A Pemberley Wedding?' Mel said, using a high ironic tone.

'Hardly. They borrowed a ring, shook hands then parted.'

'She's taken you all in.'

'No, Mel. She was entirely transparent with me. They had to work fast—just in case. She wishes you only the best. If she hadn't acted you might never have met Hassan, and God knows, he might by now be in a detention centre awaiting repatriation.'

'I just can't believe all I'm hearing... wait a minute,' Mel stammered before leaving the room in a hurry. She returned a minute later with an inhaler and her diary.

'You alright, Mel?' Anto asked. Both men had identical quizzical expressions. She took a few deep breaths and thought, *Am I milking this*? But no, she *really* thought she was going to have an asthmatic attack. It passed and she opened her diary.

'I know what you're checking,' Hassan uttered. 'That time I came to London; the trouble with the Home Office was real. But that was before, maybe two months before. I was desperate to see you. If I had told the truth, that would have blown it.' Hassan, still on his feet, an uneasy smile setting over his face, which brought out a matching one from Mel. But what else had he lied about? She didn't have to wait too long to find out.

'Okay, you two, it's time I left. Sorry to have been so brutal.'

'Wasn't you, was it, Anto,' Mel began, 'it's the truth that's brutal. By the way, what happened to the Austen Family article?'

'Final draft, almost there, honestly.'

'Don't go, Anto. Not yet,' Hassan pleaded. 'You start, then I'll…'

'Right. Mel, you once told me Hassan was under stress. But when we met that day on the boat, he appeared relaxed and happy. He had his son; he had you. It wasn't until he swam across the Thames…'

'What the fuck's this all about?' Mel gasped.

'I really must go,' Anto insisted, and without much ceremony he let himself out with hardly a 'goodnight'. Wearily, Hassan sat down next to Mel, held her hand, kissed it then looked away. For reasons she knew too well, her heart was beating too fast.

'I never wanted to bring you this pain. I always wanted you to think I was strong. But I'm weak and ashamed about it.' He was gripping her hand even harder, struggling with his words. It suddenly sounded like Royce making excuses for behaving badly, and then it didn't sound like him at all.

'It wasn't chicken pox. They tortured me.'

She rang the bell then looked away at the figures and motifs in the gravel garden.

'Come on in, Mel,' Anto said. They hugged at the threshold.

'Thank you,' Mel replied in a tone that belonged to

yesterday.

'Hassan got his train?'

'Yeah. I didn't want to let him go.'

'I know, I know. Yesterday was hard for you both. Not sure I said all the right things in the right order. I felt for the two of you. Now you have to make a fresh start. *Will do* is what I mean. Let's have some tea.'

She sat regally in an antique chair in the long lounge surrounded by the dizzying miscellany of *objets d'art*, her gaze to-and-froing and always returning to the stone buddha. What seemed an age ago now, he'd watched her pointless efforts at conception. She was already by then a no-hope case and beyond 'divine' intervention. He made her calm, though. Anto had offered to introduce her to Zen. 'There are many stages' he said. 'You don't have to go all the way; stop where you want'. She'd imagined strict adherence to rules, a demanding discipline. It sounded so much easier than having a child.

Tea was served with the usual formality. It was Mel who eventually broke the silence.

'How did you *know*?'

'I suspected something when I saw the scars—you know, when he went swimming. I'm a member of *Amnesty*. I felt a certain duty to challenge him when we were returning the boat. He stonewalled all the way back in the car then burst into tears, saying he didn't want anyone else, especially you, to know.'

'Did Fliss know?'

'No, she didn't. Possibly suspected it, though. There's another thing she doesn't know: how he got from Istanbul to the UK,' Anto replied.

'Yeah, he told me. He just got on a plane, right? He had

all the papers, including the medical evidence from a very courageous doctor. He has survivor guilt as well as all the rest. I still don't get this shame complex of his.'

'I think it's a male thing, and, of course, he'll always bear the marks. It makes him feel somehow less of a man—especially where women are concerned. We talked a lot when I was in Winchester. I think it was a mistake to do his MA in War Studies. Oh, there's something else that might intrigue you, and maybe modify your view of Fliss: I'm brokering a meeting between her and Helena. Who knows—there might be a deal in it.'

'You're kidding, that's outrageous, Anto! You're the ultimate Mr Fixer!' Mel trilled while enacting repeated salaams. 'My little go-between act has nothing on yours.'

'You did the groundwork. Don't underestimate yourself. By the way, did you ever read *Hassan's Story*?'

'No, did you?'

'How d'you think I got round Fliss?' he said with a chuckle. 'I've offered to re-write it, give it some polish.'

'It's all lies!'

'No. Hassan's escape from Syria was not without incident and risk. The rest he obtained from the charity—individual refugee's stories. If it earns any money, he wants the charity to benefit. It might help to assuage his survivor guilt. Hambledean Hall will be happy enough with the kudos.'

Chapter 28

Mel hugged Billy's monkey, Wolfgang, climbed the ladder then shot down the slide at speed. She stood up and without a word handed the monkey back. She was still in the dark as to when these outings would come to an end, their relationship alter forever. Just when she thought Jess might be having second thoughts, a realtor had visited and set a date for a viewing of the apartment. It was bound to sell fast, Jess had been told, and Mel had put herself on daydream alert. Despite the precaution, she was powerless to stop herself drifting into warm reveries, as now: she and Billy singing together while dipping by the eyot; she'd somehow been allowed to adopt him.

Billy, clasping Wolfgang, matched her as far as the top of the slide, then hesitated; she waited, crouching like a baseball catcher, ready to receive him, keeping silent. His shriek, as child and tightly clasped monkey whizzed down into her arms was delight and panic all rolled into one. It was just the beginning—he repeated the trick over and over without assistance. Immensely proud of himself, he hinted he was now on a par with Mohammed. Except, of course, that poor boy was unable to participate in any play park activities. She'd seen for herself how his cumbersome plaster caste stymied all such pleasures. He could manage only short distances with crutches and needed a specially designed car seat to travel anywhere. Indoors, he'd abandoned the wheelchair—it was too slow. Instead, he'd learnt to propel himself on a flat 'roller board' using his arms. The caste was due to come off in about a month then be re-applied for a further three months. After that he'd be allowed to go swimming and learn to walk normally for the first time in his life, also attend school. He was receiving home tutoring, his English—especially his soccer English—improving at a pace.

After that nerve-shredding Saturday, Mel decided it was unfair to put the slightest pressure on Hassan—she came some way down the list after Mohammed and his father's mental health. If only they could all be together. She recalled that while coping with her own spell of PTSD, there was always someone there pitching for her. It was an easy decision to keep Hassan out of the loop of her present troubles, the agency situation included. She'd do all the travelling now, putting in time with Winchester, Hassan and Mohammed, and then Manchester and Billy, somehow keeping the agency going in between. How realistic was she being? She would soon find out.

On their way back from the park, her phone went. It was Mr Musicals. Could she drop everything and meet him in person *now*? Still not over the shock, she stammered about 'child-minding' and the fact that she didn't have all her files with her. He didn't seem to regard any of these impediments as important.

'I can get files faxed to you from the office if you want,' she said, helpfully.

'No need.'

So it had to be about Royce, but musical theatre? That would be pushing it—his baritone singing voice was limited and Mel was certain he'd never agree to a voice coach. Besides, he'd been widely quoted as 'taking a sabbatical from the stage'. Was it simply a question of an offer he might not be able to refuse?

'The actor you have in mind isn't available right now,'

she said.

'Don't worry, I'll explain it all when you get here.'

By the time they got back to the apartment, Mel had already taken out her pony tail. She combed out the shoulder-length hair, applied some lipstick and told Billy they were going to 'Big London'. He loved travelling on the Tube and started jumping up and down.

'We're going to see a music man. He has a very special piano; maybe he'll let you play it if you ask him nicely.'

To occupy him on the journey she brought along his 'toy' keyboard. On the way to the station, she texted Jess. They changed trains at Piccadilly Circus and, at the next stop, slipped into the crowds around Leicester Square. As soon as they entered the building, Mel phoned, and the casting director came to meet them. As he grasped her hand, he introduced himself, this time more intimately, as 'Jay' and thanked her for responding so quickly.

'And what's your name, my friend?' he said, towering over Billy, who, too overcome to reply, looked up at Mel.

'It's Billy,' she replied, offering a flimsy explanation for the boy's taciturnity.

They were soon in the escalator making polite conversation. Mel's mind wound back to their previous, slightly unsettling meeting and her desperation afterwards to catch Hassan before he disappeared back to Winchester. After he confessed he'd come to see *her*, and not the Home Office, the little matter of deceit didn't add up to much.

Billy's stupefaction at the sight of the grand piano went beyond previous records. He looked underneath it, walked around it twice and then stared longingly at the pristine keys.

'Here, let me show you,' Jay said, lifting the lid, getting Billy onto the piano stool and demonstrating how the strings were actuated by the keyboard. 'You wanna play a bit?'

Billy nodded timidly. The lid was closed and the stool raised until he could reach the keys, which he began to touch at random as though he was testing them out like a piano tuner. Now he could be left and the meeting take place in easy chairs between a low table at the other end of the long room.

'How *is* Royce, by the way?'

'Oh, he's practically back to his normal self. But… as I was hinting, he has this aversion now to the stage. I think he'll get over it in time but he won't be rushed into anything. Anything except art, that is.'

'Oh, yeah, his upcoming one-man at The Barbican! The critics are sharpening their claws already. They don't like outsiders coming in, telling them how to paint,' Jay said, laughing. 'Bad publicity sells pictures though. You going?'

'Er, yeah, I'll do my bit. I'm not officially involved.'

'No? So, how's your agency gonna get through until Roycey gets his stage career back on track?'

'We can take a hit for a while. He's going to do voice-overs and poetry recitals…'

'Am I hearing right? Isn't that BB and B?' Jay interjected, reacting to Billy's efforts on the piano.

'*Please* pretend you don't know the song. He thinks it belongs to just him and me. It's just the way he is. I've gone along with it. One day I'll have to tell him—it'll be like saying there's no Father Christmas. Not sure how I'm going to do it.'

'Oh, left hand too!'

'I taught him a few chords. He loves playing chords, but he can only manage two-finger ones.'

Jay sprang out of his chair. He seemed to have lost some weight. He motioned to Mel and they approached the piano.

'You promise!' Mel whispered, and received a nod and a smile she couldn't interpret.

As soon as Billy finished the piece, there were *bravos* and clapping. He was so pleased he almost smiled.

'Love your music, Billy. Well done!' Jay exclaimed.

'It's got words too,' Billy said in a sort of confidential aside. Both he and Jay turned to Mel, the casting supremo's expression pure theatrical surprise.

'Okay,' Mel said, a small note of resignation in her voice. She touched the appropriate key on the piano and began to sing *Bewitched, Bothered and Bewildered* to Billy's simple accompaniment.

Afterwards, Mel congratulated Billy and Jay was equally enthusiastic about the 'show'. Billy was left to play and the meeting re-started.

'I owe you an apology,' Jay began as soon as they sat down. 'Last time, I was waiting for you to come out and admit you'd sent me that video.'

'What video?'

'Exactly! *Murder Ballad* at the Tabard Theatre.'

'O my God! I never sent you any video. Why should anyone do that? For a joke, I can only suppose.'

'No, it wasn't sent as a joke. I realised that after I'd run it a couple of times. When you got in touch, I was looking forward to your pitch and hearing that voice again. It has a lovely, sharp edge, by the way—don't ever lose it. I did some research—early *Rent* try-outs. I wondered why you didn't make the official premiere. I was not a million miles away at the time.'

'Fuck,' Mel half whispered, her head dropping, her whole body registering total fatigue. They'd both become mute as though hypnotized by the sound of Billy playing. He seemed to be close to exhausting his repertoire.

'I'm sorry I touched a nerve, Mel.'

'I wasn't good enough is your answer.'

'I'm not buying that. And to prove it I want you to audition. You like Sondheim, don't you?'

'You are crazy, aren't you? Or is this some weird side of your sense of humour that I still don't get?

'Negative on both counts! You held that show together. Your skillsets are a perfect fit for the countess in *A Little Night Music*, as it so happens.'

Mel burst out laughing; Jay shook his head.

'Sorry, private joke. I *know* two countesses. Well, one and a half if I'm being real honest.' She giggled at her own joke while the casting director's face remained deadpan. There followed the clearest recall of the conspiratorial humour that routinely broke out between her and Helena. It came and went in a flash. Now, a heavy silence took its place, even Billy had stopped playing. But he was evidently still in awe of the grand piano, happy in his own world, walking around it, touching and sniffing it.

'You think I'm on my ass, don't you? Need a little charity?' she said, at last.

'Wrong again! I *don't* run a social service. I like to tell people the truth; it saves a lot of time—theirs and mine. It's earned me something of a reputation. I don't care.'

'Wow! I'm truly flattered. Really, I am. Don't know what to say apart from sorry if I offended you,' Mel said, meekly.

'It's okay. But I still want to know what happened to your *Mimi Marquez.*'

'Oh… you know… life follows art. I sort of… became her.'

'Drugs?' he asked, miming a tourniquet, tapping up a vein, injecting.

'My boyfriend at the time got me smoking the stuff. Said it was safe. 'Course, we all lived with the dread of getting Aids. By the time I got out of rehab, the world had changed just a little.'

'Without Aids there'd have been no *Rent*, and without TB there'd have been no *Bohème.* Art and suffering, eh. Let's not go there. The audition?'

'It's impossible. I've got so much to take care of right now. Billy needs a lot of input.'

'They don't last long, if you remember. Here, take this; it's only 40 bars or so. You might at least look at it,' he said, handing her a small score.

Mel had a sudden sense of Jay's authority and power. It felt a little like when Fliss got her way over the garden party visit. You end up not wanting, or afraid, to let such people down. After taking up so much of his time—and his indulgence towards Billy—she heard herself promise to look at the score. It instantly pleased him and she cringed inside with guilt.

On their way back, Billy was on cloud nine. He totally ignored his keyboard, kept repeating the words 'grand piano' and moving his fingers as if he was still playing the instrument. It occurred to Mel that this might be the only consolation in his moving north: a grand piano in a grand house.

Chapter 29

Returning from the supermarket in Anto's car, Mel reflected again on the video and half-expected to feel something close to anger but really there was nothing to get mad about. Anto—for who else could the mystery sender be?—would likely deny all knowledge of it. He'd once cited professionalism as to why he'd not singled her out in his review of the show, and maybe this was his way of making amends. The subject, for the foreseeable, was closed—like his teacher days and the tragic case of his sister whose name she was yet to learn.

Her mind skipped to the present—and a curious incident at the trolley park. As she was returning hers, an elderly woman approached in some confusion.

'Can you help me get my pound back?'

Mel couldn't figure out what the problem was at first. The woman had presumably performed the simple task week in, week out. Then it hit—in the space of seven days her brain had clean forgotten how it was done. Mel quickly restored the woman's coin back to her. There was an expression of relief but no thanks were offered. As Mel came away, she detected the sweet, faint whiff of liquor.

Mel and Helena met at Bond Street Underground then walked east along Oxford Street. Despite the chill of an early December morning, they could feel the sun's warmth on their faces. The talk was desultory; neither appeared willing to risk a joke in case it misfired. How foreign it all felt, thought Mel. When they reached Harley Street, they turned to one another and smiled.

'Where it all began!' Helena exclaimed, squeezing her friend's hand.

At Mel's clinic assessment the staff had been full of positive messages. Even the term *alcohol dependency* felt neither too pejorative nor overly euphemistic. The only word that floored her was *sobriety*. It sounded posh and difficult to attain, which, she knew, it was going to be—especially on karaoke nights at the pub with Georgie. Her referral and work-up—history, bloods and physical—had decreed no more than a one day-a-week attendance programme. 'See, I'm coming in a bunch cheaper than you ever imagined,' Mel had informed Helena after the clinic had set out her individualised regime. Her friend had been generous—and clever—Mel felt under a certain sisterly obligation to come through with 'a result', as Holly in her soccer vernacular would put it.

Before confiding in her assistant about the need for treatment and time away from the agency, Mel had offered her a pay rise. Holly replied by asking if there was anything wrong. Meanwhile, her boss would take a pay cut.

Anto, when told, became emotional like when he'd fought back tears after Maria's miscarriage. He felt guilty and unnecessarily asked her for forgiveness. He begged to introduce her to Zen, but *slowly*. What had she got to lose?

'You should learn to love who you are; what you are. Try to think of the divine within you, not the one outside of you,' he preached, but softly—Anto at his most tender.

It was unsettling to discover he'd intuited at least some of her own spiritual self-questioning. And how did *she* intuit the inner Anto? For months there'd been this tiny quandary building in her head so that few days went by now without it confronting her: was Anto a grown-up version of Billy?

On a practical level, he'd agreed to dispose of the bottles and cans she'd squirrelled away. There'd be a few remaining in forgotten places. Her imagination had her ransacking the house for a drink. *Don't* go there, she ordered herself.

They'd just walked back from the swimming pool, and who should be standing by Mel's front door?

'Mummy!' shouted Billy, running towards her.

Anto took his leave, giving Mel a brief hug.

'What have you been up to, then?' Jess asked her son.

'I've been swimming in the pool with...' Billy was looking around for Anto, 'he's gone!'

'Was it Captain Anto?'

Billy nodded, by which time the two women were in a tight hug; after that, Mel unlocked the door and the happy party trouped in.

'Steve had to go away suddenly on business. I came straight on over. Can I stay?'

'Dumb question, eh, Billy?'

The two women were soon sat down with tea and biscuits, Billy putting in time on the piano.

'So, how's the swimming going?' Jess asked.

'Early days, but he really enjoys it. He wants to swim like Anto!'

'You've made such a difference. I don't know how I can thank you enough, Mel. Can't have always been easy.'

'No complaints. He's kind of reaching out in all

directions: the age of discovery!'

Jess nodded, then seemed lost for words. She ran her fingers through her hair and Mel thought she was going to burst into tears. 'It's over.'

'What!'

'He's a monster, and a control freak. And I'm a fool twice over, *and* I damn nearly sold the flat! That would have taught me a lesson, wouldn't it?'

'Oh, Jess, I'm so sorry.'

'Don't be. I feel better than I've felt for weeks. Kept giving him another chance, thinking you've got to suffer for your art. But the designing was just another illusion. I sort of knew Billy would be a nightmare—pushed it to the back of my mind. Selfish, I know. You're the one that always puts him first. I tell you, I want to write down *your* name and put it in that jar of yours.'

'Oh, Jess. Let me give you a hug.'

They shared a happy teatime together—pizzas and leftovers. Billy, after his efforts in the pool, had acquired an appetite, even attempting some pizza *and* a whole cookie.

The relentless cloud hanging over Mel—and, as it turned out, Jess too—had been blown away by the same timely wind. Billy's bath time was riotous, both women wantonly indulgent. After his much calmer bedtime, Mel apologised for being unable to offer her guest any wine, though the occasion seemed to demand it. Jess said coffee would be fine. They talked about going to 'big' London tomorrow; maybe a boat trip and should they invite 'The Captain'.

'That's two calls I gotta make. I'll be a little while.'

Almost acting like an automaton, she left Jess in the kitchen-diner, closed the door, and tapped out the phone number, waiting what seemed an age for a reply.

'Yeah.'

'It's Mimi Marquez. Hope it's convenient to speak.'

'Sure it is. I've been waiting for your call.'

'You still want me to audition?'

'You'll kill it. The countess is kind of 'real'. She's the least foolish of all the lovers, the most cynical, and the most intelligent.'

He asked if she'd looked at the score. She'd barely glanced at it, reasoning that, to do so, would have only laid her open to some half-held superstition. The calls over, Mel went to her Mason jar, fished out the fountain pen and two blank strips, which she carefully inscribed: the old ritual—waiting for the ink to dry only ever served to heighten the pleasure of the proceedings. Some things, she reflected, happen so fast they take your breath away. Hassan and Mohammed were that other thing. She knew she was their best chance, and they hers—just a question of time. There was something else though, or rather somebody else—Mohammed's mother. Mel was dimly aware, despite the difficulties, of a correspondence, which included photos, some she gathered, of herself. She thought back to when she'd posed outside Great Ormond Street Hospital in the midi dress Hassan had really, *really* loved. Was she even then auditioning for a more enduring role?

Donning her wool wrap coat, she picked up the score, played a few notes on the piano then went up to the roof terrace. Switching on her favourite lights, she began to sing.

Milton Keynes UK
Ingram Content Group UK Ltd.
UKHW011919140624
443886UK00003B/13

9 781788 648936